CONTENTS

ABOUT 'THE MYSTERY OF THE EVIL EYE'

Sir William Armand, a prominent lawyer, is found murdered, stabbed through the eyes near his country house on the Northumbrian coast. The timing appears suspicious, immediately following his order to his daughter, Estelle, to break off her engagement with the man she loves, Jack Derwick. A gruesome white 'berry' and a charm against the evil eye imprinted at the base of a tree are found where Sir William met his terrible death. Dr Eustace Hailey, a forty-something surgeon, scientist and amateur detective, investigates and succeeds in running to cover a strange and awful manifestation of distorted passion.

About the Author

Anthony Wynne was the pen name of Robert NcNair Wilson, a Scottish physician, writer and politician. Wilson began his career as a house surgeon in his native Glasgow, developed a specialism in cardiology and was the medical correspondent of *The Times* for over thirty years. He wrote over fifty books, his non-fiction under his own name and his 'Golden Age' detective fiction as Anthony Wynne. His first crime novel, *The Mystery of the Evil Eye*, was published in 1925 and introduced his principle literary creation, Dr Eustace Hailey an over-weight, snuff-snorting, Harley Street psychologist-sleuth. Dr Hailey would star in twenty-seven novels and one short story collection. Wilson died in 1963.

'Intensely interesting'
New York Times

Murder in Thin Air
'A real puzzle'
New York Times

The Mystery of the Ashes
'An ingenious story'
New York Times

CHAPTER 1
DISMISSED

"Why?"

The question came sharply in the quiet tones which Estelle had learned to love. Her eyes fell before Jack Derwick's challenge.

"I don't know why, Jack."

"But it's absurd," he declared. "We have been engaged for two months. Our happiness is complete. What right has your father to shatter it in this fashion?"

Estelle did not reply. He noticed that her fingers, which rested on the edge of the table, were pale at the tips from the pressure which she was exerting on them.

"I shall see your father at once."

"Oh, no...."

Her voice, now, had a piteous ring in it. She came to him and grasped him by the arm.

"For my sake, Jack.... Promise me that you will not speak to father about it."

She looked so terrified, that instinctively he put his arm round her waist. She did not resist him.

"Promise me."

"That means—it can only mean—that you agree with his decision. Tell me why you agree."

"I can't tell you."

He left her and strode across the room and back again. From

4

the mullioned windows a splendid view of one of the wildest parts of the Northumbrian coast was obtainable. But he had no eyes at the moment for scenery.

"There is some reason, I suppose?" he challenged.

"Yes."

Jack smiled bitterly. "I take it you are not a spy nor a thief nor... any of the things which prevent the heroines of novels from marrying till the last chapter...."

Estelle did not reply, but the misery in her eyes reproved him for his outburst. Whatever her secret might be, it was obviously a terrible one. He came to her again and took her hands.

"Look me in the face, Estelle," he demanded, gently.

She raised her head. The action gave him the full roundness of her throat, the exquisite curve of her cheek. The afternoon sunshine rushed in her golden hair filling it with light.

"Now, say you still love me."

"I still love you."

He bent and kissed her.

"Listen, little girl. I don't ask to know your secret. All I ask is that I may be near to help you. You can't send me away, because I won't go."

A moan broke from Estelle's lips. "I must send you away. If you knew how urgent it was..."

Suddenly she seemed to gather all her strength for a final effort. Her voice became more calm, but not less urgent.

"Jack, you say you love me. Do this for me without asking why and without waiting. Go away tonight, back to London, to your work. If... if things should change... if it is possible at all, I will come to you. I promise that."

She trembled as she spoke, and he saw that she was trembling.

"Estelle," he cried, "you are afraid...."

"Yes. And every hour that you delay makes me more afraid. If only you would go, I think I could bear it."

The horrible mystery gripped Jack Derwick's heart. Only an hour ago he had believed himself the special favourite of fortune with this glorious girl as his betrothed, and his career opening splendidly before him. He sank down on a chair and laid his head on his arms.

"God help me," she heard him cry, "I can't obey you."

But his weakness seemed, somehow, to give her new resolution and vigour.

"Listen," she told him in quick tones, "I have already telegraphed announcements to *The Times* and the *Morning Post* that our engagement is broken off. I have told Travers to book a sleeper for you in the night mail. Your luggage will be taken to the station at 10 o'clock.

He started up, anger flashing in his eyes.

"So that I am dismissed already, before I have even consented to be dismissed.... I tell you, I will not leave till I have seen your father and demanded..."

His voice broke. Already he was sorry. Again her eyes reproached him, so that he could not bear the pain which they revealed. He caught his breath in a sob, and then turned and left the room.

When he had gone Estelle sank down on the chair on which he had been seated. But her eyes had no tears.

CHAPTER 2 THE MYSTERY DEEPENS

When Jack left Estelle he went straight to his bedroom.

His valet was busy in the room laying out his evening clothes. He told him rather curtly that he should not require them.

"I am returning to town tonight, Bayne," he announced. "You had better begin packing up."

Bayne knew his master in this mood. He did not attempt to discover the reason of this sudden change of plan. Jack took his cap and stick and left the room.

He went out into the beautiful November evening and turned towards the shore. It was a favourite walk of his, and in other circumstances the nip of frost in the air would have delighted him. The beginnings of a great sunset already stained the western sky.

He strode on, along the cliffs, letting his thoughts rush in their turgid stream through his mind. That was his method when any big decision had to be taken—the method, as he believed, which had brought him to fame at the bar and in Parliament. Always, he had found, after the first incoherent tide had spent itself, some clear simple idea took shape and enabled him to see his problem whole.

The sunset developed as he walked, staining the sea a deep crimson in patches. Away beyond the light there was a faint mist on the water, in which he could just distinguish the outline of a ship. He paused, straining his eyes, until the vessel finally disappeared.

Then he turned and glanced back at Calthorpe Hall, Estelle's home, the place of all his desires. The old house was dark in the fading light, but it stood clear cut against the sky, a picture of rugged and solemn strength. Even the pinewoods which surrounded it seemed diminutive by comparison. Sir William Armand, he thought, had chosen well in selecting this place for his old age.

But that thought was followed by an instant stab of bitterness. For what reason of sanity or sense had this man, regarded all over England as one of the cleverest lawyers of his day, and certainly the kindest and most charming of personalities, decided to take arms against his daughter's happiness? Estelle, he knew, was the idol of all her father's thoughts and ambitions.

He bit his lip strongly as the stark truth came back to him. Whatever the reason might be, it was a sufficient one—sufficient, for daughter as well as for parent—a reason appealing as strongly to a woman's as to a man's mind. His legal instinct fastened on that fact. Again and again it had been his experience to find that objections or doubts, which seemed important to his male clients, were brushed aside by their womenfolk as quite irrelevant. Woman's mind worked in a manner different from man's.

Indeed, he had made a working rule for his own guidance in difficult cases that, when men and women saw eye to eye in any problem, the key to that problem was to be found in human nature. Money and ambition—the great "inhuman" motives of conduct—always divided the sexes.

And yet he did not believe for one instant that Estelle had ceased to love him. He knew her well enough to be quite sure that, had this been the case, she would have told him frankly. Estelle was not the sort of girl to make a mystery rather than face an unpleasant fact.

No, she was as deeply in love with him as ever. Could it be that she was sending him away for his own good?

But that idea was too ridiculous to be entertained. How

could it be an advantage to him—in the most material sense—
to lose one of the most beautiful, and certainly one of the rich-
est, brides in England. The name of her father's firm—Armand &
Blunder—was itself a passport to success at the bar, and already,
as he knew, he had profited greatly by his association with it. No
other solicitors in the world enjoyed so commanding a reputation.

He resumed his walk at a slower pace, anxiety and bewilderment possessing his mind. The path along the cliffs turned in-
land a short distance to avoid one of those deep gashes in the
rock, which are hereabouts a characteristic of the coastline.

He entered a scrubby pine wood, in which, in spite of the late-
ness of the season, the smell of resin still lingered deliciously.
Before him was the village of Calthorpe, a tiny hamlet lying in
a fold of the hills, which rise here in long slow undulations towards the main Cheviot range.

The light had grown dimmer, but this only seemed to en-
hance the beauty of the scene. His eye travelled from the square
tower of the village church, with the vicarage peeping out from
its trees behind, to the roofs of the cottages now a deep purple
colour of almost unfathomable richness. The air was cold and
vital as champagne.

He came to the church, and lingered a moment in the fresh
pain of memory which the sight of it caused him. They had
planned to be married here, Estelle and he. After the ceremony
they meant to walk back to the Hall along the cliffs according to
an old custom of the squires of Calthorpe. For an instant he saw
Estelle's face again as she asked him if he would consent to fall in
with her wishes in this respect.

How remote and impossible that glorious time seemed already! How remote and impossible even last Sunday, when they
had worshipped together in the family pew and, kneeling beside her, he had thanked God for the joy that was granted to him.

He leaned his elbows on the low wall surrounding the churchyard, and gazed vacantly at the rows of tombstones. A new grave
which seemed to have been filled but yesterday lay like a gash in

the green sward before him. That spectacle somehow made his heart quail. He covered his face with his hands.

A footstep sounded behind him. He turned sharply to find himself face to face with the vicar of the parish, the Rev Hargreave Willoughby.

"What, Mr Derwick...."

The vicar held out his hand cordially, adding:

"I suppose Miss Armand is not far away, eh?"

Jack hesitated a moment. He liked the Rev Hargreave instinctively, but his natural reticence cautioned silence. After all, he had not really abandoned hope.

"Oh, no," he said, as casually as he could, "I am alone, I was just taking a little walk before dinner. I came along the cliffs to enjoy the wonderful sunset.

The clergyman nodded. His thin, very ascetic face lighted up with enthusiasm.

"These Northumbrian sunsets are heavenly," he Declared. "Each time I see one of them, I feel how near is this earth of ours to the glory of its Creator.... Will you come to the vicarage and let me give you a cup of tea—my housekeeper would be much honoured."

For some reason, the proposal appealed to Jack. It offered, if only for a moment, escape from his bitterness of spirit. He followed the clergyman round the corner of the church and along the narrow path between high hedges which admitted directly to the Vicarage garden.

Tea was ready when they reached the drawing-room—a frugal meal of bread and butter cut, Jack noticed, rather thick and spread rather thin. He had heard that the living was a poor one.

A glance at the Rev Hargreave's clothes confirmed that impression. They were terribly threadbare and soiled—and unbrushed. Mud, splashed probably by his bicycle, clung to his trouser legs, and there were stains all over both coat and trousers. Yet the man himself somehow outshone and excused his clothes. As he spoke of his work and the hopes which inspired him in connection with it, his face literally glowed, so that it was easy to understand the love and respect in which he was held everywhere. Jack thought, indeed, that his eyes had a quality of spiritual exaltation which was unique in his experience. They were strange, deep, almost wild, eyes, that burned as he spoke. The martyrs must have had eyes of that type, and the saints.... Looking at the Rev Hargreave one realized how great may be the power of mind or soul over any material thing.... Such men surely are the strength and the glory of the Church....

When he rose to go away Jack felt a little calmer.

He held out his hand:

"I do not think," he said, "that you realize how kind you have been, Mr Willoughby. I may as well tell you now that as Miss Armand has broken off our engagement, this is perhaps the last time I shall have a chance of thanking you."

"What!"

The Rev Hargreave's eyes dilated.

"Oh," he cried, "I am sorry to hear it." He appeared to be greatly upset by the news, and paced up and down the room with swift steps.

"Do you think," he asked, "that I might offer my services as mediator. I feel sure that something might be done—there must be some mistake...."

"I fear not," Jack said. "Sir William has decided this matter, and Estelle seems to have bowed to his decision."

The clergyman stopped, and his visitor saw that his face had become very much flushed. He opened and closed his hands in a peculiar nervous manner.

"Her father has ordered her to send you away?" he cried in a tense voice. "Oh, surely that cannot be true!"

"Unhappily, it is true."

He rose to go. The vicar accompanied him to the door, but made no further comment. The thought occurred to Jack that he was a good fellow, as well as a good man, with a ready sympathy for the troubles of another. It was kind of him to offer to act as a peace-maker. His anger against Sir William rose higher when he compared his almost brutal behaviour with the consideration shown him by the clergyman. At least, he might have been furnished with some inkling of the reason for his dismissal.

His face set in a grim expression of determination. Suddenly he uttered an exclamation of amazement.

A few yards away, crossing a field towards the village, was Estelle herself.

He had a clear view of her, though the darkness was falling quickly. He hurried forward to the place where, as he knew, the footpath reached the main road. This was situated between a cottage and the village inn; for a moment as he passed the former he lost sight of the girl. Then, when he reached the stile, he saw to his astonishment that she had turned back and was retracing her steps quickly towards the Hall.

She must have seen him, of course, at the same moment as he saw her, and she would not meet him. An impulse to run after her came strongly, but he hesitated; it was only too clear that her decision of the afternoon had not altered. He wondered why she had come to the village at this late hour, and whether, when he went away, she would return again. In all his knowledge of her he had never known her act in this fashion before.

He decided to wait a few moments and then follow her back to the Hall across the fields.

CHAPTER 3 MISSING

Two days later the world learned that Sir William Armand, senior partner of the firm of Armand & Blunder, was missing.

The news caused a great sensation in legal circles, for Sir William was regarded as the kind of man who, in any circumstances, may always be relied on to do the right thing. The idea that he could suddenly vanish, leaving no trace and no explanation, seemed somehow grotesque and impossible.

At Scotland Yard, on the other hand, lively anxiety was felt, for the reports from Calthorpe were disquieting. Sir William had been last seen two days previously (that is, on the day on which Estelle broke off her engagement to Jack Derwick) about four o'clock in the afternoon. At that time he was leaving the Black Bull Inn of the village to return home along the cliffs. He was accompanied by a strange man, named Mr Sawyer, a visitor at the inn, with whom he had been closeted for about an hour previously.

"It looks bad on the face of it," the Chief declared, after reading the account sent him by the local superintendent. "What do you think, Biles?"

"I agree with you."

Inspector Biles spoke in very quiet tones, but his manner was as decided as it was gentle. He was a tall lean man, clean-shaven, with crisp hair and rather pale eyes. But his expression was good-humoured, even kindly.

"You know Sir William, of course?"

"I have met him. Before I came to see you, I sent for a record of his career. There is nothing of any sort."

"Oh nothing, of course."

"And this Sawyer?"

Inspector Biles shook his head. He had no information.

"Well," the Chief said, "do your best. I leave it entirely to your judgement. You will travel north tonight, I take it?"

"Yes. I must go over the ground."

When Biles returned to his own room, he found a further note about Sir William Armand on his desk. It stated that he had retired from active participation in the work of his firm about two years ago, though he had not in any official way severed his connection.

"Where did you get this?" the officer demanded of his clerk, who was working at a side table.

"In the Northumberland County Directory. It's a new reference which was published for the first time last year."

"There is nothing else?"

"Nothing that I can find."

Biles re-read the telegrams of the District Superintendent carefully. He tried, according to his usual custom, to make a mental picture of the mystery. The "Black Bull" would be the usual type of North Country inn, hospitable, warm, smelling a little of beer, a little of ham. The bedrooms would be on the first floor, clean, rather damp probably, with big, over-blanketed beds.

Sir William would certainly never send any guest of his own to such a place.

But why should he go out of his way to visit a stranger who had been staying at the inn only one night? He must have known that Mr Sawyer was coming; indeed, he must have had an appointment with him. Why had he not asked Mr Sawyer to Calthorpe Hall?

The description of this mysterious person was exasperatingly meagre. "A middle-aged man, well-dressed, rather stout, wearing moustache and beard, appeared somewhat excited." It might have applied to any commercial traveller. That was the worst of these local policemen. They looked only for the obvious—and never saw it.

He rested his head between his hands, gazing vacantly in front of him at the opposite wall. The more he considered this case, the more extraordinary it became. Where could an elderly man disappear to in a countryside where he was known to every inhabitant?

The possible explanations, of course, were suicide, murder, and voluntary disappearance. The first two, he thought, might be dismissed off-hand—though he never, in practice, dismissed any possibility, however remote, until he had finally investigated and disproved it. The last might furnish the key. Elderly gentlemen do not, as a rule, murder one another; but they are most apt, of all people, to depart mysteriously for other lands.... even when they enjoy blameless reputations.

"Have you sent my message to the ports?" Biles asked his clerk suddenly.

"Yes, sir."

"With a description of Sir William Armand?"

"Yes, sir."

The train left King's Cross at 9.45. It was now 6pm. Biles decided to go home at once and dine quietly in his own house. He left orders that any further information about Sir William, or about the firm of Armand & Blunder, which might be gleaned, was to be forwarded to him instantly at the "Black Bull" at Calthorpe. He drove up to Hampstead in a cab, turning over his new problem in his mind as he went. It was his invariable custom, in every difficult investigation, to think well before acting, and having arrived at some theory, to test it step by step. The method had its disadvantages, but he had proved its solid worth too often to be anxious to change it for any of the "strokes of genius" which novelists are never tired of bestowing on their detective heroes.

His house stood on the top of Holly Hill, over-looking London. From his study window a splendid panorama of spires and domes was revealed—the great city in whose darker life he found such perennial interest. A Hampstead man, he never returned to Hampstead without a thrill of pleasure.

His housekeeper, a merry little woman with a ripe apple face, had dinner ready for him. He sat down at once, but he ate little: the excitement of a new chase dominated his mind.

As he drove off to the station, he began to think about Mr Sawyer. They knew nothing of this individual at Sir William's office. Indeed, Mr Blunder had stated definitely to the detective who had been sent to interview him that, so far as he was aware, the firm possessed no client of that name. Biles could not see what reason Mr Blunder could have for being untruthful on this point. It was obvious, then, that Sir William had interests outside of his business.

But what interests? Rich men are often secretive enough about their investments. But they do not employ the kind of men as confidential agents, whom they hesitate to introduce into their own houses. The very idea of a clandestine meeting is repugnant to the legal mind—at least, in its nobler manifestations.

No, the more he thought about it, the more sure he felt that there was something in the life of the great lawyer of which he was ashamed—something perhaps which threatened his present security or peace of mind. It could scarcely be a woman— though this possibility could not be absolutely excluded—and therefore it was most probably a question of money.

Just before he went to sleep, the detective turned his thoughts to Sir William's daughter, Estelle, and her fiancé, John Derwick. Did they, he wondered, know anything of the reasons which might have led to the present mysterious events?

CHAPTER 4 A VERY SERIOUS CASE

Next morning at six o'clock Biles alighted from the sleeping car express at Newcastle. He found, to his exasperation, that he must wait here about two hours—the London time-table his clerk had consulted was mistaken, or his clerk had overlooked the matter of connections. In a very ill-humour he walked into the dingy-looking refreshment room and ordered a cup of tea.

The girl who served him seemed inclined to talk, and after a minute or two he mentioned the Calthorpe affair, on the principle that people who serve the public in railway stations often hear bits of news.

On this occasion he was destined to obtain a speedy reward. It appeared that the barmaid was a native of a village situated about two miles from Calthorpe, and had been home only the previous day. She was full of information.

This, however, amounted to no more than local gossip. Indeed, in all she said, Biles could discern only one item which appeared to him to possess significance—the statement that John Derwick had left Calthorpe Hall rather unexpectedly on the night of Sir William's disappearance.

"How do you know that?" he asked the girl.

"Because my cousin has a daughter working as scullery-maid at the Hall. She did say that Miss Estelle was crying bitter-like when Mr John went away."

"A scullery-maid wouldn't be likely to see her mistress crying?"

"That's what I said. Nor did she, sir. It was the lady's maid what told her. And the queer thing is that Miss Estelle was in her bed from before dinner-time that night. She didn't even say goodbye to her young man."

The barmaid added significantly:

"A quarrel, of course, But it kept her from knowing her father was missing till the next morning."

"It's a strange affair," Biles said, stirring his cup of tea meditatively.

"Very strange, sir. They do say the police from London is on to it already. My own notion is that they done away with the old man for his money, though they tell me there's no trace of his body anywhere to be found."

The train was very cold, and Biles had a most uncomfortable journey to Belfort. There the local superintendent was awaiting him with a motor car. They drove the five miles to Calthorpe through a wonderful North country dawn, which seemed to be all gold and crystal.

Breakfast was served as soon as they reached the "Black Bull".

When it was over, the two men went to a sitting-room at the back of the inn, which had been placed at their disposal. Biles lit his large black pipe and stood with his back to the fire warming himself while the superintendent, whose name was Robson, gave him an outline of the case to date.

The first report that Sir William Armand was missing had, he said, come from Calthorpe Hall on Tuesday morning, the day after Sir William was last seen. Miss Estelle Armand had rung up the local police herself. Thereafter search parties had been sent out over the whole neighbourhood. But so far no trace of the missing man had been found.

"What is your own view of the case. Superintendent?" Biles asked in his quiet voice, which always carried a suggestion of indifference.

"That Sir William has his own reasons for disappearing."

"Hm! But in that case he must have travelled by train or motor car. It seems pretty clear that he did not travel by train. What about his cars?"

"No. They have not been out at all."

"If he had hired a car anywhere round here, the fact would be known. I'm afraid there is no escape from the conclusion that he must have walked a long distance himself, or gone into hiding... that is, if he has really disappeared."

Superintendent Robson's face clouded.

"You think..." he began.

"No, I have no theory yet. It is quite possible that you are right. Only it seems a little difficult to explain. Now tell me, have you any information about the man Sawyer who was with him?"

"He went back to London by train from Belfort on Monday night."

"The same train by which Mr John Derwick, who is engaged to Miss Armand, travelled?"

Superintendent Robson started.

"Yes," he said, "but how did you know?"

Biles did not answer for a moment, then he asked:

"Your information came from the station-master, I take it. Did he, by any chance, mention that Mr Derwick and Mr Sawyer travelled together?"

"No. He said they travelled separately."

"You have no idea who this man is, I suppose, or where he comes from?"

"None. His name is down in the hotel register as James Sawyer, of London. But he didn't even enter it himself. He had a sore hand and got the waiting-maid to do it for him."

It was obvious that no further information could be obtained in this quarter. Biles knocked the ashes out of his pipe on the fender.

"I think, if you don't mind. I'll take a walk across to the Hall," he said. "I'll follow the path along the cliffs where Sir William was last seen, and take my own time about it. Perhaps you will make it convenient to meet me here later in the day.

He got his hat and stepped out into the village street. It seemed to be strangely empty and deserted. However, he knew that such an appearance, in the North Country, is always deceptive. After the visitor has passed, a face appears at every window. He turned suddenly, just as he reached the stile leading into the fields, and confirmed his view. The sight made him smile.

At this moment he had a small pine wood directly in front of him. Calthorpe Hall stood somewhat to the right, its chimneys being visible among the trees which surrounded it. Calthorpe Church was on the left. The path he was about to follow led straight to the wood, and then, as he guessed, swung along the top of the cliffs towards the Hall. He could see that a branch path connected hall and church directly. It appeared to leave the main way somewhere in the wood. He made a rapid sketch-map of these observations before beginning his walk.

Then he crossed the fields and entered the little wood. He stood about the centre of it, attempting to see whether or not the trees offered an effective screen. There could be no doubt that they did not. In daylight anything passing in the wood must be easily visible for a considerable distance.

Sir William, however, had been last seen just as dusk was falling. At that time of day the wood would constitute a much more effective shield from observation. He walked through it from end to end twice, and then he walked right round it. On the side next the sea it advanced quite close to the edge of the cliffs, but these were not very precipitous at this place. The theory that the lost lawyer might have fallen over and been carried out into deep water was not tenable. Besides, as Biles had verified for himself, the tide was probably at full ebb about the time of the "disappearance".

But if the missing man had not fallen into the sea, where on earth could he have gone. It was incredible that he could hide in such a place as this even during a single night.

The only explanation which seemed at all reasonable in the circumstances was that he had descended the cliffs to the foreshore, and so made his way back to the main road at a distance from the village.

Biles resolved to test this theory for himself, but as the tide was at present flowing, he postponed this piece of research work and resumed his walk towards the Hall.

His ring was answered by a tall footman who seemed very much astonished at his visit, and who told him rather curtly that "Miss Estelle" was "unable to see any visitors".

"Pardon me," said Inspector Biles, gently, "but I think she will make an exception in my favour... if you give her this card."

The footman took the card, read it and started.

"Will you come in, sir?" he invited.

Biles was shown into what he recognized as Sir William's study. It was a solidly furnished room with bookshelves lining the walls and a large desk in the centre. There was an air of established worth about every chair.

The detective examined the room quickly. He noted that the blotting-pad on the table had been used recently; it was very clean yet ink-stained. He saw, too, that the seals of a tin box standing near the fireplace had been broken and renewed within the last few days. A particle of red wax still adhered to the surface of the desk, where, no doubt, the re-sealing operation had taken place. The writing on the blotting-pad was very indistinct, but he read easily the words, "at our interview," and the signature, "William Armand". Biles prided himself on his power to read blotting paper without the use of a mirror.

He was dwelling on the significance of these discoveries when Estelle came into the room. A single glance at her pale anxious face convinced him that she was suffering great mental torture, but he put that feeling away from him.

"I am Inspector Biles of Scotland Yard, Miss Armand," he said. "I have been sent down here to assist in the search for your father which is going on. I have come to see you because I know you can help me."

He watched the girl closely as he spoke, and saw her start slightly, but she controlled herself at once.

"I wish I could," she declared. "We are in such terrible anxiety about him, and yet there does not seem to be a gleam of light anywhere."

"I am very sorry for you... especially as you have your own trouble at the same time."

Again the watchful grey eyes looked for some sign, but Estelle only nodded.

"You saw the announcement in the papers, I suppose."

It was Biles's turn to feel surprised. He had not seen any announcement. What he was working on was the information supplied by the Newcastle barmaid. Inwardly he abused his clerk for an unobservant fellow. Not once, but a hundred times, he had warned him never to overlook the social announcements in the morning papers. He hazarded:

"The breaking off of your engagement to Mr Derwick came, I suppose, before your father's disappearance?"

"Oh, yes."

"There is no possible connection between the two events?"

"How could there be?"

Estelle eyed her visitor rather coldly, but the detective fancied that an expression of fear lurked in her eyes.

"Look here, Miss Armand," he said in his softest tones, "I want to make an appeal to you. If you know anything, however intimate or personal, about this matter, it is your duty to tell me. There is no doubt at all in my mind that this is a very serious case indeed."

Estelle sighed deeply.

"You mean?..." she asked in low tones.

"That the evidence, so far as it goes—and that is not far— points to... well, to foul play. I cannot believe that a man in your father's position would attempt to hide himself in any circumstances."

"I'm quite certain that he wouldn't."

"Then tell me... everything."

Estelle did not reply for a moment. She stood looking down at her hands, which rested on the edge of her father's desk. In the deep silence the rhythm of the waves breaking on the shore was distinctly audible.

Finally she looked up into the eyes of her interlocutor.

"There is nothing to tell except that I broke off my engagement at my father's wish."

Biles thought rapidly. Then he said:

"You would not consent to that course without a good reason."

"My father gave me a reason. I promised that I would not divulge it."

"Surely that promise may be broken now—in the circumstances."

"No, I don't think so."

The detective bit his lip. He realized the kind of girl he was dealing with, and knew that, for the moment, it was useless to persist. He reached for his hat.

"There is only one question that I would like to ask you," he said in unruffled tones, "if I may."

"You may."

"Your feelings towards Mr Derwick have not changed?"

"No."

Estelle's lip quivered, but she did not flinch.

She added rather hurriedly:

"My father did not tell me that he had an appointment at the inn until a few minutes before he went there, so Mr Derwick knew nothing about it when he left here on Monday night."

"But surely he must have been astonished when your father did not return to dinner."

"He went before dinner. I did not see him again after... after our interview. I suppose he preferred to dine at Belfort."

Biles did not pursue the matter because he could see that Estelle was already near the breaking-point. Besides, he had the barmaid's information that the girl had gone to bed as soon as her lover went away. That explained sufficiently why she had not become alarmed about her father till the next morning.

"You have no guests staying with you?" he asked, as he was

leaving the room.

"No, we had some friends coming, but my father asked me to write and put them off."

Biles returned to the village by the same way as he had come. When he reached the wood he paused for a little time and searched the ground with his eyes, but so far as he could see the carpet of pine needles which covered it was unruffled.

The idea that so large an object as a human body could have been disposed of in this bare place was grotesque on the face of it. If, indeed, a murder had been committed, it must have taken place in some other locality.

He found the superintendent awaiting him at the inn. There was no further news of any sort. The various search parties had gained not a single scrap of information.

"You have not forgotten the foreshore in your investigations?"

"No, it has been thoroughly examined."

Superintendent Robson shook his head as though gloomy forebodings were entering his mind.

"I must say," he declared, "that the case begins to wear an ugly look. Since the morning I've been thinking over what you said, and it's clear to me that Sir William cannot have disappeared of his own free will. We would have been bound to have had news of him by this time."

Biles nodded.

"Quite so. I came to the same conclusion myself after I had seen the ground."

He filled his pipe slowly, pressing the tobacco carefully into the bowl.

"We've got to find Sawyer," he declared reflectively, "and we've got to discover why Miss Armand broke off her engagement to young Derwick. I fancy Miss Armand could enlighten us on both points—if she liked!"

"Did you ask her about Sawyer?"

"No."

"I've just heard that she was seen coming across the fields towards the inn while her father and Sawyer were together. But she turned and went back again before she came to the stile. And then Mr Derwick was seen walking after her. I made enquiries and found he had been to tea at the vicarage."

Superintendent Robson spoke casually. It was evident that he attached very little importance to these discoveries. Biles, on the contrary, was keenly interested in them.

"That means," he declared, "that these two may have actually been in the wood when Sir William and Sawyer entered it...."

"It's possible. Sir William left here about a quarter of an hour after Miss Armand was seen coming to the stile—so far as I can be sure about the times."

The London detective drew a deep breath.

"It's quite clear," he said, "that I must spend the rest of the daylight in the wood."

CHAPTER 5
INSPECTOR BILES
MAKES A DISCOVERY

Experience had taught Inspector Biles that, in detective work, half measures are absolutely fatal. It is better to neglect altogether than to undertake carelessly.

He determined to make his examination of the wood a thorough one in every particular; to go over it foot by foot, spending, if necessary, several days on the work.

Unhappily the weather conditions since the day of Sir William's disappearance had been unfavourable. It had rained hard on several occasions, and thus footprints had been largely obliterated. Nevertheless, as the detective often reminded himself, "You never know what you may find till you look".

He began at the end next to the cliffs, and paced the wood slowly from side to side, kneeling to examine more closely any feature which attracted his attention. He progressed in this task for about an hour before he had the least reward for his labour.

Then, close to the trunk of one of the largest trees, he observed what seemed to be the imprint of a heel.

He stooped and regarded his find with meticulous care. The heel undoubtedly belonged to a woman; undoubtedly, also, it was not the possession of a woman of the labouring classes.

But that was all. Any servant girl, "walking out" with her lover might leave such an imprint.

He examined the ground in the neighbourhood carefully, but could find nothing else of any consequence.

It was after one o'clock. He marked the place where his search had ended and went back to the inn for luncheon. An hour later he returned and resumed his task. When the light began to fail, he had scrutinized about half of the ground. He had made no discovery worthy of the name.

He returned to the inn feeling rather cold and depressed. The mystery remained as impenetrable as ever. Even his speculations mocked him by their fruitlessness.

He went up to his bedroom to wash his hands before dinner. It was an old raftered room with a low ceiling. There was no illumination except a candle. Nor had he been supplied with any hot water. The thought came to him again that in no circumstances would Sir William Armand have condemned one of his friends to this discomfort. The man Sawyer was clearly an object of dislike, or a mere go-between.

He dried his hands carefully, and put the towel back on the rail. It slipped to the floor and he bent to lift it up again. As he did so, he caught sight of a cigarette-end lying in the corner, between floor and wall. He picked it up and examined it.

The first glance made him carry his find to the candle, in order to have a better view of it. This was no ordinary cheap cigarette such as, in all probability, most of the visitors to the "Bull" at Calthorpe smoked. It was a Russian of the most expensive brand.

He rang the bell, and when the chambermaid came asked her who had had the room the night before. She told him that the room had not been occupied at all since Mr Sawyer's departure.

"You are sure of that?"

"Quite certain, sir."

"And before Mr Sawyer's visit?"

"We had no one staying for a fortnight before that. At this season we are usually empty."

Biles dismissed the girl and re-examined his find. Whoever Sawyer was he had a nice taste in tobacco. He took a small silver box from his pocket and put the cigarette end into it for future reference. Then he went downstairs to the bar and called for a whisky and soda. The proprietor, whose name was Mullins, served him. He confirmed the idea that Sawyer was a rich man with expensive tastes.

"Nothing I have in the way of wines pleased him," he declared. "Even my sherry, which is a good vintage, was unsatisfactory. But he drank two bottles of it, all the same."

"Did he ask for sherry in the first instance?"

"No, he asked for port. I fetched up a bottle of my best, 1905, but he refused to drink it. Said he was accustomed to very good wine, and had doctor's orders not to touch anything but the best. He uncorked the bottle himself for fear I didn't know my job."

Biles set his tumbler down on the bar.

"What did you do with the bottle?" he asked.

"It's there." Mr Mullins waved his fat hand towards the shelves on which his wares were arranged for the temptation of his customers.

"You have not sold any of its contents, then?"

"Not a drop. My customers don't drink port of that quality."

The proprietor reached up to take the bottle.

"Stop!" shouted Biles, "don't touch it!"

He ran round the bar to the astonished Mullins.

"I want that bottle," he explained, "but I want it unfingered. A great deal may depend on what I find when I examine it—finger-prints, you understand. Sawyer, you say, uncorked it himself. Did he use a napkin?"

"No, I offered him one, but he refused it."

The detective lifted the bottle carefully by the cork. He set it down on the bar and resumed the consumption of his drink.

"There was nothing about the fellow to identify him, was there?" he asked.

Mullins shook his head.

"I'd know him again if I saw him, of course, but he wasn't anything out of the ordinary. I reckon his age is about fifty-four, though his hair and beard are still mostly black."

"H'm!... that doesn't carry us much further, does it?"

Biles finished his drink and carried the bottle—by its cork— to his private sitting-room. He took his magnifying glass from his pocket and fitted it into his eye. The bottle was literally covered with finger prints, those, no doubt, of the proprietor and his servants, as well as of Sawyer. He turned it slowly round and round looking for separate imprints. There were a number of these, but they disclosed no special feature. He was about to conclude that this clue also had failed him, when he noticed a mark high up on the neck of the bottle which was different from all the others.

It was the imprint of a thumb, and across the middle of it was a scar about an eighth of an inch wide.

It was obvious at a glance that this mark had been made at the time when the bottle was uncorked. That meant that it had been made by Sawyer. A gleam of excitement shone in the detective's eyes. He went to his bedroom and returned with a small bottle containing very fine varnish. With infinite care he painted this over the precious mark so as to preserve it against any possibility of damage. Then be lit his pipe and fell to reflecting on the exceeding difficulty of the problem which confronted him. When he went to bed, he had advanced no further in his speculation.

The next morning before breakfast he was back at his work of surveying the wood. He pursued this tiresome search until midday, without obtaining the slightest reward. Nevertheless, as soon as he had eaten his luncheon, he returned to it. And then, almost immediately, he made a curious find.

This was a small round object, not unlike a large pearl, but of much softer consistence. Inspector Biles had never seen anything resembling it before, and at first concluded that it must be some sort of winter berry. But, though he searched diligently, he could find no shrub on which it might have grown.

Nor was there any other similar berry to be seen anywhere.

The ground in the immediate neighbourhood was rather

hard, but it did seem as if the carpet of pine needles had been disturbed—possibly by human feet. He put the mysterious object in a little specimen box filled with cotton wool, and resumed his search, but he found nothing more.

Superintendent Robson was at the inn when he returned there. Once again he had to report failure. The whole county had been searched, but absolutely no trace of the missing man had been obtained.

"It looks to me, sir, as though he must have drowned himself. The currents are strong on this coast, and his body may have been carried out to sea."

The detective nodded. "I thought of that," he said, "it may be the explanation."

He took his specimen box from his pocket as he spoke, and showed the object he had found to his colleague.

"Have you any idea what this may be?" he asked.

Superintendent Robson examined it carefully. He shook his head.

"I've no idea."

"There are no berries of that sort growing in the neighbourhood?"

"Oh, none. I'm certain on that point."

"I found it in the wood this afternoon. It may or may not be a clue. Anyhow, I shall take it to a doctor friend of mine who is a bit of a scientist and see what he thinks of it. I'm going up to London tonight to try to find that man Sawyer. I rely on you to keep me informed of anything that may happen.

When he reached King's Cross, Biles drove straight to Scotland Yard. He found his Chief as much in the dark about the whole affair as he was himself. The attempts to trace Sawyer had all failed.

"The local superintendent believes that Sir William Armand drowned himself," Biles declared. "He says the tidal currents are very strong on the Northumbrian coast, and may have carried the body far out to sea."

"Why should he drown himself? Besides, he's well over the

'suicide age'. That occurs between forty and fifty. It's the rarest possible thing to find a man over sixty attempting his own life."

"On the other hand, he forced his daughter to break off her engagement with young Derwick on the very day on which he disappeared. She confessed that herself. Derwick went back to London the same night."

The Chief raised his eyebrows sharply.

"That is certainly a new fact. I suppose you will see Derwick yourself."

"Yes. Curiously enough, Miss Armand refused to tell me the reason why her father had acted as he did, but she appeared to consider it adequate. She said that she had given a promise of secrecy."

"H'm!"

The Chief's thin fingers rested on the edge of his desk. He thought a moment, and then asked:

"Has her father's disappearance made any difference to the prospects of happiness for this young lady and her lover, I wonder?"

Biles did not know, but the question had been in his mind during the past twenty-four hours. He would certainly require to find an answer to it. Meanwhile, he wished to settle the matter of the white berry which he had found in the wood at Calthorpe. When he left his Chief, he called a cab and told the driver to take him to 22 Harley Street. A quarter of an hour later he was being shown into the consulting room of Dr Eustace Hailey, the well-known specialist in mental diseases.

Dr Hailey was justly celebrated. He was believed to be the fattest man in the medical profession, yet he did not look very fat. Somehow, Nature had compensated him for his great bulk by affording him the grace to wear it becomingly. She had given him, too, one of the kindest and most charming faces in the world.

"Ah, my dear Biles," he exclaimed, "I expected you as soon as I read in the papers that you were engaged on that fascinating Armand case. There was bound to be discoveries of a medical nature, eh?"

Dr Hailey had grasped his friend's hand as he spoke, and now stood holding it and beaming down from the serene heights of his immense tallness.

Biles chuckled.

"But this discovery," he declared, "will puzzle even you. A berry growing where no berries grow—a freak of Nature...."

He opened his specimen box and held it out to the genial doctor, who took it and set it down on the table at his side. In moments of stress Dr Hailey always took snuff before proceeding to business.

He snuffed slowly and elegantly from a silver box which he carried in his waistcoat pocket. Then he picked up the specimen box and extracted its contents with a pair of fine forceps. He carried it to the window and looked at it closely through a large magnifying glass. Biles, who was watching him eagerly, saw a look of amazement appear on his huge face.

"My dear Biles. Where did you say you found this—eh —'Berry'?"

"In the wood at Calthorpe, entering which Sir William Armand was last seen."

"Dear me... how dreadful... how shocking."

Dr Hailey turned round towards his visitor. He held the forceps in which he was grasping the berry as though he would have liked to put them away from him. His expression was unwontedly serious.

"You have no idea what this object really is?" he asked in quiet tones.

"None. Isn't it a berry, then?"

"No, my dear sir. Oh, no. Very far from that. I regret to say that this is the lens of an eye... probably of a human eye."

"What!"

"There is no doubt at all."

Biles gasped.

"But that means," he cried, "that..." He caught his breath. Dr Hailey bowed his head.

"Quite so.... The owner of the eye has almost certainly been murdered."

CHAPTER 6 THE MARKS ON THE TREE

Biles had a host of questions to ask and Dr Hailey did his best to answer them, though he gave the impression of doing this under mild protest. The pursuit of one human being by another was not agreeable to this very genial nature.

He was emphatic, however, in his opinion that the lens could not have been removed from its situation in its owner's eye except by a degree of violence which must have greatly endangered his life.

"You see, my dear Biles," he added, "we are rather firmly knit together. The eyeball is one of the strongest structures in the human body. Only a stab with a sharp knife would dislodge the lens, and such a stab must almost certainly penetrate to the brain behind."

"Yes, I understand that. But what I don't understand is the absence of all other signs of so violent a deed."

Dr Hailey took a further pinch of snuff.

"I am not a detective," he declared. "My knowledge goes no further than my own profession. All I can tell you is that on an occasion not very remote someone stabbed someone else in the eye. Probably the assault was committed exactly where you found the lens, since it is difficult to imagine that the murderer would carry such an object away with him, in the unlikely event of his noticing it at all."

"It couldn't be from the eye of an animal? Possibly a hawk

might have dropped it."

The doctor shook his head. The lens was too large to have belonged to any small creature. He was satisfied that it was not derived from the eye of a sheep or pig.

"You see, the lens of the eye has this peculiarity. It never stops growing at any age. Consequently, in old people it assumes a rather different shape from that found in young ones. This is an old lens. It follows that it cannot belong to any creature which has not reached advanced years—and we know, my dear Biles, that domestic animals never grow old. It is a mere guess, but I should put the eye of the owner of this lens at about sixty or seventy. However, no doubt the Home Office pathologist will make some microscopic sections of it. That will afford grounds for a more definite conclusion."

Biles nodded. His active mind was already busy with the steps he must take to collect further evidence. It would not, he realized, be sufficient to rely on this single clue, for experience warned him that the difficulty of proving the ownership of the lens would be exaggerated to the utmost by defending counsel —supposing that a charge was preferred. He must go over the ground again with redoubled care. He must, too, have some expert assistance.

He explained his trouble to Dr Hailey, and asked him if he could suggest the name of a medical man who would be prepared, for a substantial fee, to travel to Calthorpe and assist in the investigation. Great was his surprise when the doctor replied that he would take on the job himself, "If you will have me."

"Have you! It's more than I dared hope for."

"There is something about this case which appeals to a bizarre instinct that has been my joy and my trouble all the days of my life," Dr Hailey explained.

"A horrible something, yet, to me, as fascinating as it is horrible. I seem to recognize..."

He stopped. His face grew blank, as though a new idea had blotted out those already present in his mind.

"You had better take the specimen to Dr Ponsonby as soon as possible," he said. "I know him; he likes his material as fresh as possible. Besides, everything may depend on this clue."

The detective agreed. After arranging to meet Dr Hailey the same evening at King's Cross, he drove to Dr Ponsonby's house in Wimpole Street. The famous pathologist, a little eager man of about fifty, was at home, and received him at once.

"Well, Biles," he cried, "what have you brought me this time? Whenever I see you, I look for trouble, you know."

He opened a box of cigars, and offered them to his visitor, who selected one, bit the end off it, and lit it carefully.

"This time," he said, "I think you will not be disappointed."

Then, in his abrupt clear way, he described the investigations he had been making, and his discovery of the lens in the wood at Calthorpe.

"I thought at first it was a white berry of some sort, so I consulted my old friend, Dr Hailey, about it—quite unofficially, of course. He is an authority on so many branches of science. But he soon opened my eyes. He told me I must lose no time in coming to you."

Dr Ponsonby had taken the specimen box in his hands. He opened it and examined its contents with a large glass.

"There's no doubt about it at all," he said. "It is certainly most amazing."

"Dr Hailey said you would probably wish to examine it microscopically. He seemed to think that would give some idea of the age of the owner."

"Yes."

Biles rose to go. He promised that an official request for the pathological examination would be sent immediately.

"I am going back to Calthorpe tonight," he added, "and I'm taking Hailey with me. He's a bit of a detective himself, you know, and he is greatly interested in this case. Between us we may discover some further evidence."

He returned to the Yard and told his Chief of the discovery which had been made. His disclosure produced a sensation, but it was resolved, in the meantime, to allow nothing to be made public. Already the newspapers were busy enough with the fact of Sir William Armand's disappearance. If they learned of this astonishing find, the case would instantly become the chief news topic of the day. It is a principle at Scotland Yard to avoid alarming the criminal until the arrangements for his arrest are complete.

"You have no objections, I suppose, to my taking Dr Hailey with me?" Biles asked.

"On the contrary, there is no man I would sooner trust in the matter. We owe Hailey a bigger debt already over the Walden case, than most of us care to admit."

The finger-print on the neck of the port bottle yielded less information than Biles had hoped. There was nothing resembling it in the library of the photographs at the Yard, so that, whoever the man Sawyer might be, the police had had no previous dealings with him. Careful reproductions of the imprint of his thumb were made, however, and issued broadcast. Then the detective called a cab and drove to the Temple to call on Jack Derwick.

He found this busy young barrister in a mood of great depression. He had heard nothing from Calthorpe, but the hubbub in the papers was proving almost more than he could endure.

"I may be wrong," he declared, pacing his chambers restlessly, but I can't help associating my own dismissal with this mystery. Miss Armand told me nothing, but I know that she was dreadfully upset herself; it is quite clear to me that some terrible secret had been revealed to her."

"Yet we can find nothing to justify that idea. Sir William Armand was more than an averagely successful man; so far as is known he need not have possessed a care in the world."

The young barrister shook his head.

"There is something, nevertheless," he declared; "Estelle is the last girl in the world to exaggerate anything."

The detective watched his man closely. He felt sure that this was no feigned agitation, yet the idea crossed his mind that the cause of it might be other than was suggested. He could not forget that it was in obedience to her father's orders that Miss Armand had broken off her engagement. Jack Derwick stood to gain considerably by the old man's disappearance from the scene. He had been observed, too, entering the very wood where the murder was committed, only a few minutes before Sir William himself entered it.

"May I ask you, Mr Derwick," he said, "why you went to Calthorpe village on the night before you returned to London? And why Miss Armand came to meet you at the village?"

There was a look in his eyes as he spoke which caused Jack Derwick to stiffen in his attitude. Nothing is so difficult to endure as suspicion, however well concealed.

"There was no reason. I went for a walk after I... after our engagement had been broken off. I met the vicar and had tea with him. Miss Armand did not come to meet me. I think she came to speak to her father, who, as I found out afterwards, was at the village inn at the time. When she saw me, however, she turned back."

Biles nodded. His gesture was entirely uncommittal.

"But you walked back with her through the wood to the Hall?"

Jack's face flushed suddenly.

"If those are leading questions put to me in order to get me to commit myself," he declared, "you should know as well as I do, that they are grossly unfair."

"My dear sir, it is my duty to investigate this matter. I can only ask for information from those who were concerned directly or indirectly."

Jack seemed to control himself. The flush passed from his face.

"Miss Armand and I did not return to the Hall together," he said. "I did not speak to Miss Armand at all after she broke off our engagement."

The detective thanked him and rose apparently to go away. He turned at the door, however, and took a step back into the room.

"Please don't think that I suspect you," he said, "or Miss Armand either. So far, I am entirely in the dark. If we could find the man Sawyer with whom Sir William was last seen, we might obtain some light."

"You have no clue to his identity?" It was evident that Jack Derwick refused to re-open the question of his own share in the mystery.

"None. He is said to have travelled to London by the same train as yourself. That is all we know."

Jack started.

"The man in the long ulster! I remember him quite well, because I wondered who he was. Somehow his figure and walk seemed familiar, and yet when I saw his face by one of the station lamps, I realized that I did not know him. He had a beard and moustache, and seemed to be past middle age. I did not notice him on the train or at King's Cross."

"Would you recognize him again if you saw him, do you think?"

"I think so. His eyes were peculiar, small and rather beady, like a rat's eyes."

Biles walked across the Strand to Clement's Inn, where he had a friend, a solicitor, whom he often consulted on points of law. The boy who opened the door in response to his ring told him that Mr Humphreys was in. He was conducted through a room full of old and ageing papers to a snug office overlooking the Law Courts.

He found Mr Humphreys seated beside a big fire reading *The Times*.

"Come along, Biles," that cheerful man cried, "you find me in one of my fits of idleness. For some reason which I have never fathomed, the more I have to do, the less I feel inclined to do it. Today has been overwhelming."

The detective made himself comfortable, and in response to an eager invitation, began to fill his pipe from a tobacco-jar which stood on his friend's desk.

"Tell me," he said, in deliberate tones, "all that you know about the firm of Armand & Butler, Solicitors."

"H'm!"

Mr Humphreys pursed his rather thin lips and brought his fingers together in a gesture of great delicacy.

"You see," he said, "I know so very little. They enjoy a great reputation, of course. But it is the kind of reputation which does not invite the curious. Personally, I should say that everything in that garden is beautiful."

Biles could get no more than this. He went away feeling more despondent than was his wont. It would be possible, of course, to obtain orders to search Sir William's house and possibly to investigate his business dealings, but his professional instinct was against so drastic a course. So far, there was no convincing evidence that the missing lawyer was dead; still less that he had been murdered; for the more he thought about the find of the lens, the less he felt able to rely on it—at least for the present.

He was in this mood when he met Dr Hailey at King's Cross. The doctor, on the contrary, seemed to be full of fresh eagerness. He insisted on Biles joining him for a drink and smoke in his sleeping berth before turning in for the night.

"Has it occurred to you," he asked, "that a hatpin would be an excellent instrument with which to extract its lens from a human eye. Suppose that a woman in a fit of anger..."

"Yes. But she would then be faced by the necessity of getting rid of the body."

"Quite so. And the body has been got rid of, my dear Biles."

His gentle smile played on Dr Hailey's lips.

"A strong young man might easily lift the body of an old one and carry it—in the dusk—a long way without being detected in that operation. You have not searched for a grave, by any chance?"

"No."

Biles's eyes were growing brighter. He realized that he had been concentrating too much on the meagre details which he had so far been able to collect. It was, indeed, quite possible that the murderer, whoever he was, had buried his victim in some other part of the estate. Yet an objection to this theory presented itself to his mind.

"There would scarcely have been time for a funeral of that sort. It is certain that both Derwick and the girl returned to the Hall before dinner."

Dr Hailey took snuff.

"They had an hour, on your own showing," he declared, "and a great deal can be accomplished in that time. Moreover, Derwick dined at Belfort, whereas his train did not leave until after midnight. He could easily have returned on foot to complete his work."

It is one thing, however, to make theories; it is quite another thing to prove them. When Biles retired to his own berth, he realized that the task in front of him was a much bigger one than he had supposed, and that the odds against his accomplishing it were long. He fell asleep with his mind full of new projects.

When, however, he found himself back in the wood at Calthorpe next morning, these projects began to fade. The wood was as inscrutable as ever. Moreover, Superintendent Robson had informed him at breakfast that he had made a search of the whole estate, and that not a leaf appeared to have been disturbed. The idea that Sir William's body had been buried overnight by his murderers receded into the background.

In accordance with his usual methodical custom, he had made an exact note of the spot where the lens had been discovered. He found it at once and pointed it out to Dr Hailey, who proceeded to examine it in his rather casual way. The detective stood a few paces further on so as to give his friend a clear field.

There was a slowness about the doctor's movements which suggested an ox browsing in rich pastures. Every now and then, too, he was in the habit of raising his great head just as oxen do, and surveying the landscape with listless gaze. Yet Biles knew that no detail possessing any significance would escape these calm eyes.

He was not destined to have to wait long for confirmation of this opinion. Dr Hailey beckoned him to approach and showed him a scar on the bole of one of the pine trees. It was a tiny mark, yet it had clearly been made within the last few days.

"Observe the round shape of the break in the bark," the doctor urged. "There is only one thing which I know of that could cause such a mark."

"The ferrule of a walking-stick?"

"Exactly. Sir William, I suppose, like all countrymen, was carrying a stick at the time of his disappearance."

Dr Hailey paused and bent down suddenly, an action for which he was singularly ill-fitted by nature.

"Look here!" he exclaimed.

Biles obeyed and saw another mark on the bole not far from the ground—a mere scrape as it seemed. But what riveted his attention was a small tuft of white hair entangled in the rough bark just above it.

"My God!..."

The doctor drew a glass from his pocket and focussed it on the scrape. Then he stood erect with a sigh.

"As I feared," he said.

He handed the glass to his companion.

"If you look carefully," he told him, "you will see several tiny fragments of skin adhering to the wood. He must have struck his head on this tree as he fell. Probably the thrust with his stick was his last effort at self-defence."

CHAPTER 7
DR HAILEY'S
DEDUCTIONS

"And now," said Dr Hailey, "we must ask ourselves the question how the body, which undoubtedly fell at this spot, was carried away from it."

His eyes, as he spoke, regained their dullness, lost for a moment during the process of his investigation.

"What evidence is there," Biles asked, "that Sir William was dead? He might surely have been wounded only."

The big head shook decisively.

"If the eye alone had been injured, he would not have fallen. The wound must have involved the brain—involved it deeply, too; unless, indeed, there were other wounds, but in that case we should have discovered some blood-stains. So far, I have not detected any of these anywhere."

This reasoning seemed plausible, if not conclusive. Biles nodded agreement. His admiration for the doctor had never been greater than at this moment, yet the sceptical tendency of his mind caused him to point out that it would be difficult to hold an inquest on an eyeball and a tuft of white hairs. Even as he spoke, he felt a little vexed with himself for what struck him suddenly as an ungenerous response to his friend's effort on his behalf. Dr Hailey, however, was unperturbed. He helped himself to snuff, and waved his big hand reassuringly.

"My dear Biles," he exclaimed, "the body we seek must be near this place; very near probably. There is nothing more inconvenient, I can assure you, as a burden than a dead man. Let us clear our minds for a moment. The murderer, whoever he or she may have been, was faced with the same difficulty as we are now facing—only in a more urgent form. The body must be lifted and carried.... Where?"

Again the doctor took snuff.

"I don't know," said Biles, in humble tones. "Had I been the murderer, I should have hesitated... and been lost, no doubt. I fancy I might have thrown it over the cliffs."

"But you have already told me that the sea does not come up to the bottom of those cliffs. The body would have been discovered next morning... and it has not been discovered."

"He might have rowed it out to sea.... supposing that he had a boat handy."

"It is just possible. But the sea is apt, you know, to give up its dead. Have you made enquiries about the boats and their owners, by the way?"

Biles had made no enquiries. He promised to do so at once, but Dr Hailey had other work for him of a more urgent kind. He asked him suddenly to lie down on the ground and permit himself to be lifted and carried a short distance in order to test the probable endurance of the murderer when bearing his victim.

Biles lay down, and next instant felt himself swung up as though he had been a small child. Not until that moment had he realized the enormous strength of the doctor's huge frame. He was carried across his bearer's shoulder with his head to the back and his legs dangling in front. They went quickly for a few paces in the direction of the village, and then the rate of movement began to slacken. After a yard or two more had been covered, Dr Hailey unburdened himself.

"So," he declared, "we can conclude that the first halt was made on or about the circumference of a circle, of which the distance between this spot and the place where the murder was committed is the radius. I make that distance fifty paces.

It brings us clear of the wood on this side, and I think it would bring us to the edge of the cliffs, going in the opposite direction. Suppose we just confirm that for a start."

They walked back to their starting point, and then the doctor paced the distance from there to the cliff edge. He made it forty-five paces exactly. He stood for an instant facing the sea, as though completing a further measurement in his mind, then he turned sharply, and without moving his feet bent, and finally knelt, down. Biles saw him take his glass from his pocket and fix it in his eye in order the better to scrutinise the ground.

Apparently, however, he did not find what he expected to find, for after a few minutes he rose again and walked a short distance along the cliffs. He repeated the same performance in exactly the same way at several different places, before he rejoined the detective. Then he confessed that he had been mistaken.

"It is quite evident that we shall have to abandon the idea that the body was thrown over the cliffs," he declared. "Had that been so, I should have found traces of blood just now. You see, every wound—even a wound in the eye which has proved immediately fatal—bleeds a little. Granting that the murderer carried his victim across his shoulder, some drops of blood must have fallen on the grass at the spot where he reached his journey's end—before he threw the body over. Do you agree?"

"Yes.... But he might have carried the body in his arms, surely?"

"In that case he could not have come so far without pausing, and for the moment, therefore, we may dismiss the one possibility in order to concentrate on the other. When I was a Student Demonstrator in the Anatomy rooms, I used to watch the attendants bringing the bodies to the tables at the beginning of the session. Sometimes they lifted them in their arms from the barrows—if they happened to be working single-handed. It was as much as any man could do. Sir William Armand was a big man, was he not?"

"Oh, yes; a very big man."

They returned again to the scene of the murder, and then Dr Hailey paced the distance he supposed the body might have been carried at a stretch, in the direction of Calthorpe Hall. This brought him to an open space well outside of the little wood and well within view of the village. There did not seem to be much probability that anyone anxious to dispose of a murdered body would choose such a spot as a resting place, even in the dusk of falling night.

The ground on the opposite side of the wood was more hopeful. It sloped here towards the shore of a small creek which separated the grounds of Calthorpe Hall from those of the adjoining estate. A tiny stream ran in the dip and there was a certain amount of undergrowth. When he had determined his distance, the doctor began to survey the ground carefully, and Biles joined him in this laborious task.

They found the signs they were looking for almost simultaneously; a number of dark stains which the rain of the past few days had not obliterated. Dr Hailey rose from his knees, and stretched himself uneasily. He had a single withered leaf in his hand.

"I was not designed by Nature for work of this kind, my dear Biles," he announced, "and I fear I must leave the rest of it to your more supple limbs. I have provided myself with just one specimen which I will examine immediately we get back to the inn. I took the precaution of bringing the necessary apparatus with me." He glanced at his watch. "Do you realize that it is already time for luncheon?"

Mullins, the proprietor of the "Black Bull" had excelled himself with an admirable "spare rib" of pork, which the doctor pronounced the best he had ever tasted. He ate grandly, washing down his meal with copious draughts of the excellent beer the place provided. Impatient as he was to pursue his investigations, Biles could not but admire such detachment. He did not dare to put the questions which were on his lips—and he received no encouragement to that end. On the contrary, the talk was of music and musical instruments, in both of which Dr Hailey took a profound interest.

After lunch, however, business was resumed with energy. The doctor fetched his microscope and a case of little bottles from his bedroom. He proceeded to dissolve some of the stain from the leaf which he had picked up just before coming in. A straw-coloured fluid was the result. He conveyed a few drops of this to a slide, put on a cover glass and examined it.

"The corpuscles are scarcely recognizable," he told his companion, "but I have no doubt that it is blood. However, the spectroscope will soon settle that."

He opened a small leather case, and took out from it what appeared to be a diminutive brass telescope. This he screwed to the eyepiece of the microscope. A single glance sufficed him.

"There is no doubt about it," he announced.

He sat back and opened his snuff-box.

"A most remarkable instrument, this. The spectroscope, as you know, is able to detect blood in bulk, owing to the fact that the red colouring matter produces certain dark bands at certain definite places in the rainbow-like scheme of colours into which the prism splits up ordinary daylight. No other fluid except blood gives quite the same picture. The trouble used to be, however, that unless one had a sufficient quantity of blood, the test was inapplicable. Then, an ingenious mind conceived the idea of combining the spectroscope and the microscope in one instrument. Now even the smallest trace of blood can be detected."

Biles knew little of science, so he merely nodded acquiescence. But Dr Hailey had the born teacher's instinct to be understood at all costs. He explained in detail how the spectroscope was merely a scientific application of the familiar effect of the bevelling of a mirror in producing rainbow-like colours. These colours—there were seven of them—when mingled together made ordinary "white" light. The function of the spectroscope was to separate them out—just as a raincloud does when it produces a rainbow.

"And from that beginning of knowledge," he concluded, "we

have advanced to the possession of a new eye of justice, an instrument capable of detecting blood-stains on a single hair or a single thread."

"You think a British jury could accept this evidence as conclusive?"

"My dear Biles, we are not concerned as yet with a British jury; we should not dream of offering them such evidence. What we must offer is the body of the murdered man itself. This is merely the first stopping place on that quest."

Dr Hailey reached, as he spoke, for the case in which he had fetched his microscope. He took from it a map with which he had provided himself before leaving London. He spread it open on the table before him, and then unscrewed the cap from a pair of compasses which he carried in his pocket. He invited Biles to indicate the exact spot in the wood where the discovery of the lens had been made.

The map was a large-scale one of the kind which military men approve. The wood was clearly and accurately delineated. Biles studied it for a moment and then pointed with his finger to the place he selected. Dr Hailey set one leg of his compasses on this and opened them, so that the other leg fell on the edge of the cliffs.

"That is forty-five paces, as we know," he remarked.

He swung the instrument round, using the scene of the murder as the centre of his circle, until it reached a spot near the creek where they had found the bloodstains. He pressed the point through the sheet at this place, and then described a second circle of the same radius from this new centre.

The circumference of this second circle just reached a road leading from the main highway past the parish church to a small fishing village further up the coast.

"I'm afraid it doesn't take us very much further," said Biles. "He would scarcely risk bringing his victim on to a public way... even in the dark."

Dr Hailey did not reply. He was studying the map intently with that curious dull gaze of his.

"Suppose," he said, after a few minutes, "that we take a walk along this road ourselves and just verify the distances."

They stepped out into the sunlight of a bettering afternoon. Biles lit his pipe and turned up the collar of his coat against the keen wind which already had a nip of frost in it. Their footsteps sounded quite loud in the deep silence of the village street. When they came to the cross-roads, where the byway they were about to explore began. Dr Hailey stopped for a moment and opened his snuff-box.

"You will observe," he pointed out, "that from this spot it is impossible to see any part of the road after it reaches the Vicarage gate. No one standing in the village could therefore know what was going on round that bend—even in full daylight."

He took a double pinch deliberately, apparently well satisfied with his observation, though Biles was unable to see its import. They strolled slowly on past the Vicarage and the church to the spot where the second lap of the murderer's journey might be supposed to have ended.

The road here was without hedges or ditches; nor were there any trees near it. Its surface was rather broken.

A prolonged search revealed absolutely nothing. Biles, whose pipe had gone out, lit it again carefully as a signal, perhaps, that he thought the case hopeless. The doctor, however, was far from ready to abandon his theory.

"We must go back to the place where we found the blood-stains," he declared, "and investigate that more thoroughly."

They tramped across the grass to the bushes flanking the little stream. These now became the objects of Dr Hailey's anxious regard, and very soon he had his reward in the shape of a broken twig over-hanging a patch of rushes. The twig, as he saw at once, was stripped from the stem of the bush to which it belonged, in a downward direction. So must it have snapped if a heavy body was allowed to fall against it.

The rushes, too, though they were withered and broken enough by the rains and winds of the season, were clearly more broken than the others surrounding them. It was obvious that they had been pressed down from above. He bent and examined them, and then called Biles's attention to another and larger bloodstain on the ground beside them.

"It was here, my friend, that he dropped the body in the first instance.... An excellent place, too, where it might have rested for a long time without detection. Notice how, from this spot, you cannot be seen either from the Vicarage or from the village."

Biles looked as directed; it was true. No place in the immediate neighbourhood afforded such immunity from detection.

"Yes," he agreed, "but the body is here no longer."

"Of course not. This murderer, as you must realize by this time, is in many senses an exceptional person. He has completed his work."

"But how, where?"

Dr Hailey did not reply for a moment. Then suddenly Biles saw him start.

"How? Where? Oh, my dear Biles, how blind we can be sometimes, even when we are most anxious to see."

He pointed with his great arm to the roadway they had just left, and cried:

"Where, indeed, should one bury a dead man, but in the graveyard!"

Directly behind the road, surrounded by a low stone wall, was the village churchyard, with its rows of flattening mounds and unsteady tombstones.

CHAPTER 8 MURDER

"The right kind of experiment," Dr Hailey said, "furnishes an answer, just as the right kind of theory propounds a question. You invent your theory and then test it by application to the actual facts. Now, my theory is that the murderer of Sir William Armand left his body in the bushes at the top of the creek and went and dug a grave for that body in the churchyard. After that he returned and conducted the funeral."

Biles and he were seated in the smoking-room of the "Black Bull", drinking vermouth as a preparation for their dinner. They had relinquished their detective work for the day in order, as the doctor said, to think out the next step before taking it.

"But that would surely lead to discovery," the detective objected. "You cannot dig a grave without leaving traces of your digging."

"My dear fellow, you cannot dig a grave at all—at least, not a satisfactory grave—unless you know the way to do it."

"In that case…"

The doctor had his snuff-box in his hand. He closed it with a snap.

"Did you notice," he asked, "that there was a new grave in the churchyard… a very new grave? Now, any full-grown man could re-open a grave which had been recently dug sufficiently to add to its contents…. And there would be nothing left behind, if he exercised even average care, to indicate his handiwork."

"Good heavens…!"

"No; we must not go too fast. It is by no means so clear as all that. In the first place, we have to ask ourselves how the murderer could have known that the churchyard did, in fact, at that time contain a new grave. He must have known this, I think, or else he would not have attempted the plan at all."

Biles frowned as though trying to jog his memory. Suddenly he started.

"Why," he exclaimed, "Jack Derwick had tea with the vicar about an hour before the murder was committed. He must have crossed the very ground we have been working on, for he told me that he came from the Hall along the cliffs. And he must have walked past the churchyard...."

Dr Hailey's eyes narrowed a little, but otherwise he made no sign.

"That may possibly dispose of one objection," he said; "but there is another. You cannot dig a grave without a spade, and sextons are not in the habit of leaving their tools lying about in the churchyard."

"Presuming that Derwick was the murderer, he might have gone back to the Hall and got a spade. There must be plenty of them in the gardener's tool-house, which is probably not kept locked."

Dr Hailey nodded.

"It is possible," he said. "There was plenty of time, certainly. Meanwhile, before we do anything, we must make quite sure that the body really does lie in that new grave. I propose to carry out certain investigations myself tonight. After that, we can institute a public search."

Biles secured a spade from Superintendent Robson, who was continuing his own search, and who came each evening to report progress. He obtained the key of the hotel from Mullins, telling him that, in all probability, his work would detain him most of the night.

"You have no clue, as yet?" said that amiable man, repressing his curiosity with difficulty.

"The mystery, on the contrary, grows deeper every day."

Mullins lowered his voice.

"I did hear," he said, "from one young customer in the bar, Jim

Deiry, that Mr Sawyer, the gentleman who met Sir William here on the night of his disappearance, was quarrelling terrible with him when they left the inn. 'There is no other course open to me as an honest man,' Sir William said to him. He cried out, 'For Heaven's sake, don't rush to such an extreme now when there's no need for it.' That was at the stile leading to the fields. Jim was at his own back door at the time. But after that they moved away, and he heard nothing more."

"H'm!" Biles assumed his most sophisticated attitude. "And did your customer see whether or not they went into the wood together?"

"No, I asked him that; but it was too dark. Mr Sawyer came back within twenty minutes, though, as I know myself...."

Biles retailed this conversation to Dr Hailey, who showed great interest in it, without, however, offering any comment. They dined together, and at dinner the doctor returned at once to the subject of his beloved music, as though he had no other concern in life. He put the proposition to the detective that, strictly speaking, it was erroneous to describe Beethoven as one of the classics. That term ought to be reserved for such composers as Bach. Biles shook his head in dismay.

"I enjoy music," he said, "but I know very little about it."

"My dear sir, that is the position of us all. How can we know much of any mystery so great as this one? When I listen to the fire music in 'The Valkyrie' for example, I feel as though I were looking at the very essence of life, and yet the complete revelation is always denied me. Strangely enough, though, it is different when I hear some of the folk-songs of our own country, things like 'The Raggle Taggle Gipsy'. Then I seem to understand perfectly, without knowing what I understand. Sometimes I wonder if the soul of a nation is not enshrined in its folk music."

He opened his snuff-box. Biles eyed him with a mixture of awe and delight.

"You see, detective work is nothing more nor less than the understanding of human nature. Once you have put yourself completely in the criminal's shoes, his crime becomes more or less obvious; so that music, which reveals the depths of our nature, is the finest of all trainings for this business. It helps us to feel, and so to understand."

After dinner they smoked in silence for a long time. Dr Hailey was in the habit of sleeping a little at this period of the day, but tonight he remained alert and wakeful. Now that he had, as he believed, found the victim, his thoughts began to turn to the murderer. They became concerned with the man Sawyer.

It struck him as astonishing that no one had obtained the slightest information of real value about this strange individual —for his practical mind discounted the finger-print on the port bottle, and the cigarette-end about which Biles had told him. These were identification marks, nothing more. It was necessary, in the first instance, to "catch your hare". He wondered whether a more careful study of the bedroom Sawyer had occupied might not yield some information. Failing that, there was the possibility that intelligent questions addressed to Miss Armand or some of her servants might prove fruitful. It seemed quite certain that this man had had many dealings with the dead solicitor.

At eleven o'clock the two men separated to get their hats and coats. They let themselves out of the front door of the hotel as quietly as possible. Biles had the spade wrapped up in a spare coat which he carried in such a way as to disguise its contents as much as possible. They took the main road down to the village street.

There was a half-moon in the sky and a light mist lay in the hollows, suggesting the presence of water. Dr Hailey stopped, when they approached the church, to admire the scene. He declared that such effects of atmosphere and light were as characteristic of the North Country as are its minglings of outlines of the Fen district.

"And this air, my dear Biles, so strangely resembles champagne in its effect on the spirits!"

The Vicarage was dark and silent behind its hedges. Over its roof they saw the square tower of the church with its four corner-turrets clearly outlined against the pale sky. Their footfalls on the moist surface of the road had an eerie sound.

They came to the gate of the churchyard, passed it, and climbed the wall. Biles going first and helping Dr Hailey to mount. The grass was very wet and slippery, but in spite of this they arrived without mishap at the new grave which they had observed in the afternoon. The doctor took an electric torch from his pocket and switched it on.

The grave appeared to be undisturbed. On the top of it was a glass jelly jar containing some half-withered chrysanthemums which pious hands had placed there. There were no other flowers. Dr Hailey examined the jar carefully; then he moved the beam of light over the raw mound. Suddenly he stooped to make a closer inspection.

"Look!" he commanded his companion.

Biles bent down and saw, on one of the upturned clods, the imprint of a round object. He started.

"The jar!" he exclaimed.

"Just so. That was its original resting place... before the second funeral. No doubt, this detail escaped attention in the darkness."

The doctor stood back, leaning against a tombstone, while Biles took his spade from its cover. The implement gleamed dully in the moonlight. Then the detective began to work at what seemed to be the head of the grave.

He had removed only two or three spadefuls of earth, when he uttered an exclamation of horror. The doctor strode across to his side and ignited his torch.

The yellow beam fell on a mass of white hair dabbled with the graveyard earth.

"My God! it's horrible!" Biles whispered in hoarse tones.

Dr Hailey knelt down, and with his hands broke the soil away from the dead man's brow. Then he asked his companion to dig again a little further down the grave, so that they might expose the features. He remained kneeling while this operation was in process of completion. When it was finished Biles knelt also, and assisted in removing the last fragments of earth.

Then a sight truly appalling met their eyes. Sir William's eyes had been stabbed through with a ferocity which surely was without equal in the annals of crime. His face, too, was bruised and discoloured as though it had been struck with a heavy fist.

The doctor touched the edges of the wounds, and then examined them with his eyeglass.

"It is impossible to decide at once," he declared, "whether or not they were inflicted after or before death."

He rose up and brushed the mud from his knees.

"I fancy we need no further confirmation," he remarked. "You had better replace the earth."

He took snuff rather more freely than usual while Biles was engaged on this task. When it was completed, he examined the grave again with his lamp, suggesting one or two finishing touches. Then they made their way back in silence to the inn. Dr Hailey poured out two stiff glasses of whisky from the bottle which Mullins had left for them by his direction. He handed one of these to the detective.

"Well?" he asked.

"It's more horrible by far than I expected."

Biles took a big mouthful of the whisky. His face was distinctly paler than usual.

"And also more interesting. I confess I was not prepared for so much bruising."

"But the eyes.... Why should he put out his eyes in that... awful... manner?"

"My dear Biles, once a man has committed murder he is very apt to become a demon. Fear is the cruellest of all the human emotions... and the most senseless. You must have seen that for yourself many a time. Some murderers—quite gentle people at other times—positively hack their victims to pieces—after they have killed them."

"I can scarcely believe it of Derwick, though. A man of his education..."

Dr Hailey shook his head.

"Above all things, do not let us jump to conclusions. Derwick may be the murderer, but at present that is a mere guess. Before we can afford to suspect anyone, we must find the man Sawyer…."

CHAPTER 9
BROKEN GLASS

The discovery of Sir William Armand's body thrilled the whole country. The London evening papers of the following day contained full accounts of the "exhumation" which had been carried out during the early afternoon. The Black Bull Inn positively hummed with local and special correspondents, each intent on his own explanation of the mystery.

Mullins supplied those enterprising gentlemen with plenty of clues and very soon the public learned all about the mysterious Mr Sawyer, and the other actors in the drama. Happily, it learned nothing whatever about Dr Hailey, who took the precaution of absenting himself from the village during the whole day.

He returned late at night to find Biles in a very cheerful state of mind. The detective had been able to secure the exclusive use of a small room on the ground floor, and so was safe from the attentions of the journalists. He greeted his friend most heartily.

"I had enormous credit," he declared, "for your work. But I kept my word and never so much as mentioned your name. I don't mind owning, though, that I felt a cur. They took the body to the mortuary at Belfort. The inquest opens tomorrow."

"It will be adjourned, of course?"

"Oh, yes."

"And then...?"

Biles shook his head.

"I can't see any light," he confessed. "We can't arrest anybody as yet, but now, of course, there will be a fearful hue and cry. The place is full of journalists tonight, and more are arriving tomorrow. It's what the papers call a first-class sensation."

"You've taken possession of everything, I suppose?"

"Not yet. I'm going to search the house tomorrow morning first thing. Miss Armand will be a witness, and Mullins here. Later on we shall summon Derwick and Blunder, Sir William's partner."

Dr Hailey went to the sideboard and poured himself out a glass of whisky. He turned to his companion with his drink in his hand.

"I fear I have an unpleasant surprise for you," he said, in his calmest tones. "Miss Armand has been missing since the early afternoon."

"What!"

"While you were all busy in the churchyard, she seems to have driven off with some stranger who came to the Hall just after midday in a big car. She had not returned at nine o'clock."

Biles had become rather flushed while the doctor was speaking.

"Why the deuce didn't we keep an eye on her," he cried. "These local police are worse than useless. I told Robson early in the week that he was to have the Hall watched."

"But, my dear Biles, the lady is a free agent."

Apparently, that fact had, for the moment, escaped the detective's mind.

"Still, we could have seen whom she travelled with—and followed her to her destination. Now she's probably in London… anywhere. It will be another case of Sawyer. How did you find this out?"

"By the simple process of calling to inquire. I went for a long walk today to Bamburgh. On the way back, it occurred to me that I might possibly be of some service to the poor lady in her most tragic circumstances, but she had already gone when I reached Calthorpe Hall. I met the vicar on the same errand as myself, and returned with him to dinner... a most interesting man!... We went back to the Hall about nine o'clock, but she had not returned."

Biles declared that he must inform Scotland Yard immediately. He ordered out the hotel car and drove off to Belfort to send a telegram. Dr Hailey began to open a large roll of newspapers which had arrived for him by post that afternoon.

The roll contained back numbers of *The Times* and the *Morning Post* for a whole month. He addressed himself to the work of studying these carefully, page by page and issue by issue. Occasionally he cut out items of news which interested him and placed them in his pocket-book. He had made but little progress by the time Biles returned.

"I drove round by the Hall on the way back," the latter told him. "She has not returned. It seems that the car was a hire from Newcastle, but there's no description of its occupant worth listening to." He added bitterly: "I've left a policeman in charge now. Poor old Robson nearly had a fit when I told him; he would have sent the entire constabulary of the district."

"The thing that is puzzling me at present," Dr Hailey said, "is why Miss Armand should have published an announcement of the breaking off of her engagement in both *The Times* and the *Morning Post*. She must have been very anxious to let the whole world know, and yet you say that she told you her feelings for Derwick had not changed."

"She told me that."

"If we believe her it can only mean that she did it for Derwick's good. In other words, there was some ugly revelation coming."

Biles nodded. "I thought of that."

"Connected, undoubtedly, with the man Sawyer, but not connected with Derwick."

"That was what I hoped we should be able to get some light on at the inquest. I am certain that Miss Annand knew the nature of her father's trouble."

Dr Hailey took snuff.

"So we arrive," he said, "at the conclusion that she has probably run away in order to avoid answering questions, and not because she fears being accused of murder. Clearly, we must answer the questions ourselves in her absence."

"I only wish we could."

"I took the liberty," the doctor said, "of making a rather careful search of your bedroom this morning before I went out. You told me it was the room which Sawyer occupied during his visit here. I made one small discovery."

He felt in his waistcoat pocket as he spoke, and took out a small paper parcel. This he opened, disclosing two very minute fragments of brown glass. These were bent circular fashion. He fitted them together to make a ring and pushed this gently across the table to Biles.

"They are not yours, I take it?" he asked.

"No; have you any idea what they are?"

"I know exactly what they are.... Any doctor must know. They are portions of a phial which contained hypodermic pellets. Brown glass is used in order to exclude the light. I can even go further than that and say that the phial probably contained atropine, morphia, or strychnine. It is too small for the size of pellet in which most other drugs are made up. Unhappily, I have not, so far, been able to discover any more of it. These portions, as you can see, were broken off when the cork was taken out; they are from the very top of the tube."

"So Sawyer is a drug maniac."

"Possibly."

Dr Hailey drew the fragments of glass back towards him, and gazed at them for a few seconds in silence.

"The presumption is quite strong," he remarked, "that this was a new tube. Once a tube has been opened, it seldom gets broken at subsequent openings... at least, that is my experience. Did you notice that one or two small threads are still adhering to one of the pieces of glass?"

Biles had not noticed, but on re-examining the glass with a magnifier, he agreed.

"They are from the cotton-wool plug with which these phials are always sealed. Now, my own dealings with drug-takers has led me to think that most of them are exceedingly careless. I expected to find the plug of cotton-wool in the fender where I found the glass—but it was not there. The chamber-maid, too, is quite sure that she did not notice it. It would seem to follow that it was carefully replaced before the cork was re-inserted."

The doctor paused and again took snuff.

"You mean," Biles said, "that you suspect it was not for his own use that Sawyer opened this phial."

"I confess the idea has occurred to me."

Biles frowned slightly, as though this new complication disturbed him.

"I don't see," he remarked, "why even a murderer should wish to do his work twice over. If Sawyer meant to knock out his victim, why should he try to poison him as well?"

Dr Hailey did not answer this question. Instead, he asked whether the detective had made any further examination of the body after its arrival at the mortuary. Biles told him that he had, and that a post-mortem examination had been ordered for the following morning.

"The coroner did not think it necessary to send for the Home Office people, so one of the local doctors is going to do it. I suggested that you might care to be present, and I have to tell you that no objection will be offered to this."

"I shall avail myself of that permission."

"Those bruises on the face which you thought were made by the murderer's fists," Biles added, "did not look so bad when we examined them carefully. They might even have occurred when the old man fell against the tree trunk. The real mystery is the condition of the eyes. In all my experience I have never seen anything to approach that for sheer ferocity."

Dr Hailey rose to go to bed. Very carefully he wrapped up the pieces of glass and returned them to his waistcoat pocket. When he had gone, Biles lit a final pipe and tried to collect his thoughts.

In his own mind, he had already decided that the burden of evidence was against Jack Derwick. The disappearance of Estelle Armand, he felt, strongly supported that idea. She knew why her father had objected to her engagement, and she admitted the validity of the objection. But at the same time she was in love with the young barrister. What more natural than that she should try by all means in her power to shield him from justice.

It was not easy to argue with Dr Hailey, who seemed to have a theory of his own, but Biles had already constructed what seemed to him a plausible story of the crime. He supposed that some discreditable episode in Jack Derwick's life had come to the knowledge of Sir William, perhaps through the agency of the man Sawyer. Sir William's austerity was well-known, and his natural inclination would be to order his daughter to break off her engagement at once. No doubt, the girl had given her lover some idea of the charges against him and urged him to try to set himself right with her father.

What followed seemed obvious enough from this point of view. Derwick, the rejected lover, threatened with a terrible exposure, must have lost control of himself. It was certain that he had wandered about the estate in the most irresponsible way immediately after hearing the news. It was also beyond dispute that he had been hanging round the hotel where Sir William and Sawyer were closeted together. He went into the wood a very short time before the murdered man entered it....

And then there was the damning fact that he had walked over the very ground across which, later in the day, the corpse was carried. He, alone, of all the actors in the drama, certainly knew of the fresh grave in the churchyard.

That circumstance seemed to Biles to exclude the possibility of Sawyer's having committed the murder. Whoever this individual might be, he was a complete stranger to Calthorpe. There was the authority of Mullins for the idea that he had not left the inn during the whole day of the murder, until he went out with Sir William. He had returned, too, almost immediately on that occasion and remained indoors until he was driven off to catch his train at Belfort. It was utterly impossible that he could have carried out the funeral of his victim even if he had committed the murder.

Moreover, the words overheard by Mullins's customer suggested that Sawyer was pleading for Derwick, against Sir William's determination to ruin him.

"There is no other course open to me as an honest man."

"For Heaven's sake don't rush to such an extreme, when there's no need for it."

No doubt the fellow was a vulgar blackmailer, who had expected to make a few pounds by his disclosures, but not to precipitate a violent upheaval. He had lost his nerve at the end and cringed—probably because he feared the vengeance of Derwick.

Biles wondered whether or not that vengeance had already overtaken him. A man who has murdered once does not, as a rule, hesitate to repeat the crime when the same or a greater incentive urges him to that course. Then he wondered whether or not Estelle Armand had positive knowledge that her lover was a murderer. She might or might not have discovered him. In any case it was clear that her suspicions must be strongly aroused....

The only real difficulty seemed to be the horrible nature of the crime. Biles could understand one man knocking another down with the intention to kill; he could not understand any man deliberately putting out the eyes of his victim. Such cold barbarity was foreign to his conception of human nature. He resolved to discover whether or not there was a history of insanity in the Derwick family.

CHAPTER 10 THE INQUEST OPENED

The first surprise of the inquest on Sir William Armand, was the appearance in court of Jack Derwick. He had arrived by the night train and gone, in the first instance, to Calthorpe Hall, where he learned of the disappearance of Estelle. His anxiety, when he returned to Belfort, was evident.

His presence surprised Biles exceedingly. However, he had plenty of experience of the daring of criminals, and determined not to allow the fact to influence the manner in which he presented his evidence; but during the whole course of that evidence he watched the young barrister as closely as possible.

The story he told was listened to by a crowded court with the very closest attention. He described his preliminary investigations at some length, dwelling especially on the fact that Miss Armand had told him that, though she had broken off her engagement, her feelings had not changed. Then he traced, step by step, the search which had led to the finding of the dead man's body. Finally, in describing Miss Armand's disappearance, he contrived to make it quite clear in what direction his own suspicions lay. Judging by their expressions, the jurymen appeared to share his views when he stood down from the box.

The next witness was Superintendent Robson. His evidence was largely of a confirmatory nature. Then, at his own request, Jack Derwick was sworn.

His features, Dr Hailey noticed, were haggard, and his hands trembled slightly, but he answered the questions put to him by the coroner, in a clear strong voice and with complete frankness. It was quite true that he had seen the new grave when he passed the churchyard on the afternoon of the murder. He distinctly recollected seeing it. It was also true that he had observed Miss Armand coming to the inn, and that she had turned back when she saw him. He did not speak to her again before his departure.

"Did you meet Sir William Armand in the wood on your way to the Hall?" the coroner asked.

"No, sir."

"Do you know the reason why Sir William desired his daughter to break off her engagement to marry you?"

Jack shook his head sadly.

"No. I begged Miss Armand to tell me, but she refused absolutely, on the ground that her father had exacted a promise of secrecy."

The coroner leaned forward.

"Are you prepared to tell the jury that you have no idea whatever of the nature of the objection to your proposed marriage?" he asked, in slow tones.

"Yes, sir."

One of the jurymen interposed to ask whether the witness had by any chance seen the man Sawyer at Belfort Station, and Jack told him that he had noticed a man whose figure and walk seemed somehow familiar, but when he happened to obtain a glimpse of his face, he realized that he had been mistaken.

"I fancy," he added, "that this must have been Sawyer, from the descriptions I have since read."

Again the coroner leaned forward. He asked:

"You have no idea why Miss Armand left home yesterday, or who her companion was?"

"None. I came this morning in the hope of being of some service to her in her trouble. I have not heard from her at all since our engagement was broken."

The Vicar of Calthorpe, the Rev Hargreave Willoughby, was

the next witness. He gave formal evidence, about the grave and its rightful occupant, and confirmed the statement that Jack had taken tea with him on his invitation on the evening of the murder.

"Did he tell you that his engagement had just been broken off?" the coroner enquired.

The witness moved uneasily, clasping his hands in front of him, and again unclasping them.

"He did. He appeared to be very much depressed. I concluded from his manner that Sir William Armand was dissatisfied at the match in some way, for he told me that Miss Armand was obeying her father in sending him away."

"He said nothing to suggest to you that he might bear Sir William any great ill-will?"

"Nothing at all."

The vicar was followed by Mullins of the "Black Bull" and then the coroner called Dr Williamson, who had that morning performed the post-mortem on the body of the murdered solicitor. He asked him to what he ascribed death.

"To a penetrating wound of the brain in the region of the left eye socket," said the doctor.

The answer seemed to surprise the coroner, who apparently had already formed the idea that Sir William had been struck down in the first instance, and mutilated afterwards.

"So," he said, "the bruises on the dead man's head and face were not so serious as they appeared."

"They were not serious. It is my opinion that they may have been caused when Sir William fell and struck his head on the trunk of the tree. Two of the bruises were certainly caused in this fashion, because small pieces of bark have been driven into the skin."

"What about the wound in the right eye?"

"No, it does not appear to have reached the brain at all."

The doctor further stated that he believed the wounds might have been caused by a large pocket knife.

"But how, in that case," the coroner asked, "do you account for them? Surely it would be difficult to stab a man in the eye while he retained possession of himself?"

"It would be very difficult. As it happens, however. I am in a position to offer an explanation which, to my own mind, at any rate, is satisfying. *The fact is that, before he was murdered, Sir William Armand was drugged!*"

To say that this statement created a sensation in the tightly packed court room, would be to minimise entirely its effect. The reporters looked up sharply from their notebooks; the members of the public gasped. Even the policemen on duty craned their necks. The coroner's clear voice when he spoke came as a relief.

"You are really in possession of evidence to that effect?" he asked.

"Indisputable evidence. On the back of Sir William's left thigh, about three inches above the knee, I found a small swelling with the mark of a needle-puncture in the centre of it. I have satisfied myself that this represents what remains of a hypodermic injection administered shortly before—but still an appreciable time before—the death of the recipient. I may say that I am supported in this view by my colleague, Dr Hailey of Harley Street, who was present and assisted me at the autopsy this morning."

There was a moment of profound silence; then the coroner asked:

"Will you explain to the jury how you believe this crime to have been committed."

"So far as my examination goes," the doctor declared in his emotionless, practical tones, "I imagine that Sir William Armand was knocked down, in the first instance, either by a blow or by being jostled. As soon as he fell, his assailant plunged the needle of a hypodermic syringe, filled, of course, in advance with a suitable drug, into his thigh, and pressed home the piston."

"But surely such an operation would present tremendous difficulty?"

"No, sir, it would not. It could be accomplished in an instant with but little pain to the victim."

Dr Williamson added, however, that he felt in duty bound to explain to the court that Sir William himself was possessed of a hypodermic syringe.

"As his doctor, I was called pretty frequently to attend him for a severe form of neuralgia which came on very suddenly. Sometimes I was not immediately available, and so I instructed Miss Armand how to give him a hypodermic injection of morphia, and left her a syringe and a supply of tablets. I am of opinion, however, that this dose in the thigh was not administered in that fashion."

Again a rustle of excitement betrayed the feelings of the spectators. The coroner's brows narrowed.

"It is certainly a most extraordinary case," he declared. "In view of what you say, the wounds in the eyes become almost inexplicable. Indeed, there is so much mystery about the whole affair that I feel the only course open to me is to adjourn the inquest for a week."

Dr Hailey returned with Biles to Calthorpe. The latter was rather depressed because he found it difficult to fit the drugging of the murdered man into his theory of the crime. He confessed to himself that nothing was more unlikely than that Derwick should have taken Miss Armand's syringe or attempted to use it.

He communicated those doubts to his friend while they drank their aperitif in the inn before dinner.

Dr Hailey nodded.

"We shall have to think again," he said, laconically.

"But how? If Derwick is not the murderer, who is? It is impossible that Sawyer could have buried the body in the time at his disposal. Besides, we have failed to discover any clue to the man's identity. At one time I thought he might be Blunder, Sir William's partner. I sent a man round to his office to make observations, but it was a wild goose chase."

"In what way?"

Biles lit his pipe with care before he replied.

"Mr Blunder has no scar on his left thumb—or either of his thumbs. You remember how I found a scar mark on the finger-print I discovered on the port bottle here. It can be said for certain that Mr Blunder did not open that bottle, whereas we know that Mr Sawyer did. Moreover, Mr Blunder does not smoke Russian cigarettes."

The doctor inclined his head slightly. He appeared to be satisfied.

"You don't happen to have kept one of the photographs of that finger-print, do you?" he asked.

"Oh, yes."

Biles opened his pocket-book and handed a card across the table. Dr Hailey examined it closely with his magnifying glass.

"May I keep it?"

"Certainly, I have another."

CHAPTER 11
SCOTLAND
YARD ACTS

Dr Hailey returned to London the next morning. He had spent longer than he intended on the Armand case; nevertheless he promised Biles to return for the adjourned inquest.

Left to himself, the detective began to hark back to his first theory. After all, he argued, there was no absolute certainty in the matter. It was possible, if not probable, that Miss Armand had herself supplied her lover with the syringe. Generally speaking, women were not the instigators of crime, but there were, as he knew well, exceptions to that rule. Faced with a choice between her father's scruples and her lover's safety, many a girl might become a criminal.

The more he considered this aspect of the matter, the more it appealed to him as the probable solution. Miss Armand had come to meet her lover at the inn and had turned back towards the wood on seeing him. They must have met in the wood, and she could then have supplied him with the syringe, ready filled. That, perhaps, was an afterthought on her part, a kind of sop to her conscience, so that she might console herself with the reflection that, at any rate, her father had not suffered.

The idea of delivering the fatal blow in the eyes became more understandable on this assumption. It avoided the real danger of shedding much blood, and it was, perhaps, the most instantaneous way of accomplishing the murder. Granted that Estelle Armand hid beneath her frank appearance of girlishness the heart of a Lady Macbeth, this surely was exactly how she would have planned her father's death.

The idea of burying the body in the village churchyard was worthy of the rest of the scheme. It betrayed, Biles felt, the master criminal mind. But for the single chance that one of the eye lenses had become detached, it must assuredly have succeeded, for, brilliant as had been Dr Hailey's work on the case, it could not even have been begun had not the clue of the lens been discovered.

If the specimen which had been sent to the Home Office for analysis really contained morphia, the case would be strengthened, because the contents of the phial found in Sawyer's room were unknown, whereas it was certain that Miss Armand possessed a supply of this drug.

He had just reached this conclusion when Superintendent Robson called to tell him that the walking-stick which the murdered man always carried, had been found washed up on the shore below Calthorpe Hall. That was not, of course, proof that it had been thrown into the sea at the same spot. But it served in a way as confirmatory evidence.

The rest of the day was spent at Calthorpe Hall, in a minute examination of every possible source of information. Biles excelled at the work and enjoyed it. He found, as he had expected to find, that the sealed deed-box in Sir William's study was missing. That, he made no doubt, had been taken away by Miss Armand. Nor could he discover any trace of the hypodermic syringe or the pellets of morphia. This latter fact removed his last doubts.

When his survey was complete, he began the examination of the servants. This took place in the study, each member of the staff being introduced separately by a policeman who had been told off for the duty. The head gardener came first on the list.

He was an old man who had been a very long time in the employment of the Armands. It was obvious that the tragic events of the last few days had distressed him greatly. Indeed, Biles found it difficult to engage his attention to the questions he asked him, and even more difficult to get satisfactory answers.

One fact, however, was easily obtained: the shed in which spades and other tools were kept was never locked. Anybody who knew the place could easily enter it at any time. Work in the garden, of course, stopped at sundown, and after that the place was deserted.

"You didn't miss a spade on the morning after Sir William disappeared?"

"No, sir. There was no spade missing."

The chauffeur was positive that the car had not been used for two days before the crime. The last time he had taken it out was to fetch Sir William himself from Belfort on his return from London.

Biles started slightly at this information, but immediately controlled himself. He had not known that Sir William had been away from home recently.

"How long had your master been in London?" he asked the man.

"Two days. I drove him to the station when he went away."

"Did you notice anything peculiar about him when he came back?"

"Well, sir, he usually spoke to me before we drove off, but this time he never said a word. I remember thinking that he must be very tired or unwell."

"The car has not been out since the murder?"

"Only to take Mr Derwick and his valet to Belfort. I left him at the 'Queen's Head' in the town."

Biles looked up and fixed the chauffeur with his keen eyes:

"You didn't happen to see the car in which Miss Armand went away yesterday, did you?"

"No, sir. Yesterday was my day off, and I was in Belfort most of the time. That is where my parents live."

The butler, however, had seen the car, and spoken to the driver. It was a hire from a Newcastle garage. The visitor whom it brought to Calthorpe Hall was a stranger to himself, but, as he had been but a short time in the service of the family, this was not a matter of surprise.

"A short man, sir, with a grey moustache and wearing broad-rimmed spectacles. Looked to me a little like a foreigner, he did, but spoke English perfectly, if I may say so."

"Did he stay to luncheon?"

"Oh, no, sir. He was 'ere only about half an hour." The butler added that his opportunities of observation had been limited, as Miss Armand dispensed with his services as soon as her visitor arrived.

"You didn't happen to notice whether or not he was smoking?"

"Yes, sir. He was smoking a big cigar when I opened the door to him."

The rest of the servants' evidence merely confirmed what was already known. On the afternoon of the murder Jack Derwick had been seen going out alone along the cliffs. Miss Armand went out later. None of the servants saw them return; indeed, none of them, except the butler and chauffeur, knew until late in the evening that Jack had left the house.

It is one thing, however, to have a theory; it is quite another to present it to a jury. The really weak point in the charge against Derwick was, as Biles clearly recognized, the absence of any clue to the reason why Sir William had objected to him as a son-in-law. Information on that point had been shared by three people, of whom one was dead and two were now missing. He turned over the possibilities in his mind as he walked back to the "Black Bull".

It was a clear night with all the glory of a Northumbrian sunset in the western sky. The sea lay like a mirror towards the horizon, a great stillness possessed the earth. When he came to the pine wood, he stood still to listen to the faint lapping of the swell on the rocks at the foot of the cliffs. It seemed strange, grotesque almost, that this serene loveliness should have been the scene of such an appalling crime.

The next morning found him closeted with his Chief in Scotland Yard. He recounted in detail exactly what he had found and the inferences he had drawn, watching, while he spoke, the cold clear face of this master detective. The Chief remained silent until he had finished; he gave no sign of agreement or dissent, but before the whole story was told, his decision had been taken.

"It is enough to justify an immediate arrest," he said. "I think, myself, it is enough to hang any man. Remember, we are not concerned with motives, except in so far as they help to explain conduct. That is a first principle of law."

Biles felt a thrill of satisfaction. During the night, in the train, he had passed through a fresh period of doubt, and had felt his chain of evidence snapping in his hands. But this practical brain was not likely to make a mistake. The number of men Scotland Yard has placed in the dock on the capital charge, and failed to convict, is very small.

"The way it strikes me," the Chief said, in his abrupt, incisive tones, "is this: Derwick was rejected as Miss Armand's lover in the afternoon, for a reason we need not trouble about. But it was Sir William and not the girl who rejected him. He was seen entering the wood a few minutes before Sir William and the man Sawyer entered it. Miss Armand was with him or near him. Sawyer returned to the hotel within a few minutes. Nobody knows exactly when Derwick returned—but in any case he had ample time to bury the body as it was found to have been buried. Moreover, he had access to a hypodermic syringe and morphia, and to a spade.... You'll be interested to know that it was morphia —a very large dose of it too—which was administered hypodermically to the murdered man. I have just had a report from the Home Office people. In the circumstances, we can definitely exclude Sawyer, who could not possibly have carried out the full programme, however active he might have shown himself. Who remains? Not a breath of suspicion, so far as I can see, attaches to anybody else. Moreover, there is the disappearance of Miss Armand.... I fancy they made absolutely certain that the body would never be discovered."

"As you put it," Biles said, "it does seem to be pretty damning. I confess I hesitated a little over some of the details."

The Chief smiled. "One always does that when one has to bear the strain of deduction and search. The case is so strong that I propose to arrest Jack Derwick just as soon as I can get out a warrant. He will be taken to Newcastle tomorrow, and handed over to the local police. In the meantime, I fancy you had better make a careful examination of his rooms in The Temple as soon as he is out of them."

Two hours later Biles was seated at a window overlooking the gardens of King's Bench Walk. Before him, spread out on a card table, were a collection of miscellaneous articles which he had discovered in various drawers and receptacles of Derwick's flat, and which seemed worthy of further scrutiny. The collection included a cane with a loaded head, a large pocket knife, and a tiny dagger of Italian workmanship. So far as could be seen, both knife and dagger were entirely free of stains of any kind.

When he had completed his survey, Biles rang the bell for the valet, Bayne, who remained on the premises by his express order. This young man was very pale, and appeared to retain his self-control with great difficulty. He protested that at no time had he entertained the slightest suspicion of his master.

"Do you remember the night on which Sir William was murdered," Biles rapped out sharply.

"Very well, sir."

"When your master came in from his walk, were his clothes soiled in any way."

"I did not notice any soiling, sir."

"Think again, if you please. Think very carefully."

"Possibly there may have been a little mud on one of the sleeves.... I remember now brushing it off the next day."

Biles raised his eyes in a glance of warning.

"This is a very serious matter, remember," he said.

The valet wilted.

"There was mud on the left sleeve, at the elbow," he declared.

"Mr Derwick told me he had been leaning on the wall of the churchyard."

"You still have the suit, I suppose."

"Oh, yes, sir. Shall I fetch it?"

The valet went out of the room and returned in a few minutes with a brown tweed knickerbocker suit. Biles glanced sharply at the shoulders. They were quite unsoiled. He noticed, however, a dark stain at the back, low down, near the hem.

"How long has that been there?" he asked.

"I don't know, sir. I didn't notice it before."

If this was a bloodstain, then the case against Derwick would be complete, for so must blood have fallen from a body carried on the wearer's shoulder, presuming the body to be wounded about the head and to be carried feet foremost. Biles felt his pulses quicken with excitement.

"I put it to you," he declared, "that that stain was not present until after the murder of Sir William Armand. Use your memory again on that point."

Once more the valet wilted visibly.

"I certainly don't remember noticing it before then," he stammered.

"But you have noticed it before now?"

"I... yes, sir."

Biles took the coat away with him and sent it direct to the Home Office. Next morning he had a report on the nature of the stain.

His suspicions were confirmed. The stain was blood.

CHAPTER 12 A BOW
AT A VENTURE

Dr Hailey practised his profession in a desultory sort of fashion. He was a man of some independent means, a bachelor, able to gratify his personal tastes. Consequently when he returned to Harley Street it was not to see large numbers of patients. The fascination of the Armand case possessed him too completely for that, and so far, the most fascinating observation which he had made in connection with that case was one which he had kept to himself.

It pleased him to know this as, for the tenth time, he turned his magnifying glass on the photograph of the finger-print with which Biles supplied him. There could be no doubt whatever about it; the scar on which so much store was set by his friend was a fake. Whoever Sawyer might be, he was clearly an artist.

But he had not been quite clever enough. In cutting out the tiny piece of material which he had used to disguise his finger-print, he had made one slip. He had left a single ragged point, and that point had got bent over. No scar of Nature's handiwork ever possessed such a break in its continuity.

It followed that the acquittal of Mr Blunder of all share in the mystery was not justified. The solicitor might, of course, be innocent; but the fact that his two thumbs were intact did not, as Biles imagined, constitute a proof of this.

Dr Hailey reached for the telephone book which lay on his desk, and looked up the number of the firm of Armand & Blunder, Clement's Inn. He gave this number and was answered by a voice which he guessed to be that of a clerk.

"You may remember he said in quick tones, "that I rang up last Monday week to ask for an appointment and you told me that Mr Blunder was ill."

"Oh yes, sir.... But who is that speaking?"

"My name is Smith, Albert Smith. Is Mr Blunder back to work yet?"

"Oh yes, sir. He was only away for a day...."

Dr Hailey hung up the receiver very quietly, so as to convey the impression that the line had been cut off. A smile flickered for a moment at the corners of his mouth. He consulted the telephone book a second time and then gave another number—that of Mr Blunder's private house in Camden Hill. A woman's voice answered him.

"Is that Mrs Blunder?"

"No, sir, I'm her maid. If you hold the line...."

"No, no, please," Dr Hailey cried, "I only rang up to ask if Mr Blunder is better. I heard he had been confined to the house two days ago."

The girl's voice took on an eager tone:

"Oh yes, thank you. But he's quite well again now. Who shall I say rang up?"

"Mr Albert Smith."

So Blunder had been confined to the house on both occasions when mysterious strangers visited Calthorpe. The fact seemed to merit some further investigation.

Dr Hailey chuckled as he thought of the moment when the lawyer returned home, to learn of a further enquiry after his health by Mr Albert Smith. It was just possible that on receipt of that news he would do something foolish—but probably not. Wise men always wait as long as possible before doing anything. He wondered if Estelle had been taken to Camden Hill; if so, she was probably safe for the moment. If not...

He got up and rang the bell. His butler, a man almost, though not quite, of his own dimensions, answered it.

"Jenkins," he said, "I want the car immediately."

A new Daimler came to the door. Dr Hailey gave the address of Armand & Blunder in Clement's Inn. Then he lay back on the deep cushions and closed his eyes. Driving in London was one of the new delights of his life, but the delight was not complete unless he was able to enjoy it in somnolence.

He mounted the stairs to the lawyer's office slowly, and handed his card to the clerk in the anteroom, who took it into his employer's room at once. A moment later he re-emerged and opened the door for the visitor to pass in.

Mr Blunder was seated at his desk with a pen in his hand, but Dr Hailey saw that he had not been writing. He rose at once and bowed.

"Dr Hailey, of Harley Street," he said, using the phrase which had been employed at the inquest at Calthorpe the day before, and reported in all the newspapers.

"Quite so. I ventured to trouble you, because I have been helping my friend, Inspector Biles, of Scotland Yard, during the last few days, in connection with this tragic affair of your partner. There are one or two matters which puzzle us very much and which you may possibly be able to clear up.

He watched the lawyer carefully as he spoke, but his eyes seemed utterly listless.

"I am at your service, of course," said Mr Blunder, with an expression of deep concern which, it had to be admitted, was entirely unforced.

"The first point is this...."

Dr Hailey fumbled in the tail pocket of his morning coat and produced a memorandum book. He turned over several of the leaves hurriedly.

"Sir William's life seems to have been insured for a very large sum... judging by a memorandum which was found in a sealed box in his study...."

He glanced up from his notes as he spoke. The face opposite him had changed so that he scarcely recognized it.

"You are ill, my friend...."

"No.... It's nothing...."

The round pebbly face of the lawyer was suffused suddenly with blood, changing from pallor to redness. He mastered himself with a supreme effort which won the doctor's admiration.

"I believe what you say is correct," he managed to ejaculate. "The exact sum was £50,000."

Dr Hailey made a note.

"Unfortunately," he declared, "the box has now disappeared with Miss Armand. It was she who opened it and gave us this information, and consequently we were anxious to have it checked if possible."

Again he glanced up, but this time his victim was forewarned. Whatever relief he experienced was hidden under an appearance of unruffled calm.

"Your partner was a healthy man, wasn't he?"

"So far as I know."

Dr Hailey replaced his notebook in his pocket.

"One question more, if I may," he said, "and then I shall apologize for troubling you and take myself off. When Sir William visited you here, a few days before his death, he did not, did he, require to send for a doctor?"

Again there was not a quiver of the lawyer's eyelids.

"Oh, no," he said. "On the contrary, he appeared to be in excellent health."

The doctor bowed himself out. He descended the stairs as slowly as he had mounted them. He returned at once to Harley Street. So far, his investigation had yielded the results he expected, but he realized now that the task he had set himself was more difficult than he had supposed. Mr Blunder and Sawyer might be the same individual, but that would take a great deal of proving. He had to confess himself nearly as much in the dark as before.

He tried to imagine the effect on a jury of such evidence as was at his disposal, and perceived that it would be negligible. Even supposing that Mr Blunder had been absent from business on the days of the stranger's appearances at Calthorpe, what did that signify? And how, as Biles had asked, could he have killed and buried Sir William in the space of twenty minutes? Moreover, where was the certainty that the pieces of glass found in the fender of the bedroom at the "Black Bull" really belonged to Sawyer at all? Numbers of people, after all, used hypodermic syringes. His question about the insurance policy, too, might well have been misunderstood. It might have appeared as a direct accusation since, in all probability, Blunder was the executor of Sir William's will and a beneficiary under it. Very few men can bear even a hint that they may have been concerned in a criminal action... murder especially.

Compared with the case against Derwick, this one was, he recognized, merely contemptible.

But there was a tough quality in Dr Hailey's character, which resisted all argument when argument was opposed to instinctive feeling. The great detective, after all, is born, not made. He spent an uneasy night examining again all the points in the case and attempting to fit together in a new way all the conflicting items of evidence. It was consequently nearly eleven o'clock when he breakfasted. At three o'clock in the afternoon, just when he was about to enjoy a short siesta, his butler announced Inspector Biles.

Biles entered the consulting room briskly, with the air of a man who has achieved his immediate purpose. His tall figure seemed to have straightened. His muscles were braced. Even the usual kindliness of his features was a little tinctured with severity.

"Well," he declared, "he's arrested at last: and we've issued a second warrant against the lady. I owe you, my dear doctor, an immense debt of gratitude."

Sleep was in Dr Hailey's eyes. He tried to rub it out, and looked, in the process, uncommonly like a bad-tempered baby.

"What do you say, my dear Biles?" he enquired petulantly. "Whom have you arrested? I fear I am very dull-witted this... eh... afternoon."

"We've arrested Derwick. What is more, we've found blood-stains on the coat he was wearing on the fatal night—right down at the bottom of the coat, at the back. The chain of evidence is complete… against both of them, I think."

Dr Hailey opened his snuff-box, but did not take any snuff.

"Do I understand you to say, then, that Miss Armand has been found?" he asked.

"No; she has not been found. We are circulating a description of her to the Press this afternoon. I don't suppose her arrest can be long delayed…"

Dr Hailey shook his head.

"I fear," he said, "that her arrest will never occur at all, unless someone takes action. You are terribly precipitate, my dear Biles. It seems to me that we are only at the very beginning of this strange crime."

Had any other man ventured to reprove him in this way, Biles would have been immediately resentful. But with the doctor it was different. Though he scarcely admitted the fact to himself, he recognized in his friend a greater detective than any other he had ever met. Dr Hailey met his rather puzzled look with a crisp description of his investigations of the previous day.

"Are you quite sure about the finger-print?" Biles asked anxiously.

"I am quite sure. Look for yourself."

The detective opened his pocket-book and extracted his own copy. He examined it and then laid it down on the table.

"There's no doubt about it. What a fool I was not to notice it sooner."

He thought for a moment, and then added:

"But after all that does not prove much, does it?"

"Not much. But enough to make it worth while enquiring into Mr Blunder's movements during the past few days, I think."

Biles bit his lip.

"He couldn't have committed the murder."

There was a challenge in the words. The doctor accepted it with alacrity.

"My dear friend," he declared, "it is the duty of an investigator to investigate."

"But we believe we have got our man. The case against him is overwhelming."

A slight frown gathered on Dr Hailey's broad brow. He spread out his hands.

"If I were a barrister," he said, "I should like to have the job of defending young Derwick."

Biles went away pretty soon, for he was travelling to Newcastle that night to be present in the police court the following morning when Derwick would be charged.

Dr Hailey drove down to the Strand end of Chancery Lane, and then told his chauffeur to ask where the nearest garage was. He found one behind the Law Courts.

"Drive in," he told the man, "and fill up with petrol."

While the petrol was being obtained, the doctor made a tour of the premises. A number of cars were standing in the place, but none of these tallied with the ideas he had formed of the kind of vehicle Mr Blunder might be expected to possess. He was about to conclude that he had drawn blank, when he saw a very smart coupé, painted electric grey and heavily silvered, coming up the alleyway to the garage. Blunder himself was driving it. Dr Hailey got into his car on the off-side and bent down while the vehicle passed him.

From his position, he could see without necessarily being seen. The grey coupé was splashed with mud… yellow mud, too, of the kind which is not to be picked up in London streets. It was manifest that it had just returned from a run in the country.

That run, too, must have taken it away from the main roads, which are covered with tar-macadam, to byways, where the old top-dressing of dust remains.

He had just observed this fact, when the plump body of Mr Blunder descended into the garage. The car lurched a little as he stepped down, giving the impression that it was glad to be rid of him. Dr Hailey chuckled. He bent again as Mr Blunder passed him on his way out of the shed.

"Had a good run, sir?" asked the man who was engaged in filling the doctor's petrol tank.

"Oh yes. Pretty muddy, though. You needn't clean her, by the way, as I am likely to be going out again tonight."

"Very good, sir."

The little man waddled out of sight. Dr Hailey descended again, and strolled towards the coupé. He noted instantly that the mileage recorded stood at 2,415½ miles. He made a quick note of that figure on his cuff. Then he scraped a little of the mud from one of the panels, and received it into a tiny pill-box which he had brought with him.

The window of the coupé was open. Just beneath it was a pocket in the upholstery of the door, covered by a loose flap. The doctor glanced round to assure himself that he was not observed, and then slipped his hand into this receptacle. It was empty, except for a handkerchief. He seized on this, and squeezed it to a ball in his palm. Then he walked carelessly round a few of the other vehicles, and so back to his car.

As soon as he was back in the daylight of the Strand, he looked at his booty. It was a fragile absurd thing "all lace and empty space", as he had once heard a lawyer describe such articles. Nevertheless, he searched its margins with an eagerness he could scarcely conceal. He discovered what he was seeking in an instant, a name neatly printed on the fine cambric.

"Poppy de Vere."

He sighed. He had half-hoped, in spite of the scent of Parma violets, that the name might be Estelle Armand. Then he examined the handkerchief more closely, and realized that it probably possessed considerable value. The lace which trimmed it was surely very old.

Who was Poppy de Vere, and what, in any case, was her handkerchief doing in Blunder's car? When he got home, he consulted a directory of the stage without avail. It was two years old, however, so he rang up *The Times* Book Club for a new one. When he got it, he found what he was looking for in the following entry:

DE VERE, POPPY:
  Played Lead in:
  THE GIDDIES, THE GIRLIES,
  Address:
  1 The Wayside Lane,
  Hampstead, NW3

She was in the telephone book, and he rang up her number at once. There was no reply. Either Miss de Vere did not employ a maid, or the place was shut. He glanced at his watch. It was already five o'clock. He walked round to the garage in Harley Mews, where he kept a small car which he usually drove himself. His chauffeur had already filled and oiled it in readiness. It was a closed vehicle, one of those semi-coupés which became so popular just after the war. He drove it round to his house, and left it standing by the kerb.

Then he ate a hurried meal of two courses, and went upstairs to change into his very warmest clothing. Before he left the room, he slipped a tiny automatic pistol into his pocket, after making sure that it was fully loaded. The car was provided with a number of tools which his former excursions into the world of crime had suggested as convenient accessories of the amateur detective.

He drove very carefully down to the city, going by Portland Place and Regent Street. The traffic in Piccadilly Circus was very dense, and he had to sit inactive at his wheel for about ten minutes till an Olympian constable, who was making a free-way up Shaftesbury Avenue, deigned to lower his white-gloved hand. Then he turned down the Haymarket, and so to the Strand. He drew up just opposite St Clement Dane's Church, and stopped the engine. Then he lit a cigar and lay back with his coat well muffled round his face.

It was a bow at a venture, of course, but his calculations had been carefully made. Blunder would scarcely leave his office till six o'clock. He would probably go and dine somewhere before calling for his car—probably at the "Cock Tavern" at the top of Fleet Street, which was popular with the legal fraternity.

It was a cold night, but, happily, the coupé was fitted with an electric foot-warmer. Dr Hailey was not uncomfortable. He watched the egress from Clement's Inn as a ferret watches the rabbit which it is stalking.

Presently, he saw a fat figure emerging from that egress into the swollen stream of the Strand.

CHAPTER 13 INTO
THE WILDS

Mr Blunder wore a big overcoat and a cap well pulled down over his ears. He turned at once in the direction of Fleet Street. Dr Hailey touched the self-starter button on his dash-board, and set his engine purring. He moved slowly along the kerb like a taxi-man looking for a fare.

His quarry evidently did not intend to dine, for he kept along the left-hand pavement till he passed the Law Courts. Then he turned into the narrow close which separates that great building from the premises abutting on Chancery Lane. Dr Hailey lost sight of him for a moment in the crowd. He could not follow directly, of course, for the close is a footway only. He quickened his pace, and turned into Chancery Lane, hoping to be in time to see Blunder emerge again into the public street.

Unhappily, a traffic block delayed him. When he came to the place he desired to reach, Blunder had disappeared. He drove on towards the garage, determined to take what risk of exposure there might be, rather than abandon his quest at the beginning. When he passed the entrance, he saw that the lawyer must have arrived, for there was no sign of him in the passageway. He halted his car again and looked out through the back window. It commanded a clear view of the whole street; no one could leave the garage without being observed by him.

About ten minutes later, the grey coupé poked her nose out, and slipped quietly into the street. She came purring past the place where he was standing, and turned up at the first corner towards Holborn. Dr Hailey made haste to follow her; so much so, indeed, that he very nearly collided with her when she drew up to await a chance of entering the main stream of traffic. Blunder drove with great assurance. He went straight up to Oxford Circus and then by Portland Place to Regent's Park. At the bridge over the canal, he turned into Avenue Road.

The thought struck Dr Hailey that possibly this was an excursion to Hampstead to visit Poppy de Vere, but that surmise was quickly disproved. The coupé mounted through Hampstead to the top to the Heath and thence sped away down the steep hill to Golder's Green Station.

The road was nearly empty now, and it was necessary to exercise greater caution. Dr Hailey just kept his quarry in sight. He drew up halfway down the hill to allow for the inevitable stop at the Tube Station. The grey coupé turned into the Finchley Road. From this point it made rapid going to Barnet, where the Great North Road to Hatfield was chosen. Dr Hailey found that all his wits were required to sustain the pace.

At Hatfield, he imagined he had lost the game altogether. When he rounded the bend through the town, he found a clear road. But then he saw a tail light disappearing along the way to Hertford. He drew up, reversed and turned. The tail light had vanished altogether. He opened his accelerator to its widest.

The road is narrow here, and he had a most exciting escape from death at one of the corners where he encountered a big limousine. The experience sobered him somewhat, but nevertheless he was determined to sight the coupé again before they reached Hertford. He continued to drive "all out", discovering in the process how very much even a couple of minutes' start signifies to a swift vehicle.

He had his reward: at the steep hill which leads to the outskirts of the county town, he caught a momentary glimpse of a red light. He saw it again just as they came to the first street lamp. Caution was necessary now, lest Blunder should stop for dinner at one of the hotels. A minute later, as the coupé drew up at the "Stag's Head", the doctor congratulated himself on his foresight. He passed quickly on to the "White Bear" where another car was standing.

The bar of the hostelry commands the street, so that he was able to order himself a whisky and soda, and at the same time keep an eye on the grey car. Mr Blunder was evidently in a hurry, for only about twenty minutes elapsed before he reappeared. He drove off at once in the direction of Ware.

The night was very dark, and it had begun to snow. The roads were distinctly dangerous. Nevertheless, the grey coupé maintained a pace which Dr Hailey's speedometer showed to be not far short of thirty miles an hour. They took the sharp bend into Ware giddily, and then went out on the hill-road to Bishop's Stortford.

This was new country for the doctor who, like many other Londoners, was imperfectly acquainted with Essex and the ways of reaching it. The tremendous hairpin bends in the road, which soon occurred every few furlongs, made him catch his breath. Once he thought he had lost the grey coupé altogether, and twice he very nearly ran into it.

Possibly the latter fact determined Blunder, who apparently knew the country well, to take the short cut from Muchadam village to the main Stortford road. To the occupant of the car following him, it seemed as though he disappeared suddenly into the side of a house—so abruptly does the road turn off. When he came to the turning point himself. Dr Hailey hesitated a moment, for his headlights revealed a very bad surface. But he decided finally to go on. A minute later his car was ploughing a quagmire, and a minute later still, it was in a ford.

Happily, the water was not deep, but the mere fact of this road having been chosen, made the doctor uneasy, and his uneasiness increased when, a little later, he reached the high road again and read a sign-post to the effect that this "short-cut" saved less than a mile and led through water. Obviously, his quarry had been "trying it on".

He followed at a greater distance for a mile or two, until he judged that they must be approaching Bishop's Stortford. Then he drew a little closer. Blunder scarcely slackened his pace at all; he drove right through to the Cambridge and Newmarket road, which he followed through Stanstead-Mountfitchet and Newport. Just beyond this latter village, he turned right-handed to Saffron Walden. Dr Hailey saw that they had travelled upwards of forty miles.

Saffron Walden was passed without a stop. It was not yet nine o'clock, but this little market-town was as empty of life as if the hour had been midnight. The road they followed led away from it in an easterly direction, towards that bare and sombre plateau which is known as the Essex Uplands, upon which no fewer than four small rivers have their source.

The snow had stopped, and a half-moon peered from the broken cloud. Dr Hailey had a vision of wide empty fields, and long watery distances. The road was extremely muddy and rough. They mounted for a mile or two, passed a hamlet on the hill-top, then, farther on, mounted again and descended steeply to a tiny village with a big church, set in the very centre of it. After that, the road ran straight for a short way.

The doctor confessed himself entirely unaware of his whereabouts, but the longer this strange chase continued, the higher mounted his hopes. This country, above all others in his knowledge, lent itself to secrecy. The inhabitants of these scattered villages would take but small interest in any but the most local affairs. They seemed to go to bed at sundown, leaving, for the whole stretch of the night, their world to any who might care to use it. He had heard that the great Dick Turpin himself was a native of one of these hamlets. That, he thought with a grim smile, explained much in his adventurous character.

The thought was still in his mind, when suddenly, on rounding a sharp bend between the high banks, he saw the grey coupé standing still in the middle of the road, immediately in front of him.

Not a chance existed of avoiding dire calamity.

CHAPTER 14 MR BLUNDER HAS A GUEST

He could not recollect afterwards what he did. There was so small a fraction of time in which to do anything. All he remembered was a terrific dizzy swerve, a tremendous crash, and the spectacle of his car rearing wildly under his feet, like a shying horse.

A long, fierce grind of machinery followed, and then, with a sound that was half-explosion and half-sob, the engine stopped. He remained holding the wheel, and then suddenly and swiftly ran his hands over his legs.

Could it be possible that he was uninjured?

The car had mounted the off-side bank. It had not turned over, because the front wheels had become fixed in the low hedgerow which crowned this eminence; but it was buckled about him so that he seemed to be seated in a concertina. He tried the door on his right hand, and was unable to open it. Then he noticed that the left-hand door had been wrenched entirely from its hinges. He got out and stood looking down on the cause of his misfortunes.

The grey coupé had not moved. As his impressions of what had just happened clarified in his mind, he realized that he had not injured it by more than a few scratches at most. The first instinct of every driver, to avoid the vehicular obstacle at all costs, had asserted itself to good purpose. His swerve had certainly carried him clear. Then he saw a most extraordinary sight. Blunder was standing some distance behind his car, coolly surveying the disaster he had brought about.

They observed one another almost at the same moment. The little solicitor threw up his hands and shouted as though he were welcoming someone back from the dead. He ran forwards across the white road, looking like a waddling duck on his short legs.

"My dear sir, oh, my dear sir, thank God you are safe!"

Dr Hailey remained on his vantage ground. He restrained a strong impulse to go down and strangle the wretch with his hands.

"It was a near thing," he declared, in deep tones; "an object lesson, if I may say so, on the danger of stopping suddenly near a blind corner."

"Alas, yes."

The doctor was not so far thrown off his usual balance that he failed to observe that Mr Blunder showed no anxiety lest there might be other occupants of the shattered car. Evidently, he was well aware that it had only one occupant—well aware, too, doubtless, who that occupant was. But he gave no indication of his knowledge. On the contrary, when he had climbed the bank, he began to renew his protestations of sorrow and regret.

"In this part of Essex we are apt to forget that anyone else in the world owns a motor car. I don't think I have seen a dozen cars on this road after dusk since I first came here ten years ago."

Dr Hailey had turned to examine the wreck of his coupé. He was trying to make up his mind what to do, what to say. He remembered that Colchester lay somewhere in this direction, and resolved to make that place his destination. He declared that he had lost his way at Bishop's Stortford, but hoped he would pick it up again by reaching the Cambridge-Colchester road.

"Oh, my dear sir," said Blunder, "that is several miles away."

He appeared to consider for a moment, and then his tones changed to those of friendliness.

"I do indeed hope that you will let me make what amends are in my power by accepting my hospitality for the night. I have a little place, not half a mile from here, at the village of Hempstead. My wife will be charmed to see you, and tomorrow my man will drive you to your destination."

Again, Dr Hailey found himself gasping. He was convinced that Blunder knew who he was; yet this bold invitation, this daring "my wife". In spite of himself, his heart warmed to a man who combined, as he believed, the will to crime with the instinct for a workman-like style in the commission of it. He accepted the invitation at once in spite of the obvious danger which it threatened.

"I do hope you have suffered no injury," said Blunder, as they climbed down the bank to the road. "The shock must have been terrible."

"No, I'm none the worse."

They came within range of the grey coupé's headlights. Blunder turned, with an appearance of curiosity which did credit to his powers as an actor. Then he exclaimed:

"What! Dr Hailey?"

"Mr Blunder," said the doctor, without any emphasis whatever.

The lawyer enlarged on the amazing nature of this coincidence. His companion cut him short by asking whether his car had received any injuries. He answered his own question by going round to the back of it to inspect it for himself. The off-wing was slightly dented. He glanced at the road behind, and saw that at this place it widened like the neck of a bottle approaching the body. The spot was chosen with remarkable insight. Any one of a thousand drivers could be trusted to swerve, just as he had swerved, and so to mount the bank, just as he had mounted it. It was long odds, too, that the car would turn over and fall back on the road. Nevertheless, he felt a further thrill of admiration at the daring which had conceived and executed the plan. The only pity was that Blunder had not so completely trusted his judgement as to remain in the driving seat of his coupé. The fact that he had got out, detracted in a small way from an otherwise most distinguished performance.

They got into the car, and Blunder set the engine running. The coupé glided away, as it seemed, among the shadows of the road. Dr Hailey tried to make up his mind whether the man beside him had really intended to kill him, or merely put him out of action. He rather favoured the latter idea, though he could not be sure. Probably, at the moment, the publicity of an inquest, even on the victim of an accident, would be inconvenient.

The car slowed down and turned into an avenue through an unostentatious gateway. A moment later it drew up in front of a long, low-built house, the front of which seemed to be entirely covered with ivy. Blunder opened the door beside him and got out. He then hurried round to assist his visitor to alight.

"I'll take the car round to the garage later," he said. "Meanwhile, let me assure myself that you are in some sort of comfort."

He ran up the steps of the house and opened the front door with a latchkey. He advanced some way into the hall and called "Mary" twice in a loud voice. A door opened, filling the hall with light.

Then Dr Hailey had one of the sharpest surprises of his life. He saw an elderly woman with a plump, matronly figure appear in the doorway.

"Oh," she cried, "it's Dad."

This information was intended, evidently, for her daughter, who followed her into the hall and ran towards Blunder with an expression of obvious pleasure on her very pretty face. Dr Hailey, standing behind his host, gasped. What he had expected to see, and what he now saw, were worlds apart.

"Mother," said the lawyer, "here is a gentleman whom I have very nearly killed. He will tell you all about it while I'm putting the car in. But I wanted to tell you to be specially kind to him."

His face looked more like an apple than ever as he spoke, one of those pippins, the doctor thought, which do not acquire much colour even when they are quite ripe. He waddled away to the front door. Mrs Blunder and her daughter helped their visitor to take off his coat and muffler, then they ushered him into a very cosy drawing-room.

It was furnished in a way which delighted Dr Hailey at the first glance. Everything was so exceedingly good and yet so very comfortable. He glanced from an exquisite little Queen Anne clock on the mantelpiece, to a fire-screen which had assuredly done service once upon a time in nobler surroundings. Then his eyes fell approvingly on a huge, deep Chesterfield of that kind which a few modern cabinet-makers have had the wit to place once again on the market.

"What can we give you?" said his hostess in her rather faded voice, which suggested an unequal struggle abandoned long ago. "James always has a plate of cold beef and some cheese, but it will be quite easy to get some hot soup as well."

"Thank you," said Dr Hailey, "but the cold meat will be quite enough for me. I'm not hungry."

"Dearest," said her mother to the pretty girl, "bring the decanter and syphon of soda. I'm sure Mr——"

"Dr Hailey."

"——Dr Hailey must be needing a little stimulant." She turned again to her visitor. "I don't know. I'm sure, what James has done to you, but he's so reckless with that car that I can believe anything. I scarcely ever go out with him now because all the time I have my heart in my mouth...."

There was a trace of complaining in the faded voice which suggested that possibly, though defeated, Mrs Blunder was not yet entirely reconciled to her fate. Dr Hailey watched her closely while he described the accident. He noted that such exclamations as she uttered during his narration were purely formal. This woman lived, as he had once heard an American express it, "a mile inside herself". He concluded that the furnishings of the room were not her work. Women of this sort are all slatterns at heart.

Miss Blunder clearly took after her father. She poured out his whisky for him without asking his consent, and she sent the soda down among it with the deftness of a potman. He felt that her prettiness was curiously misplaced—unless, indeed, she married a hunting squire or some other horsey young man who would know how to subdue her. She was not pitiful like her mother, but she had the same negative quality—the lack of subtlety, of *alure*.

It was strange, because the drawing-room in which these women presumably spent much of their time was full of this indefinable charm. It suggested the feminine, as leisure and taste has evolved that delicious human quality. These women were foreigners in their own house. With a sudden, clear distinctness, Dr Hailey realized the whole tragedy of Blunder's life. For the first time he pitied him. It is not wickedness in a woman, as that quality is generally understood, he reflected, which usually drives her husband to the devil. It is emptiness of spirit.

He raised his glass and bowed to the two women. Mrs Blunder was telling her daughter over again about the accident, and re-expressing her certainty that "Dad" would soon come to an untimely end. There was a wistful tone in her voice as she said this, which was not without its significance. She added, for Dr Hailey's benefit:

"But Dearie's just as bad as her father."

Mr Blunder came in, all rubs and wiggles, as though he sought to shake off the cold which he had left behind him in the yard. They went into the dining-room—another impressive apartment—where supper had been laid for them. Mr Blunder instructed his manservant to bring him a bottle of his 1900 port from the cellar.

"A vintage, my dear doctor," he declared, "of which I am sorry to say there are now too few survivors."

He talked further about wine, revealing the fact that his knowledge was superficial and his taste dubious. Dr Hailey led the conversation to furniture and, when he had accomplished his object, was rewarded. The solicitor was a real collector, one of those rare beings, moreover, a collector with a point of view. As he spoke, the delight of the man in that quality of beauty which is just a trifle too obvious, was revealed again and again. Furniture, perhaps, is the only material in which sensuousness can be expressed without any restraint.

When they returned to the drawing-room, Mrs Blunder was seated behind a big coffee-pot from which she instantly began to pour out cups of coffee. Miss Blunder carried those to their destinations; then she brought brown sugar in a silver bowl and jingled her bracelets while she served it. Dr Hailey helped himself and then took out his snuff-box—a gesture which made both the women stare. He took snuff. Then he turned to his host and said in his soft tones:

"I know, my dear sir, that you play the violin-cello. Do you think that I might ask...."

Mr Blunder started slightly.

"How can you know that?" he exclaimed in evident bewilderment.

"I guessed it. If I may be permitted to guess again, I will say that your favourite composer is Gounod."

The solicitor's eyes narrowed. This man by some means or other had read his heart. He did not like it.

"The 'Ave Maria', for example...?"

"Oh, yes, Dad plays that beautifully. It is so sweet, don't you think?"

After all, then, there were points of resemblance, other than superficialities, between father and daughter. But horsiness and sentimentality are often bedfellows... and crime.

The 'cello was produced by the girl from its big case. She brought it to her father, who caressed it after the manner of amateurs. A moment later the cloying sweetness of the "Ave" sobbed through the room. Dr Hailey closed his eyes. At least, this man knew how to play. He began to form a mental picture of Miss Poppy de Vere. She would be like a nun... assuredly like a nun.

It was certain that as soon as the music stopped Mrs Blunder would go to bed. Women of her type always retire early, as soon as they have served the last meal of the day. There is, too, an uncomfortable sense of early rising and the preparation of breakfast about their "Good nights". Though others may indulge in late hours, the work of the world must go on. A second pang of pity for Blunder smote the doctor's heart.

Miss Blunder soon followed her mother, but without the same suppressed righteousness of manner. Mr Blunder indicated the decanter which stood on the tea-table. He was obviously anxious to play again. This time he rendered the "Salut d'Amour", then he put his 'cello back into its case and lit a cigar.

"So they have arrested young Derwick," he said in smooth tones.

"I believe so."

"It seems rather premature, doesn't it? Especially as they have not found the girl yet. You didn't know Estelle Armand, did you?"

"No; I know none of the people in the case, I'm afraid, except Inspector Biles. He is a patient of mine, and occasionally indulges my passion for amateur detective work, by calling me in. He came to see me this afternoon. He appears to be very confident of obtaining a conviction."

Again Blunder's eyes narrowed. But his visitor caught the gleam of satisfaction in them nevertheless.

"Really! Possibly they have evidence which has not got into the papers. I confess, thought, that the whole story seems to me complicated and difficult to a degree. Armand, I assure you, was one of the simplest and gentlest of men—the very soul of honour. I cannot conceive why anyone should ever have borne him a grudge."

Dr Hailey did not reply. He drank his whisky reflectively as though awaiting the passing of an unpleasant topic. His host asked him if he wished to go to bed, and assured him that he would find a suit of pyjamas and shaving material placed at his disposal in his room. It was obvious that he himself wished to retire.

He conducted the doctor to the bedroom which was on the first floor, at the end of the house, remote from the carriage way.

"Tea will be brought you in the morning," he announced. "But don't hesitate to order your breakfast in bed as well, if you like. This is Liberty Hall, you know. When we come down here we put all ceremony aside. In fact, I can scarcely get my wife and daughter to leave the place. They came down yesterday, in the Ford car my daughter drives, and mean to stay till after Christmas." He turned away, and then from the doorway added: "The village here, Hempstead, is Dick Turpin's birthplace, you know."

When he had gone, the silence of country houses in winter, descended. Dr Hailey raised the curtain, and saw that snow was again falling. It seemed to muffle the world so that every sound was muted.

He stood in the middle of the room and tried to take stock of the position, but a great weariness was upon him. He sat down on the couch at the foot of the bed; then he lay down. In a moment he was asleep.

Two hours later he started up, listening with every faculty strained and alert.

CHAPTER 15 A CRY IN THE NIGHT

The sound which he heard was the buzzing of a telephone bell.

He glanced at his watch. It was just after one o'clock. He went very softly to the door and opened it with great care. The bell rang again, and then he heard footsteps at the far end of the corridor. They seemed to descend the stairs, though he was not sure of this. Then he heard Blunder's voice speaking, though he was unable to detect any words.

He crept out into the corridor, which was faintly illuminated from a window at the far end, against which the setting moon was now shining. He moved noiselessly towards the staircase. He was just in time, as he reached this, to hear the lawyer say:

"Very well. I'll come at once."

The receiver was replaced with a click. Dr Hailey hurried back to his room and closed the door. He sat down on the bed to try to think things over.

It was obvious that Blunder was going somewhere immediately. That he was going on any ordinary errand—unless indeed some wealthy client was dying and wished to make a will—seemed out of the question. His parents were both dead, and he had no brothers or sisters, so that a family emergency was scarcely possible.

Suddenly the truth dawned.... The doctor found himself gasping again. Wherever he went, for the next twelve hours at any rate, there would be no danger of pursuit. He had the hunter safe abed in his own house.

Was there no possibility of acting as stowaway on this journey? But no, the coupé was too small. Even if he managed to scramble undetected on to the dickey, his weight would affect the steering and make discovery absolutely certain. Besides, Blunder would see him through the back window of the hood. If only they had been nearer Saffron Walden, he might have obtained a hired car, but walking there was out of the question even if he started an hour before the lawyer. Besides, what assurance had he that this route would be chosen?

He got up and walked to the window. He was about to lift the curtain, when he remembered that by doing this he would probably illuminate the branches of the trees in front of the house, and so disclose the fact that he was awake.

He switched off the light, and then looked out. The snow lay evenly on the lawns; the sky, however, had become quite clear. It was possible to see a wide sweep of the country. He made up his mind that, at any rate, he must get out of the house immediately and use such means as might present themselves to get away also from the neighbourhood.

And then suddenly he remembered the Ford car in which Blunder had told him his wife and daughter had travelled from London. It must be in the garage still....

He waited anxiously at his door till he heard the door of his host's room open again. This time the lawyer's footsteps were loud and firm as though he had nothing to hide and was not in a mood to hide anything. His boots sounded heavily on the old wooden staircase which creaked under them.

Dr Hailey left his room and tiptoed to the stairhead. He heard the lock of the back door click and then the sound of bolts being withdrawn. He came down the staircase as quietly as he could, and turned in the direction which he took to be that of the servants' quarters.

Blunder went out and shut the door behind him, but he did not re-lock it—probably because there was only one key, and because the chances of burglary in this quarter were so infinitesimal. The doctor came to the door a moment afterwards, and stood behind it listening.

He noticed that a small pantry opened off the corridor just to the right of him. It had a window looking out on the yard, because there was a patch of moonlight on the floor. He crept into it and gently drew the door half-shut behind him.

The next instant he had reason to be thankful for this precaution. Blunder had evidently forgotten something, and came back to fetch it. He passed within touching distance, and went lumbering away into the darkness of the corridor. The doctor waited until his steps became fainter, and then slipped out by the open door into the yard. He congratulated himself that fortune, this time, was playing into his hands.

The house had evidently been a farm at one period, for there were numerous sheds and outhouses surrounding it. One of these, as he could see, had been rebuilt as a garage. The others appeared to be empty. He chose the interior of that which seemed to be the darkest and entered it. It was a roomy place, used evidently by the gardener, for it was full of all sorts of odds and ends of apparatus—seed boxes, forcing frames and the like. He crouched down behind a number of these latter, and watched the door, which was clearly illuminated by the moon.

Presently Blunder returned. He was dressed in his full motoring kit and wore a large muffler round the lower part of his face. He carried a key in his hand—possibly the object for which he had re-entered the house. When he crossed the yard, the doctor lost sight of him, but he heard him in the garage next door, opening petrol tins and filling his tank. These occupations appeared to distress him a good deal, for he puffed and blew while engaged in them. The sounds changed, and the listener heard the creak of the big doors of the garage. Then he heard a carriage-door slam, and immediately afterwards the whirr of the self-starter. The engine began to purr. Blunder drove out into the yard, stopped the car, and came back to shut his garage. Then, very quietly, he drove away into the night.

There was not an instant to be lost. The doctor had already

possessed himself of an iron stake he had found lying beside the forcing frames. He ran out and without a moment's hesitation inserted the end of it, jemmy fashion, between the doors of the garage. A single wrench of his powerful shoulders broke the lock and opened the place to him.

He nearly cried out for joy at the sight of the Ford car, which immediately greeted his eyes. It was the work of a few seconds to find the switch and light the place up. There was an abundance of petrol and he lifted a couple of cans into the back seat. Then he jumped in and switched on the engine.

The car was a new one and started at once. He had driven Fords on many occasions and felt no uneasiness. Within five minutes of the departure of Blunder, he was actually on the road in pursuit, but those five minutes were, in fact, a long start, for Blunder enjoyed the inestimable advantage of knowing the district. Moreover, it was out of the question to use any lights during at least the early period of the chase. The moon alone must be his guide and protector.

Happily, there was the snow, which recorded faithfully the tracks of the coupé. It declared that Mr Blunder had taken the road to London.

The Ford made good easy going. In a few minutes it came to the place where the accident had occurred the night before. There was the smashed car, still perched on the top of the bank, but covered now with a shimmering white mantle. It looked lonely, disconsolate, its owner thought, as though making silent protest against the evil design which had wrought its ruin.

The tracks led straight back to Saffron Walden. They lay clear in the middle of the road, uncrossed by any other wheels. Even when the Newmarket road was reached, their possession of this midnight world remained unchallenged.

Dr Hailey let the Ford out and went down to Stanstead much faster than was at all safe. As he approached the village, he caught a glimpse of the tail light of the coupé.

Mr Blunder drove into London by Epping. As he neared the city, the difficulty of keeping him in view became much greater, so that Dr Hailey began to despair of his task. Nevertheless, when they reached the Strand, he was still following. The coupé ran up the Haymarket and turned into Piccadilly. It reached Putney Bridge by the Fulham road, and then took the Portsmouth road. Here again, the snow was thick and but little disturbed. When Kingston had been passed, following was as easy as it had been in Essex.

Dr Hailey was just congratulating himself on his success when, with a sudden gasp, the Ford came to a standstill. He knew that sound. The petrol tank was empty He climbed out from his seat, and realised as he did so how exceedingly stiff and cold he was. Even in his thick gloves, his hands were frozen. He worked his arms cabman fashion to warm himself, and then opened both the tins he had brought with him.

About a quarter of an hour elapsed before he started again, but he had no difficulty in following the tracks till he reached Guildford. There, unhappily, another car had come to complicate matters, for while one set of tracks remained on the Portsmouth Road, the other mounted towards the Hog's Back.

He got out to examine the tread-marks, but unfortunately he had not looked carefully enough at those made by the coupé. There was nothing for it but to retrace his way to the outskirts of the town to the point where only the coupé's tracks lay on the road.

More than half an hour was spent in this work, but at last be learned that Blunder had stuck to the Portsmouth road. He hurried back through the steep little town, where so many motorists have paid, in the past, the price of their excessive speed.

There was no further check, and he came quickly to the place where the Hazlemere road takes off from the main highway. Blunder had gone in that direction. He made good going over the steep uplands and through the silent, snow-laden pine-woods which give to this part of England, in winter, a magical quality not found in any other district. The tracks led straight into the little town, and then turned off towards the heights of Blackdown,

A moment later Dr Hailey came to the open gates of a large private house.

It was his destination.

He ran the Ford a short distance farther up the road, and drew it into the side, out of sight of the gateway he had just passed. Then he got out and walked back to reconnoitre. This was not easy, for the moon had set, and it was very dark.

The house apparently stood well back among thick trees, for he was unable to catch a glimpse of any light from where he stood. He entered the gateway, and at once passed among the trees, using his electric torch to follow the direction of the avenue, but taking care not to debouch upon it. The way was uphill, and once or twice he slipped, and only saved himself from falling by using his hands. He turned the torch on the carriage-way and saw that the coupé had had a difficult climb and must have given its driver considerable anxiety. Just when he had begun to wonder whether there was any house at all—so long was the approach—he caught the glimmer of a light. A few yards farther on, he realized that this proceeded from a window on the first floor of the house.

He crept forward carefully, using his torch as little as possible. The house was evidently surrounded by a wide expanse of lawn, for his view of it became more and more uninterrupted as he approached. He changed his direction and moved round it, keeping still within the shelter of the shrubbery. As he came abreast of the façade, he saw the outline of the building against the clear, star-filled sky.

It was evidently a very large house indeed. Moreover, though he supposed that this was an illusion of the darkness, it had a deserted appearance, like that of a great mansion in the hands of caretakers. The carriage-way, he could see, ran round this side of the building to the others, and a hurried inspection with his torch revealed the fact that Blunder had driven round. He walked on, and came to a wall which evidently enclosed the yard behind.

It was necessary now to emerge from the cover of the trees

and find the gateway in this obstruction. He felt his way along the wall and soon came to it. Very cautiously he glanced within. The red taillight of the coupé gleamed at him from a distance of a few yards.

He waited, in case by any chance the man he was following had not yet entered the house. But the yard was silent. He stole forward and came behind the car. Its headlights had been switched off, but the side lamps were burning. They showed him a back door in full illumination. Some distance to the left of this door was a window, which was less brightly lit.

He advanced to the window, and gently tried the sash with his thumbs. It resisted him. He turned his light on it and saw that the catch was fastened. He felt in his pocket for his knife, and with a deftness which must have astonished his patients had they seen him, inserted the blade between the sashes and pressed the catch back.

It opened with a slight click, which sounded very loud in the utter stillness of the night. He waited anxiously to hear if there was any response. Then he gently raised the lower sash and climbed into the house. He shut the window carefully and quietly behind him.

The room he found himself in was a pantry of some sort, for it smelt of food—he thought—of food which had been eaten a long time ago. There was an indescribable musty dampness in the air which was, somehow, rather horrible. He moved to the place where he conceived the door must be, and found it closed. He switched on his light for an instant.

The small apartment was hung with hooks—doubtless for hams or game. There were a few sacks in one corner, and he observed a table set against one of the walls. Otherwise the place was quite empty.

Happily, the door was not locked. He turned the handle and crept out into the passage beyond. Then, suddenly, he turned back and removed the heavy coat he was wearing; he also bent down and took off his shoes. His hand travelled to the pocket where he had placed his pistol before leaving home.

He passed back into the passage and followed it till he came to a door covered with green baize. He pushed this open and found himself in the main hall of the mansion. It was dark, but he caught a gleam of light from somewhere overhead.

Then suddenly a terrible cry, which horrified even his cool, professional nerves, rang through the emptiness of the house.

CHAPTER 16 MR BLUNDER EXPLAINS

The cry was repeated.

Standing in the darkness, it seemed to him the most piteous sound he had ever heard, something between the whimpering of a child afflicted by night-terror and the wail of an animal in pain.

Yet it was not a cry of fear. That unmistakable note was quite absent from its shrill cadences.

The deep silence of the house fell again, and muffled all sound, so that he found himself wondering whether his senses, in the eerie darkness, had not deceived him. He passed through the door and came out into the centre of the hall.

There was no further sound. In front of him, as his torch showed, was the main doorway behind a wide oak staircase. The light of the stars, when he switched off again, was visible through long mullioned windows set behind it. He crept up the stairs and had reached the landing which divided the two flights, when the cry was repeated.

It came from some room on the left side of the house. Heard at this greater nearness, it sounded rather less terrifying, rather more, piteous. He hurried up the remaining steps, and came to the first door. The carpet was thick and soft, and his passage made no sound. He stepped quickly along the corridor in the direction from which the cry had come.

And then, suddenly, the sound of voices talking in hurried

tones came to his ears.

He approached the door from which these sounds emanated. He stood still, holding his breath in his eager excitement; but the door seemed to be very thick and he could hear but little.

"Tomorrow... the police... arrest."

That voice, he thought, was Blunder's, though he could not be quite sure. Another, softer voice answered it, but what was spoken was inaudible. He pressed his ear to the door and listened again. Then he heard the first voice say:

"Even so, we cannot delay and the danger is small."

Again the soft voice answered, and again he failed to catch what it said. But one thing was clear. Estelle Armand was in this house, and these two men were deciding her fate. Then a terrible thought came to him. The cry he had just heard must have been hers.

It was repeated at that instant. It came, undoubtedly, from the next room to that in which the conference was going on. As it died away, the loud voice exclaimed:

"You hear? Surely that is sufficient?"

What was he to do? These men were desperate, and there were two of them. How could he hope to rescue the girl against their united opposition. On the other hand he was armed and they, possibly, were not. But that was a desperate course, at best. It would be better and wiser perhaps to steal away and rouse the Hazlemere police.

On the other hand, time might be more vital than he supposed. What if they had given the girl poison and were awaiting the effects of it? He shuddered as the idea crossed his mind. But no, that could not be the explanation, for they were speaking about handing her over to the police. What could have happened then?

Again the cry....

It was different this tune, longer, wilder. Suddenly, as he listened to it, Dr Hailey knew that his question was answered.

There could be no possibility of doubt. Estelle Armand was mad.

By their treatment of her in these tragic days of her young life, the villains had robbed her of her senses. A burning fury of indignation drove all thought of his own safety, even of caution, from the doctor's mind. He plunged his hand into his pocket and drew out his pistol, then, with a swift movement of his hand and arm, he flung open the door.

The scene which greeted him caused him to hold his breath.

Seated round a table in the centre of the room were Blunder, a young man with fair hair, and a young woman in a nurse's uniform with a huge red cross on her breast. Blunder appeared to be weeping.

At sight of Dr Hailey brandishing his pistol, they all sprang to their feet. The woman screamed and the man, instinctively, it seemed, ducked down under the table. Only the little lawyer maintained his sang-froid.

"What, my dear doctor," he cried, "have you actually followed me from Hempstead...!"

He looked up without a tremor of fear into the muzzle of the gun. His eyes, reddened as they were, did not flinch.

"What is the meaning of this?" the doctor cried, "and what have you done with Miss Armand? What damnable villainy is afoot here?"

"If you please...." Mr Blunder raised his hand in a deprecating gesture. "I cannot really talk to you while you flourish that weapon in that exceedingly... shall I say?... theatrical manner. There is, as doubtless you perceive, a lady here and she is naturally alarmed."

"I mean to have no nonsense..."

"Of course not. And let me say, I admire your zeal nearly as much as I deprecate your lack of judgement. Permit me to introduce to you Dr Parsons and his wife, who are rendering me and, incidentally, Miss Armand, a very great and heroic service."

Dr Hailey glanced at the doctor. His weak face was still full of anxiety, but he certainly looked innocuous enough, though there was a cunning gleam in his eyes.

"I don't understand," he declared bluntly. "What was that terrible cry I heard just now."

"That?... That was Miss Armand, my patient. The poor lady has lost her reason, I fear."

"Where is she?"

Dr Parsons pointed to a door leading into the adjoining room.

"There," he said. He signalled to his wife, who immediately left them to go in beside the patient.

"So I was right in my suspicion. You have driven her out of her wits."

"My dear doctor," Plunder cried, "why will you jump to conclusions in this frantic style? Is it necessary always to impute the worst, the most villainous motive to your fellow-men. I know you are a detective, of course, but even detectives allow that some men are honest."

Blunder's round face wore a slightly cynical smile. In spite of himself, Dr Hailey felt his admiration for the man increasing. Only honesty, or genius, could maintain such an attitude in such circumstances.

"I insist on an explanation," he declared in tones which, as he felt himself, lacked the conviction of his first assault.

"You shall have it. You may even keep your gun if you wish. I should not care to rob you of that safeguard. But I do ask, as a matter of common politeness, that you lower the muzzle of it. After all, you might, inadvertently of course, pull the trigger, and I am not yet anxious to quit this wicked world."

Dr Hailey lowered his pistol, but he refused the invitation to sit down which followed this concession.

"Go on," he declared, "I'm listening."

Blunder cleared his throat.

"You may or may not have observed," he said, "that last night, when I spoke to you of Sir William Armand's death, I adopted the most casual tones?"

He paused. Dr Hailey inclined his head.

"I noticed it," he declared.

"You would, of course. Very well, my reason was not, as perhaps you concluded, lack of affection for my dear partner—"

again to the bewilderment of the doctor, the little man's eyes filled with tears—"but to the fact that I had already done all that lay in my power to save his name from dishonour and calamity."

He paused, and wiped his eyes with his big white handkerchief.

"You are aware, I know," he continued, "that a warrant has been issued for the arrest of Miss Armand. I foresaw that warrant when I heard of Sir William's disappearance, and before even his body was found—for I knew that he could not have disappeared of his own free will. It was inevitable, surely, on the face of it —just as the arrest of that poor young man was inevitable on the face of it. The police of this country are not the fools which some people, I understand, suppose them to be."

There was a wealth of sarcasm in this last statement which made Dr Hailey redden in spite of himself. But he did not reply.

"And so, perhaps wrongly, I determined to do what I could to defeat the ends of justice, by furthering those of a higher justice and conveying the poor girl to a place of refuge."

"Ah, so *you* were the mysterious stranger with the motor car who came to Calthorpe Hall, were you? I may congratulate myself on my perspicacity."

"Undoubtedly, you are entitled to do that."

Mr Blunder rose and pressed the points of his fingers on the table, a gesture, no doubt, which he often employed in the course of his professional practice.

"When I made that journey," he said, "I found, as I had reason to expect to find, that this poor girl was sorely tried. I could see then, though I lack, perhaps, the professional eye, that it was but a matter of time until she broke down altogether. In other words, there was not a moment to be lost if her reason was to be saved."

He paused again, and again wiped his eyes. There were, the doctor observed, tears on both his cheeks.

"This house, as you may, or may not, know, is a private home for cases of incipient insanity. Dr Parsons who conducts it is an old personal friend of my own. I brought Miss Armand straight here from London by private car. Unhappily, I was too late. The breakdown, as you know, has taken place in spite of us. It was because I received a message to that effect from the doctor at Hempstead, that I made this night journey."

Dr Hailey contracted his brows.

"I do not see," he said, "why so much haste was necessary. Even in these tragic circumstances, you. might, surely, have put off your visit till the morning."

Blunder waved his hand impatiently.

"I know. You think I was anxious to improve the chance given me by your safe bestowal in my own house. I agree that, had I planned the execution of some villainy, the opportunity was a good one. My dear sir, the reason why I made this night journey is far simpler than you imagine. It is that Miss Estelle Armand is an epileptic—and my friends here do not possess the necessary means of controlling such a case. When you entered the room we were actually discussing what we should do in the very difficult and terribly tragic circumstances. You will agree that action is imperative—unless indeed you favour the view that I should hand over the daughter of my old friend to the police."

Dr Hailey's face was blank. He thought he had been prepared for anything; he found himself unprepared for this.

"Can you be serious?" he said in tones which afforded a grudging admission of his miscalculated action.

"I am indeed serious. Dr Parsons will tell you that before Sir William's death I paid him a visit for the express purpose of arranging Miss Armand's transference to his care in order that what I understand is a new and hopeful treatment might be given her. My late partner was in a state of deadly anxiety about her condition, and no wonder. On two separate occasions she had made determined attempts on his own life."

"What!"

"There is, unfortunately, no doubt whatever about it, though naturally the matter was kept a profound secret. Only Sir William himself and I knew anything at all about it, for it so happened that both the attempts were made at night when the father and daughter were alone together in their drawing-room. It was only after the second attempt that my advice was sought, and that, I believe, only because, in the interval, Miss Armand had engaged herself to young Derwick. Not even the family doctor was consulted in the matter."

The lawyer's voice had dropped to a whisper. He seemed to be greatly moved, but nevertheless Dr Hailey's critical faculty was re-awakening after the shock it had received.

"I confess," he said, "that it sounds to me a most improbable story. I cannot imagine that Sir William would not at once, in these circumstances, lay the matter before his doctor."

"You did not know him, as I knew him. To begin with, the late Lady Armand was an epileptic. She left a special request in her will that her husband would shield their daughter in every way against the terrible consequences of this disease, should it ever break out in her case. He regarded that as a trust from the dead. Moreover, he was terribly anxious that Estelle should be happily married. It was his one hope to avoid all local publicity and seek a cure, if such could be obtained."

"Then why did he order his daughter to break off her engagement? I presume you mean to suggest that her illness had some relation to that step."

"It had, of course. The reason was that he felt that he was bound in honour to save Derwick from the consequences of such a marriage. You would not surely, as a physician, question the rightness of that step?"

"I certainly should not question it."

"Sir William was murdered because he came to this honourable decision… a decision from which I confess I tried myself to dissuade him only a few minutes before he met his death."

"Good Heavens, so you are the man Sawyer."

"Of course. Is that not sufficiently obvious from what I have been telling you."

CHAPTER 17 ON THE WRONG TRACK

To say that Dr Hailey was convinced by this astonishing narrative, would be to do less than justice to his critical faculty. On the other hand, he was made uneasy by it. Blunder, emphatically, had startled him. He glanced down at the pistol in his hand and experienced, as he did so, a feeling of some regret that he should have acted so violently.

He put the weapon back in his pocket. As he did so, he saw a smile, which was capable of various interpretations, none of them very complimentary to himself, on the lawyer's lips.

"May I add," said Blunder, "that my disguise was worn at Sir William's own request. I have stayed on former occasions at Calthorpe Hall, and might have been recognized. In the present instance, it was desirable—or so my late partner felt—that no inkling whatever of his trouble should be obtained by anyone."

"But I don't see...."

Blunder waved his hand in indication of his desire to be absolutely frank.

"My dear sir, Sir William, as perhaps you know already, came to London in the week before his death to ask my advice. I saw Dr Parsons after his visit, and arranged for Miss Armand's treatment. The doctor gave me his views of the case, and these I laid before my friend as soon as possible. My visit was made for the express purpose of doing this. I confess that the news of the broken engagement came as a great surprise, yet I would not dispute its fairness, though, as I have said, I tried to mitigate its severity. When I left Sir William, he was profoundly disturbed and agitated."

When he stopped speaking, a heavy silence filled the room. They heard the doctor's wife moving about beside her patient. Far away, in the village, a clock chimed the hour of five. Dr Hailey sat down and took out his snuff-box.

"It is a very strange story," he declared. "It does not seem to help us much with the solution of the mystery, does it?"

"Except that Miss Armand's mind may well have become unhinged when her happiness was threatened. I speak subject to correction, but I believe that if there is insanity in a family, a severe shock is apt to bring it out. The girl set immense store by this love affair. I can imagine that she might be ready to go to any lengths to safeguard it—even the length of murder. Remember, she had already tried on two occasions to kill her father."

Blunder was now at his ease. He got up and came towards Dr Hailey, waving his fat hands as he did so in a manner which suggested the efforts of a swimmer. There was the plain suggestion in his attitude that he meant to bear no ill-will against a mysterious, though misguided, upholder of the law.

"Of course," he added, "in telling you all this, I am placing myself in your hands; but I believe I speak as one gentleman to another. Meanwhile, come and see Miss Armand for yourself."

He led the way to the door of the bedroom. Dr Parsons followed him. A moment later Dr Hailey found himself face to face with tragedy.

Estelle lay back on the pillows, over which her beautiful golden hair was spread in disorder. Her face was very pale, but red spots burned in each cheek. She had an unnatural, wild loveliness. Her lips kept moving to frame a torrent of incoherent sound, and her hands, free of the bedclothes, wandered over them in great restlessness. The doctor advanced to the side of the bed where Mrs Parsons stood with a cup and spoon in her hands. He bent over the recumbent figure, watching the twitching eyelids and ever-shifting hands in silence. He could doubt no longer that some terrible disorder of the mind afflicted the poor girl, but he realized also that he could give no name to the picture presented to him. Her wonderful beauty seemed to intensify the tragedy.

Estelle opened her eyes, and gazed up vacantly into his face. For a moment he seemed to see fear in that glance, but her lips smiled and she muttered something about having enjoyed herself very much. Then she laughed outright, and turned over on her side. Dr Parsons had joined his professional brother, and said:

"I am not quite clear about the nature of the case. It is delirium, of course, but from what cause arising is difficult to say. I have given her some morphia."

Dr Hailey nodded. He knew enough to know that the textbook descriptions of insanity are seldom accurate for any individual case. So it was with all descriptions of disease. Always the patient possessed his or her own inflection—just as each human voice is subtly different from all the others. He turned away from the bed and came back to the door. Blunder opened it and passed out with him into the anteroom.

"Are you satisfied?" he asked in low tones.

He appeared to be greatly overcome again. A sense of utter bewilderment took hold of Dr Hailey. He nodded slowly without speaking.

"In my place, you would have acted in the same way?"

There was just a trace of urging in the lawyer's voice.

"I don't know. Perhaps I should have.... I think if I had really believed that she killed her father, or helped to kill him, I certainly should have."

"Thank you."

The lawyer smiled in a watery, chastened manner. Then he indicated the sideboard on which were several bottles and syphons and some sandwiches. He said that he could offer port or sherry, or a whisky and soda. Dr Hailey, however, was in no mood for eating or drinking. His bewilderment had dulled the edge of his humour. Every idea which he had formed of this case seemed to have been incorrect from the very beginning. The force of Biles's contention that Blunder could have had no part in the murder, on the mere, obvious ground of time, struck him anew. He had been too subtle and so had failed where a more practical mind had achieved success.

In his hurry to be gone from the house, he so far retracted his suspicions as to assure the lawyer that he would not, personally, communicate to the police the whereabouts of the missing girl. He promised, too, to leave the Ford car in the garage behind the Law Courts, and apologised for having borrowed the use of it. He went out by the back door, having found his coat and shoes in the little pantry.

On the way back to London a great weariness came on him, the consequence, perhaps, of his despondency, as much as of his exertions. He could scarcely keep awake, until the difficulties of the city traffic roused him. He drove straight home from the garage, and went immediately to bed. It was nearly dinner-time before he woke in response to a telephone call.

He had a switch to his bed. It was Biles, just arrived from Newcastle, where the proceedings against Derwick had been opened. He asked him to come to dinner, and rang at once for his man.

Biles was, if possible, more satisfied than ever with the progress of the case. Fresh items of evidence, he declared, were being collected. They all bore out the central thesis of the prosecution that Derwick was the murderer, and that Estelle had helped him—probably after the event.

"We don't think that she actually gave him the hypodermic syringe and the morphia," he explained. "Probably she had spoken of her possession of these and he knew where they were kept, and so was able to obtain them before he went out. I fancy he lacked the nerve to kill the old man outright, and so planned to trip him up and, as it were, anaesthetise him in the first instance. The rest was easy, and of course he counted on the certainty of the body remaining undiscovered.... That, my dear doctor, was where you were too clever for him. The more I think of your work at Calthorpe, the more intensely I admire it."

It must be confessed that, in his present chagrin, Dr Hailey found this tribute rather gratifying. He would have dismissed his more recent adventures from his mind if he could, and accepted wholeheartedly the plausible, if rather clumsy, explanation of the tragedy which Biles was offering, but even as he listened, the knowledge came again to him that such acceptance was impossible. That dogged instinct of his rejected the argument with an energy which surprised him.

"My dear Biles," he said, in his most deliberate manner, "would you attempt to administer a dose of morphia in that fashion?"

"Certainly not."

Biles's tones were brusque. It was his experience that the worst way of approaching a crime, was to attempt to place oneself in the position of the criminal. The tendency to do this which Dr Hailey habitually exhibited, seemed to him a fatal bar to success. It was the streak of amateurishness in an otherwise supremely capable detective. He tried to explain this in language which would not afford the least ground for offence. Dr Hailey's spirits revived a little in the face of opposition.

"If Derwick committed the murder," he said, "he did so in a moment of passion, during, that is to say, an altercation with the old man. No other explanation seems to me to be even a possible one."

"In that case the fatal dose of morphia—for it was a fatal dose —must have been administered by the girl before her father left home. It is just possible, of course...."

"It is just possible...."

Dr Hailey lifted his wineglass, which contained some choice old Burgundy, to his lips, and drank thoughtfully. His dull eyes travelled round the beautiful dining-room, to every detail of which he had given his closest personal attention. He asked the detective to tell him about the scene in the magistrate's court when Derwick was charged.

"It was purely formal, of course. The prisoner seemed very ill at ease."

"No wonder."

"I fancy he will be defended by Sir Abraham Smith... at least there was mention of that."

"H'm."

The butler served the last course, and then withdrew. Dr Hailey pushed the port towards his companion, who was engaged in cutting a large cigar. He helped himself to a tiny glass of old brandy.

"You mentioned some further clues," he said.

"Oh yes; it appears that Sir William visited London a few days before his death, and had an interview with his partner. That, I take it, was his avowed reason for the journey. The real reason, probably, was connected with the other matter which brought Sawyer to the 'Black Bull' and led to the breaking off of the engagement. There is no doubt in my mind that a connection exists between those events."

Dr Hailey remained silent. He could not now mention that his own suspicions about Sawyer were correct. If what Blunder had told him, however, was even approximately true, Biles's reading of the case in this direction, at any rate, did him credit. He raised his brandy to his lips.

"And then we found a letter in Sir William's desk—or rather I should say, the beginning of a letter. I don't attach much importance to it. It was addressed to Lady Windwest—'My dear Lady Windwest'—and consisted of but two lines in which he said he had heard with deep regret of her illness, and wished to take an early opportunity of seeing her. The letter broke off at that point...."

"Lady Windwest!"

Dr Hailey's expression had changed in an instant. Biles observed the alert manner which had so far been conspicuously absent. He felt a real thrill of joy in seeing his friend evince further interest in a case which seemed to have lost all its attraction for him.

"She is the widow of the Earl of Windwest, you know," he explained. "Armand & Blunder are the family solicitors."

"The deuce they are…."

Dr Hailey rose and asked his guest to excuse him a moment. He went out of the room and returned presently carrying a file of *The Times*. He cleared a place for it on the table and laid it, open, before him. Then he turned up the number corresponding to the day of Sir William's murder. There was a paragraph in the column of society news, stating that Lady Windwest's recovery was being well maintained. He turned back a week and found the following, which he showed to Biles in the same column:

"Lady Windwest's condition gives rise to very grave anxiety. The pneumonia from which she is suffering has invaded both lungs, and her pulse continues to show signs of weakness."

"That would reach Calthorpe, I fancy, the day before Sir William left for London."

Biles drew out his notebook and consulted the table of dates he had made in connection with the case.

"Yes," he said, "that is certainly accurate."

Two days later *The Times* announced that a turn for the better had taken place in the patient's condition. The doctor directed his guest's attention to this item also.

"You do not know," he asked, "whether Sir William's visit was made in connection with some change in the lady's will?"

Biles shook his head.

"Impossible. She lives in Herefordshire, near Ross. Sir William certainly did not travel there."

Dr Hailey took out his snuff-box and snuffed vigorously.

"Then, in all probability, he came to town to satisfy himself that everything connected with the estate was in good order."

"Yes, possibly."

Dr Hailey leaned across the table towards the detective. His eyes gleamed.

"Supposing… that everything was not in good order."

CHAPTER 18 THE LAST CLUE

The jury, at the adjourned inquest on Sir William Armand's body, returned a verdict of wilful murder against Jack Derwick. Dr Hailey had expected that, and because of his expectation had refrained from going to Calthorpe. He felt that the time given him to probe this mystery was all too short to permit of his wasting a single hour of it.

Unless he could produce evidence of a convincing kind within the next few weeks, Derwick would assuredly pay the penalty of his life.

It was a horrible thought, for, in spite of all that Biles could urge, the doctor was unconvinced. His instinct refused the whole theory of the crime which the prosecution had built up; and yet, he was forced to confess that his suspicions of Blunder had found no confirmation in the investigations he had made.

He spent wakeful hours testing the story which the lawyer had told him. He was compelled to admit that, whether true or untrue, it held together. Estelle Armand was undoubtedly insane. There was nothing even improbable in the story of her epilepsy—his professional experience had furnished him with examples of the same kind of thing on many occasions—carefully guarded secrets of mysterious "fits" which fathers and mothers, or brothers and sisters, persisted in regarding as mere fainting attacks, but of which they never spoke to any outside person.

It was certain, moreover, that Blunder had not buried the

murdered body. The idea that he possessed an accomplice was ridiculous on the face of it. That a man should begin a crime of that sort, a crime evidently premeditated and thought out in every detail, and not finish it, was absurd.

And yet there were suspicious circumstances connected with the lawyer which could not be overlooked. Why, for example, had he been at such pains to hide his identity during his stay at the "Black Bull". He had worn a false beard, adopted an alias, and even taken the trouble to disguise his finger-prints. It was comprehensible that some steps to avoid village gossip might have been necessary, but these minute precautions suggested, surely, a deeper, more sinister purpose.

And then there were those pieces of glass which he had found in the fender of the bedroom. Blunder did not look like a drug-taker himself. What, then, was he doing with a phial of hypodermic pellets?

He had omitted to ask him that question, but the omission did not signify much. The lawyer would merely have disclaimed all knowledge of the matter, and it could not be denied that the fragments of glass might have been dropped in the fender by some previous visitor.

Did Blunder, then, really believe that Estelle Armand had helped to murder her father? He did believe, on his own statement, that she had tried to kill him on two earlier occasions, but the events were not strictly comparable. In the one instance epileptic attacks had overwhelmed her; in the other, she was possessed of her faculties. Yet, he had seen with his own eyes how fragile was her sanity, how easily unhinged her mind in the face of disaster.

Suppose that she, and she alone, had committed the crime. But no, that was impossible. No girl of her build could have carried the body to the churchyard and buried it there. Her part, if indeed she had played a part at all, must have been that of accessory before or after the fact.

That brought him back again to Derwick, for obviously he was the only person whom the girl could have assisted. They had been together, too, in the pine wood a few minutes before the dead man entered it....

His brain reeled. He got up and paced his consulting room restlessly. So impenetrable a mystery had never before disquieted him. Whichever way it was looked at, grotesque improbabilities met the vision.

He reflected that there was only one clue remaining to him to follow up—that furnished by the letter to Lady Windwest, which Sir William had left unfinished in his desk. Behind that letter lay the remote possibility that Blunder had been a dishonest steward and had misappropriated trust funds.

It was a slender chance enough, for the firm of Armand & Blunder was by common repute an exceedingly wealthy one. The partners in such an old-established firm would be the last people on earth to run risks of this kind.... Moreover, Blunder lived frugally enough. His establishment at Hempstead was by no means bigger than might have been expected in the case of a man in his position, nor was his town house at all suggestive of extravagance. There was no reason to suppose that he was addicted to gambling.

Could Miss Poppy de Vere, the actress, supply the key to the riddle?

Dr Hailey's mind was singularly romantic for a man of his wide experience of the darker side of human nature. In a sense he idealized all women; it was the hardest possible thing for him to believe evil of any of them—though he was a shrewd enough judge of woman's character when it was actually before him. Somehow, he did not believe that a very pretty young girl —he had seen a photograph of Poppy De Vere in one of the illustrated papers—would have dealings of any kind with such a man as Blunder.

The clue, however, was his last remaining hope. He must meet this young woman, and if possible attempt to discover whether or not she was on intimate terms with the lawyer—in any case, why her handkerchief had been found in the pocket of Blunder's coupé. He decided that his first step should be a visit to his old friend, Rhoda Romney, whose knowledge of the stage seemed to grow more extensive with each year of her separation from that scene of her triumphs.

He drove to her flat in Cheyne Walk, just before tea-time. She was alone in her strangely furnished drawing-room, which suggested, he always thought, a museum combined with a high-class curiosity shop. Relics of the wonderful past jostled there against pieces from the drawing-rooms of Old Versailles and the Faubourg—pieces collected haphazard, without much care, but always with discrimination. Yet the room lacked nothing of comfort. Indeed, its comfort transcended and embraced its motley furnishings, making them, somehow, a proper background for the personality of their owner.

Miss Romney was busy writing when he discovered her, but the tea-table was already set. He caught the gleam of wonderful silver, the indefinable suggestion of deliciousness in store. His hostess rose with the enthusiasm of a girl and came to him, both hands extended in welcome.

"My dear, good Eustace, how delightful of you...."

She took his hands and looked up into his face, and he saw again the woman whose beauty was proverbial. Sixty years had but slightly, he thought, tarnished that lustre.

"Ah, dear Rhoda," he said, "already you make me feel ashamed of myself, of my mission."

She stood away from him, smiling.

"I know what that means," she cried; "you have come on business. You men... you men! When we are young and when we are old, it is the same thing. Always you come with a purpose, never just for the joy of coming. And yet, you know, we are glad to see you, however you come."

She installed her visitor in a great arm-chair, covered with a royal robe of silk which, in spite of its age, possessed still much of its ancient splendour. He was aware immediately of the sense of well-being which her presence always induced in him; the charm which had captivated every audience almost from the rise of the curtain, was as potent as ever.

126

"You shall talk to me," she declared, "when I have given you tea—and not before. But don't be afraid. I know what it means to be busy and I can guess how anxious the work of unravelling this case must be. I have read all the reports of it, you see. Your name has been mentioned again and again."

She lifted the big teapot which cunning hands had shaped, a century before, in the form of a dragon, with fierce muzzle and terrible claws. The exquisite, wide cups, were filled with meticulous care. Dr Hailey possessed himself of one of them, and at the same time lifted the cover from a muffin dish and presented it to his hostess. The muffins, he noticed, were buttered to perfection.

"Do you happen to know a girl whose stage name is Poppy de Vere?" he asked in his gentlest tones.

"Yes."

Miss Romney's voice was crisp. Her monosyllable seemed to compromise between a desire to say much, and an even stronger wish to say nothing at all. Dr Hailey sipped his tea.

"I understand," he remarked at length, "or at least I think I do."

"My dear Eustace, you certainly do not. Poppy de Vere is exactly the kind of girl whom a man like you is incapable of understanding.... And so men like you come, sometimes, to great disaster. I have seen it."

"From which I may infer that you do not like the young lady."

Miss Romney's lips parted in sudden hesitation. It was an expression which, when she was a girl, had been described again and again by enthusiastic admirers in the Press.

"No... you must not infer that—at least, not quite that. There is something about Poppy... I believe that if there were no men in the world, I should like her very much indeed. But that is not fair to you, is it?"

"I confess it leaves me a little bewildered."

"Poppy is a man's girl—in the strictest sense of that horrid expression. She drives some men quite crazy."

Dr Hailey handed his hostess the cake basket. She selected a sponge-finger and began to nibble it.

"Do you understand now?" she asked.

"H'm, yes, in a way. I suppose that means that she is as greedy as the proverbial sparrow?"

"Not greedy—spendthrift."

Dr Hailey laid his cup on the table and took out his snuff-box.

"I see," he declared; "the sort of girl who doesn't mean to ruin the men she makes friends of."

"Exactly."

"Still, extravagance is an elastic term, you know. In Tooting, I am told, it is reckless extravagance to possess ten hats."

"Poppy de Vere is extravagant after the fashion of the *Rue de la Paix*."

Miss Romney refilled her visitor's cup. She watched him take snuff with the fascinated interest of a child who has been expecting the exhibition of a mannerism, and crows inwardly with delight when expectation is realized.

"Hats in her case are a cure for melancholy."

"Curious," said Dr Hailey, "but I have observed myself that women of that sort are always the victims of depression."

"Because they are always the victims of *ennui*. Buying happiness is so much more difficult than buying hats."

Dr Hailey stirred his second cup of tea reflectively. This was the kind of girl who might, after all, supply him with the motive he was looking for. Yet he found it more difficult than ever to associate her with Blunder. He wondered whether or not he should pursue the matter further.

"One more question," he said, "and I will apologise for my curiosity. Does Miss de Vere earn a good income by her acting?"

"About £4 or £5 a week—not a penny more."

"Yet she played the lead in… I forget the name of the piece."

"My dear Eustace, you said 'earn'. I have no doubt she has been paid very much larger sums on many occasions."

"In that case I want to meet her."

Miss Romney opened her eyes, but before he had time to observe this expression she had changed it. The actress died hard in the woman.

"I shall ask her to my next 'at home' then—on Friday. Will that do?"

"Today is Tuesday. I haven't much time to spare; but we can't force matters, I think."

"And I shall introduce you as the eminent Harley Street specialist. Poppy likes eminent men, especially if they are rich as well as distinguished. And now tell me this, just to satisfy an old woman's curiosity: is it in connection with the Armand case that you are making this... this move?"

"Yes."

"Then I shall tell you something which I am quite sure you will like to know. The last time Poppy de Vere played lead in a West End production, Mr Blunder, of Armand & Blunder, found the money for the show. People who understand these matters put his total loss at about £10,000."

CHAPTER 19 A SUM IN ARITHMETIC

Miss Romney's "at homes" had this in common with the British Museum—that they brought together times past and present. They were at once an anachronism and a joy. The older actors and actresses who came to them caught, once again, the spirit of their first successes; the younger found success of a sort in having been invited. In addition, there were always a number of people whose interest in the stage accounted for their presence —queer people with queer names and ambitions.

In this company Poppy de Vere looked surprisingly modest. She did not look like an actress, but, as Dr Hailey had anticipated, like a nun. He observed her very carefully before he was introduced to her, and was frankly astonished. He had expected a degree of flamboyancy as well as of saintliness; he saw a girlish figure in the simplest possible style. It did not immediately occur to him that that simplicity had cost more than all the bizarre raiment in the room put together. Miss de Vere's face was greatly intelligent. Her brow was broad, her eyes widely set, her nose and mouth excellently proportioned. She possessed, too, very charming hands... the hands of a well-bred woman. He turned away, and then looked back again. There was a dreamy quality in her big eyes which appealed to him in spite of himself.

When Miss Romney introduced him, he became acutely conscious of this quality. It dominated the girl's expression, giving her an air of remoteness from her surroundings.... She seemed to look on the world from a distance, and there was the suggestion that this vantage ground was infinitely to be desired a place of enchantment and wonder. Nevertheless, there was a shyness, almost a *gauche* quality in her manner, which maintained the girlishness of her appearance in spite of her siren glances. It would be possible, he felt, to believe all the good in the world of her, while at the same time abandoning oneself to her bewitchments.

That impression, however, did not endure. When he had talked to her for a few minutes on indifferent topics, he found himself becoming aware of another feeling—which he could only characterize as the effect of an overwhelmingly feminine temperament on a purely masculine one. Miss de Vere made love with her eyelids. She promised understanding and sympathy in conventional phrases about the weather. As he watched her, there arose in his mind the memory of the family circle at Hempstead as he had seen it on the night of his motor smash—Mrs Blunder, incurably virtuous and hard; the girl, hard without any other quality whatever except her high spirits; Blunder, with his obvious, pitiful hankering after the pretty things of life—the feminine things. How overpowering must be the effect of such a girl as this on such a man.

He looked down—into the depths of the velvety-grey eyes, which were smiling up at him. Miss de Vere said:

"You are not really listening to me, are you, Dr Hailey?"

"I was thinking about you, though."

"What a little fool I am, no doubt."

"On the contrary——"

He led her through the crush to the refreshment room and found a seat for her in a quiet corner. He fetched a cup of tea and sat down beside her.

"Tell me about your new part," he said.

He saw her cheeks flush quickly. The velvet eyes grew discontented.

"My new part? Oh, that's all off now."

"What!"

He affected a note of pained astonishment.

"Yes. It's a beastly nuisance, but my luck this year is all out. Do you know, this has been the very worst year of my whole life—everything has gone wrong."

It had, apparently, because the girl pouted in a sulky fashion, of which he would scarcely have supposed her capable. Yet the feminine quality which radiated from her suffered no diminution in the change of her expression. It seemed, indeed, to grow in intensity. He could imagine the devastating effect on a lover of this show of feeling.

"I suppose," he said, "that it is difficult to finance any play just now. Times are bad, you know."

She bit her lip.

"That doesn't make disappointment any easier to bear, does it?" she exclaimed. "Men never seem to think how much a girl like me counts on her work to keep her spirits up. When I heard that the play must be dropped, I felt so utterly wretched that I could hardly bear to live".

There was fresh resentment in her voice. Evidently she considered that the reasons for the abandonment of this enterprise —whatever it might be—were inadequate. Dr Hailey drew a bow at a venture.

"Mr Blunder was to have financed the play, wasn't he?" he asked in casual tones.

"Who told you that?"

"Oh, it's common talk."

The grey eyes searched his face. He bore the scrutiny with what indifference he could command.

"I wish," said the girl sharply, "that people would mind then own business. It's disgusting, I think, the way everybody keeps prying and nosing into my affairs."

"My dear, it's human nature."

Her mood changed suddenly, and the sulky look in her eyes cleared away. She showed him a very charming smile—so charming that he felt genuinely sorry for her disappointment.

What Rhoda Romney had said about this girl was true in every respect.

"Bring me another cup of tea," she asked, "and then I shall be quite good-tempered again."

She held out her cup to him, and again he admired her hands. He made a special study of hands, and these showed both character and sympathy. They were, however, rather too fine for the hands of a really successful woman. Miss de Vere, he thought, would never get much farther in life than love affairs.... Perhaps in her heart she did not really wish to get any farther; so many pretty girls pretended to be ambitious.

She was pensive when he returned with the tea, as though her mind was already far away from the things they had been talking about. Her fine eyes seemed gentler, too.

"It is kind of you," she said sharply.

He sat in silence, not knowing what to say. After a few minutes she suggested that they should return to the drawing-room.

"May I come and see you some time?" he asked.

"Of course, any time. You know my address."

He was aware that her interest had reawakened suddenly. Probably she was still thinking of her leading part; one man would be as good as another to adventure his money in theatrical enterprises. And yet, she did not strike him as particularly worldly.

He waited behind when the other guests had gone away—a privilege he often exercised at Miss Romney's.

"You were right, of course—as you always are—about that girl," he told her. "She is exactly as you described her."

The actress lay back in one of her great chairs, with her arms extended before her. She seemed to be very tired, though he could not decide whether this was real or only make-believe.

"My dear Eustace," she said in weary tones, "I almost forget my own description now. These people exhaust me more than they used to do." She added after a moment, lest he should think her ungracious, "She is charming, isn't she?"

"Very charming."

"Did you discover what you wanted to discover?"

"Some of it."

There was another pause. Then Miss Romney smiled, in her half-cynical fashion which never conveyed any real impression of cynicism.

"You will not rest content until you have discovered all," she declared. "I know you. Tomorrow, or the next day, poor Poppy's secrets will be dragged from her. It must be terrible to be a detective—even an amateur detective—I think."

"And yet, you know, curiosity is a quality of art. As an artist...."

He did not finish his sentence. Miss Romney nodded.

"We are all hag-ridden," she declared. "It would be better to break stones."

He walked home, through a mist which lay lightly on the pavements, like the foam of some ghostly sea. Exercise cleared his brain and enabled him to think. When he reached Harley Street, his mind was restored to the activity which the adventure at Hazlemere had, for the moment, almost brought to a standstill.

Whatever might be the truth of that affair, it was certain that Blunder was spending a great deal more money than any of his acquaintances supposed him to be spending. He did not know very much about the theatre, but he knew enough to realize that financing plays for the purposes of friendship is one of the high roads to ruin. Only a millionaire can continue to pursue that hobby.

It followed that the lawyer was probably in monetary difficulties already. When a man of that type begins to pander to a woman's fancies, he is very far gone indeed. As a rule, he is quite incapable of stopping in time. The fact that a halt had been called to the expenditure meant, without a doubt, that sheer necessity dictated that course.

In other words, Blunder was ruined. The question remained to what depths of disaster he had sunk. Had he, for example, spent other people's money as well as his own—Lady Windwest's money? If so, then Sir William Armand must have experienced the greatest shock of his life when he visited his office during his last stay in London.

Dr Hailey accepted that idea as true for a moment, in order the better to arrive at the consequences which must have followed. Sir William was, beyond all doubt, a man of very high honour. He would be appalled, stricken. There is no darker crime which a lawyer can commit, no crime which lawyers, from the oldest to the youngest members of the profession, hold in greater detestation.

His first impulse would certainly be to find the money himself, and so at least secure his client against loss.

He was a rich man, but his total fortune probably did not exceed £100,000. Suppose that this sum was inadequate to cover the defalcations? Rhoda Romney, who was no financier, had put the losses on one play alone at £10,000. And there had been two plays at least. He consulted his theatre guide again. The first was called *The Giddies*, and had been produced in 1920. He could faintly remember seeing the bills. It had run just ten weeks. *The Girlies* followed in 1922, and ran a fortnight. This last was the £10,000 adventure clearly; he wondered whether its predecessor, in its ten weeks' course, had not cost double that sum. Both were exceedingly expensive plays....

And that, of course, was only the beginning of Poppy de Vere's extravagance. If she had managed to wheedle £30,000 from her lover for plays, how much had she not obtained in the last four or five years for clothes and jewellery, for hats, for houses, for motor cars, for visits to fashionable resorts, for eating and drinking...?

Moreover, it was possible that Blunder had been the victim of this infatuation for a decade. Poppy was not a child, and Mrs Blunder must have been almost unendurable from an early period of her wedded life. He had observed that many men will bear an unhappy marriage about fifteen years—after that, they were apt to break loose.

It was therefore quite possible that Sir William's whole fortune was inadequate to make good the embezzlements of his partner. His course, in that case, would not be difficult to determine. He would pay what he could, and put the matter at once in the hands of the police, lest bad should become worse in the process of time.

But that meant absolute ruin for himself, as well as for Blunder. He was a partner of the firm, jointly responsible for all its dealings. He must have realized with deadly clarity that his name was bound to be covered in disgrace.

Nor could his daughter escape a share of this tragedy....

Dr Hailey got up, as the thought expanded in his mind, and began to pace the floor of his consulting room. Estelle Armand's shame would cover also her future husband, Jack Derwick, MP. It would lead inevitably to his retirement from politics—to the ruin of his career, both as a politician and a barrister. Unless, indeed, he could make good his escape from the entanglement. But a decent man does not break off his engagement in such circumstances....

Was that, then, the reason for the mysterious order to Estelle to get quit of her lover as speedily as possible—an order which she obeyed immediately? On the other hand, it must be admitted that the theory supplied Derwick with a fresh motive for the crime of which he was being accused. If Sir William's mouth was sealed in the mysterious way attempted, the shame of exposure would be delayed and very greatly lessened. The law does not proceed against dead men.

Next morning a fresh consideration occurred to him. It was just possible that Sir William might have refunded the money, and yet in addition to that have felt it his duty to inform the police. In that case, his death would save the situation for everyone concerned—Blunder among the number.

But these were suppositions. He must possess facts. Immediately after lunch he called his car, and drove out to Hampstead to redeem his promise to Miss de Vere.

The outside of her house, as he saw it when he approached,

did not suggest extravagance. It was a Georgian house, with long windows and a severe beauty of line which enchanted him. But the rent, he guessed, could not exceed £200 a year.

He sent his car away and rang the bell. It was answered by a maid, who showed him through a panelled hall to the drawing-room.

The room was empty. A single glance at it made him gasp with amazement. Never, anywhere, had he seen such splendid, such prodigal luxury. This luxury spread itself everywhere. The very walls were hung with tapestries which, he knew, must be almost priceless—glorious scenes executed in the grandest style of a period which created beauty for the enjoyment of kings and queens. The carpet was another miracle of loveliness—an old French texture of the early Versailles period. The curtains over the window were of exquisite rose brocade. He glanced at the furnishings, the tables of bric-à-brac, the huge piano, the exquisite little bronzes which flirted with the light, the enamels, the inlays—there was not an article of them all which was not perfect in its own way, not an article which had not been chosen with the loving care of enthusiasm and experience. In the light of this artistic triumph, the drawing-room at Hempstead seemed like a crude sketch.... But they bore, nevertheless, the imprint of the same hand....

The door opened. Poppy de Vere came into the room.

CHAPTER 20 A WOMAN IN THE CASE

Her appearance was a fresh surprise. She was dressed in a blue teagown, which on some women would have looked dowdy. Worn by Poppy de Vere, it looked ravishing. Her fair hair and delicate complexion contrasted exquisitely with its deeper colour. Her slight figure made its looseness an artistic triumph.

Dr Hailey glanced at her in admiration which he could not disguise. No wonder men were found to gratify the whim of so lovely a creature.

"I didn't think you would come so soon," said the girl in tones which left him doubtful whether or not she welcomed his visit. He felt suddenly as awkward as a schoolboy.

"I'm afraid," he declared, "that my visit is not... what perhaps it may seem to be."

The big eyes opened wider.

"How funny!"

"You see, I am a doctor. A doctor hears a great deal which does not reach the ears of other people...."

He paused again, trying to think how he should handle a situation which had been made unexpectedly difficult for him.

Miss de Vere bit her lip.

"Don't say you've come to feel my pulse," she exclaimed, "because I can assure you I'm quite well, thank you."

He decided swiftly. He would be frank with her—up to a point.

"You may have seen in the papers," he said, "that I am helping the police in the Armand case. I believe you are a friend of Mr Blunder, who was Sir William Armand's partner, and I believe you can help me."

The girl's face became grave.

"Mr Blunder is not a friend of mine," she declared.

"Then I have been mistaken."

Her eyes were troubled. He thought that he saw a hidden fear in them.

"Will you go away now," she said simply.

He turned to the door. He was just about to open it when the street bell rang sharply twice. The sound drove the blood from the girl's face.

"Oh," she cried, "he's there.... He will find you. What am I to do?..."

Her voice challenged and appealed to him at the same time.

"I will say..."

"No, no! He must not find you—not on any account! You don't understand...."

She glanced round the room with tragic eyes. They heard the steps of the maid going to open the door. Suddenly, she sprang to the curtains and drew back; the heavy folds of one of them. There was just room for a man to stand within those folds.

"Quick!" she urged, imploring him in her distress. He obeyed her. She drew the curtain about him with deft fingers, arranging its folds so that even an observing eye would detect nothing amiss. In his sorrow at having so deeply compromised her, he did all that his inconvenient size would allow to facilitate the process.

A moment later the door opened, and he heard Blunder's voice say:

"My dear child, I had to come at once to tell you the good news...."

There was a pause, a gasp of admiration, then the voice exclaimed:

"Aren't you lovelier than loveliness itself?"

"Am I?..."

"Babs, there is nobody like you in the world!"

Miss de Vere was evidently accustomed to this kind of talk. She urged her visitor to come to the point and disclose the object of his visit.

"It's about the play," he declared; "we can go on with it."

"What!... Oh you dear thing!"

"I found the money."

There was a pause. Dr Hailey imagined that the girl was rewarding her benefactor with kisses, but could not be sure. Then Blunder said:

"Never mind about the details, little puss, they wouldn't interest you a bit. You get busy on the production. This time I mean to succeed—for I know we can succeed. We must get the very best crowd obtainable. As Lady Di, you should set the town on fire."

Miss de Vere clapped her hands.

"I'll begin making plans today," she assured him. "I'll have the car round at once and go and see Marston. We must have a Shaftesbury Avenue House, of course... and... and..."

Her voice lost itself in her anticipations.

Blunder declared:

"And I'll come back after dinner, if I may. I can't wait now because I'm up to the eyes in work at the office."

He seemed to the listener to move about the room. Then, in a changed voice, he asked:

"You will not bring David into it?"

"Oh, why not?..."

"Because..." suddenly the tones grew deep and violent; "because, by God, I won't have it. Do you understand, child, I won't have it. The fellow's in love with you!"

"You say that of everybody...."

"And it's true... of everybody."

In the silence which followed, Dr Hailey could hear Mr Blunder's breathing. Then the girl's clear voice declared:

"I've told you before that I will not have my friends interfered with. If I want David in the play I'll have him—or you can find another girl to be Lady Di."

"You are in love with David…. My God, I can't bear it!"

"I'm not in love with anybody."

Blunder's temper broke loose. He raved so that it was difficult to recognize the cold clever lawyer in this wild man, driven crazy by jealousy.

"No," he shouted, "that is the abominable thing. You are not in love with anybody, because you are incapable of love! You love only yourself—you are ice, steel. The men you know are only things to be used and thrown away. Look at you a week ago when I was afraid I could not finance this new toy! You hated me then, abused me, sneered at me. What did it matter to you that I had ruined myself in satisfying all your whims. I might go to the gutter and be hanged. Now, when I find the money, you will kiss me again. Ha! and you will kiss other men, too—just as easily. You have no heart, no soul. How I hate you! How I would like sometimes to take your pretty neck in my hands and strangle you…!"

"Please try to control yourself."

Her words only fanned his exasperation.

"I won't control myself. I have controlled myself long enough; controlled myself to the tune of thousands, hundreds of thousands of pounds. I have brought myself to the edge of ruin. And all the time I have had the knowledge that you cared nothing —that you were unfaithful in thought if not in fact; oh, you are poisonous, poisonous…."

The girl laughed softly.

"You know you don't mean that," she said in quiet tones.

"Mean it? I mean every word of it. But, believe me, I mean also to draw the line here and now. I mean to have my money's worth in submission, if not in affection. I warn you that if I find you fooling about with David—or anybody else—anybody else, mark you—I'll close down on the whole show. You can go to the devil for all I care!"

"So you don't really love me?"

141

His voice broke so that Dr Hailey could scarcely listen to it. The madness of the wretch was strangely disagreeable, strangely piteous.

"You know that I love you with my whole soul, Babs. Oh, my God, how I love you!..."

"If you loved me, you would wish to make me happy."

There was no reply for a moment. Then the lawyer spoke again in calmer tones.

"I know you don't mean to vex me," he said, "but you're strange, wild, impossible, and I'm crazy. Oh yes, I'm stark mad where you're concerned. For pity's sake try to play straight with me, and I swear you shall have all you want—all."

"I always play straight with you."

"I believe you do—in your own way. Perhaps it isn't your fault that men worship the ground you walk on...."

Mr Blunder went away. When the door had closed behind him, Poppy de Vere came and released Dr Hailey from his prison. Her face was flushed and her deep eyes held a strange quality of resignation.

"It was your own fault," she said coldly, "that you heard what you heard. I think your visit a monstrous insult—in the circumstances."

"You have the right to think that. Yet, believe me, the reason which brought me here is serious beyond any exaggeration. That is my only excuse."

She walked to the fireplace and stood before it, a picture of girlish loveliness.

"You heard what he said about me," she declared. "I have no soul. I am utterly selfish."

"Yes, I heard. May I say that I pitied the man?"

She looked down into the fire, showing him the delectable lines of her neck and shoulders.

"I suppose you may. I do myself... sometimes. And yet I like him too—and fear him."

Her manner had changed entirely. She seemed anxious now to talk, as though another nature had taken possession of her. Dr

Hailey had not met any woman quite like this before—and yet he was surprised to find that her inconsistencies did not puzzle him. In a sense she was womanhood itself, an embodiment of all the worst—and perhaps of all the best—qualities of her sex.

"You will have some tea?"

He protested that he must go, but she rang the bell. Then she asked:

"Did you find out what you came to find out?"

"Yes."

"That Mr Blunder has been spending a great deal of money on me?"

"No. I knew that before."

She frowned. Then she shrugged her shoulders.

"I can't see what you came for, in that case," she said.

"I came to discover whether he possessed any more money."

"He does, evidently."

"Evidently."

She looked up into his face with eyes suddenly troubled.

"Do you mean that that fact tells against him in some way? Because, if it does, it would not be fair of you to use it. You got it by a trick—on a girl."

He nodded slowly. He had been thinking the same thing.

"I promise you that I will not use it," he said. "As it happens, there are other bits of evidence which amount to the same thing."

Possibly his tones were a little severe. In any case, they alarmed his companion. She came to him and put her hand on his arm.

"I feel that something terrible is going to happen," she whispered; "I feel it. And that you are going to make it happen. Oh, please, tell me, have I been vile in getting this money out of him."

"I don't know."

She uttered a little cry and covered her eyes with her hands.

"Has he... has he done something... awful?" she cried, brokenly.

"I don't know."

"But you suspect... oh, I feel that you suspect, and it makes me terrified.... I wish now that I had refused to let him pay for the new production...."

Dr Hailey was silent a moment. She left him and sat down on a sofa near the fire. Her maid brought in the tea-tray and arranged it. When she had left the room again, he said:

"You see, a young man's life is in danger. They have arrested Jack Derwick on the charge of murdering Sir William Armand, and I feel almost certain that he is innocent of that crime."

She started up:

"You mean... that he... Blunder, is guilty. Oh, my God!"

"No. That is scarcely possible."

"I should not like him less than I do, if he were guilty. I don't mind what people do—only what they are."

Her face, as she said this, glowed with a resolution which transformed it. Dr Hailey felt a new interest in her.

"What is more," she added, "I am going to warn him that you are after him. It is only fair. After all, he has been my pal."

He bowed his head.

"I can't prevent you doing that," he said. "But Mr Blunder knows already that I am after him. We have met... often."

"Then I needn't have minded his finding you here. He would not have suspected... anything?"

"I don't think so."

"I shall tell him," she repeated. "Perhaps it's all I can do now to help him."

CHAPTER 21 BEHIND PRISON BARS

Sir William Armand's will appointed Mr Blunder sole trustee. He left the whole of his fortune to his daughter. The will had been made rather more than a year before his death.

This information was brought to Dr Hailey by Biles on the day following his visit to Miss de Vere. It occasioned him no surprise. Until the girl was found, Blunder would have the disposal of £100,000; and the girl, for reasons which he knew, would not be found. Yet his lips were sealed. He could not even tell his friend Biles, without prejudicing his honour.

For, after all, he had no real evidence that his theory was correct. Blunder had spent large sums on Poppy de Vere; but he was a rich man. He might have come to some belated arrangement with his bank which enabled him to finance the new venture. On the other hand, if any inkling of Estelle Armand's whereabouts reached Scotland Yard, the result would be her immediate arrest.

If only he knew whether or not Blunder was acting honestly in relation to his partner's daughter. Dr Hailey had a deep respect for the law, but nevertheless he would not stir a finger to betray the whereabouts of that unhappy girl, of whose complete innocence he felt convinced. Even if he had not, tacitly, promised to respect the lawyer's secret, he would, he told himself, have felt bound in honour to shield a broken woman from the fresh horrors which awaited her.

Biles assured him that a verdict against Jack Derwick was a matter of certainty. The case, even in the absence of Estelle, was complete. The proceedings in the magistrate's court would finish that week and the trial might be expected within a fortnight —at the next Assizes.

"The prisoner," he added, "means to conduct his own defence; but that will not help him, clever barrister as he is."

"On the contrary," said Dr Hailey, "it is madness. How can he collect the necessary evidence from his cell in Newcastle gaol?"

"What evidence is there for him to collect? We shall put all the available witnesses in the box. All he can do is to cross-examine them."

"He might be able, surely, to authenticate his movements on the night of the murder."

"My dear friend, the only person who could possibly give evidence on that point is Miss Armand herself, and she is still in hiding. I don't think I can ever remember a woman eluding the police so successfully for so long a period."

"No. It is extraordinary. You haven't discovered any clue to her whereabouts?"

"Not an inkling. We know that she entered the London express at Newcastle in company with a man—and that's all. Our people were warned in time to meet the train at King's Cross, but they saw nothing of the couple."

"The train stops at Grantham, doesn't it?"

"Yes. Unfortunately, there was not time to cover that possibility."

They were seated in the doctor's consulting room. He brought a box of cigars and offered it to his friend, who selected one. Then he asked:

"Would I be permitted to see young Derwick in prison if I went to Newcastle?"

Biles opened his eyes in astonishment.

"Why on earth should you want to do that?" he demanded sharply.

"Because I think I might be able to help him. Somehow, I cannot quite feel about this case as you feel."

"You don't believe he is guilty?"

"Frankly, no."

Biles thought a moment.

"It's irregular, of course," he said, "but we have no desire whatever to stand in the way of his obtaining an absolutely fair deal. Scotland Yard, as you know, prides itself on giving the men it prosecutes every possible chance to save themselves. When do you want to go?"

Dr Hailey considered. "Would Saturday be convenient?" he asked—"the day after tomorrow?"

"Yes, quite convenient. I'm going back tomorrow for the final proceedings at the police court. I'll see the Governor of the prison myself."

Dr Hailey did not enjoy his visit to Newcastle. His enthusiasm for detective work ended always at a prison's gates. Indeed, he never entered these terrible buildings without a shudder. The utter futility of the whole system bore dismally on his spirit.

Biles had been as good as his word, and the Governor, Colonel Whitestar, a kindly man with the spirit of the Army in his nostrils, received him most graciously. But in the short interview they had in the office, not a word passed which was not directly concerned with business. This man, the doctor realized, had acquired a habit of reticence, just as a surgeon acquires what the unthinking often call "callousness". It was his shield against the world in which he lived.

A warder with jingling keys conducted the visitor across the prison yard, where men dressed in the raiment of shame were marching in aimless circles round unhallowed patches of grass. The expressions on their faces were the expressions of beasts of burden—of the less well-conditioned variety. Again the thought sprang to his mind: "What is the good of it? What can it accomplish?"

They passed into a large building, which somehow reminded him of the lion house at the Zoo. It seemed to be constructed of cages joined together with concrete. Other warders in their severe blue uniform were standing about, and convicts were hurrying along the corridors. Once an order rang out—and then the convicts seemed to hurry a little faster. A bell rang sharply.

"What is that?" the doctor asked his guide.

"Somebody ringing for a whisky and soda, I expect," the man explained, with a grin which was not lacking in kindness.

He was an old man. Probably he lamented the passing of the severer discipline of his youth. Even prisons, apparently, were being demoralized by the modern spirit.

They came to the block reserved for prisoners awaiting trial. The warder led the way into a fairly large room, furnished with a table and chairs. He left the doctor here and went to fetch Derwick. A few minutes later the latter entered. The warder went out, but left the door ajar behind him. Dr Hailey heard his footsteps passing out of earshot in the corridor.

Jack Derwick was dressed in his own clothes. He looked undaunted, but anxious. His face was thinner than it had appeared at the inquest at Belfort and his eyes held a haggard expression.

"Dr Hailey, I believe," he said, in tones of some surprise.

"Yes. I have taken a liberty of forcing myself upon you, I know, but I have done so because I feel I may be of some use."

He paused.

"You assisted the police, did you not, to find Sir William's body?"

"That is so. Beyond that I have not been able to help them. May I say at once that I do not share their views about yourself."

A look of slight suspicion crept into Derwick's eyes. Had this man been sent to him as a kind of spy? But immediately afterwards his expression cleared. He held out his hand.

"Thank you," he said.

"On the other hand," said the doctor, "I don't disguise from myself the fact that the evidence is rather damaging—so far as it goes. What I came to tell you, I'm afraid, does not remove that difficulty, but it may possibly be of greater assistance to you than I am able to realize at present.... May I sit down?"

Derwick apologised for his rudeness in not having anticipated this wish. He took another of the wooden seats round the table. He rested his head on his hands while his visitor recounted, step by step, his investigation into Blunder's activities. Not until the scene in the house at Hazlemere was described did he utter a syllable.

But at that disclosure he sprang up suddenly, with a cry of horror.

"My God! they mean to kill her. Oh, tell me that you know she is safe?"

"I have reason to think so, my dear fellow," said the doctor gently. He continued his narrative, reporting as nearly as he was able the statement made by Blunder. Derwick controlled himself with what was obviously a very severe effort. At last he interjected:

"It's all rubbish, of course. Estelle never had an epileptic fit in her life!"

"But his point was that no one except her father knew about the fits. As a doctor, I am forced to admit that this may be true."

"What! Do you mean to say people can be mad without their most intimate friends knowing it?"

"Epilepsy is not madness. Between attacks, its victims are often specially sane. Both Napoleon Bonaparte and Julius Caesar were epileptics."

Jack Derwick frowned.

"I can't believe it," he declared.

"Recollect that Miss Armand was certainly out of her mind when I saw her. There is no doubt whatever about that."

A look of great weariness came into the young man's eyes.

"So you think it was because of these fits that she broke off our engagement?"

"You will admit, anyhow, that the reason was an adequate one —one, I mean, which would seem adequate both to her father and herself?"

"Ye-es—it may be so."

"Moreover—you see, I am defending my own conduct to some extent—one could not quarrel with Blunder for rescuing her from the police—always supposing that his object in doing so was her own good."

"No."

Dr Hailey moved round a little in his chair so as to face Derwick.

"In any case," he said, "it is quite certain that Blunder, or Sawyer as he called himself at Calthorpe, did not murder Sir William. He hadn't time to do it. He would not be likely therefore—or so I have argued—to do any injury to Sir William's daughter. If he had a quarrel, it would be with the father."

Derwick inclined his head. He did not speak.

"Therefore I left Miss Armand where she was, and devoted myself to inquiring into Blunder's private affairs."

He described his visit to Poppy de Vere, and the information he had gathered about the lawyer's expenditure, adding:

"You see, there might be—I say might be only—a motive for murder there, but the case breaks down at once when we come to the actual circumstances. By no hook or crook could any man have accomplished the burial of Sir William's body in the time during which Blunder was absent from the Black Bull Inn."

He paused again and took out his snuff-box.

"You have no theory of the crime, then?" said his companion.

"At present, none."

"Naturally, I have thought a great deal about it. It is certainly baffling in the extreme; all that evidence about morphia, for example. Believe me, I never owned or used a hypodermic syringe in my life."

"Yes, that is one of the most mysterious features."

Derwick got up and began to pace the room. He was wearing prison shoes and they fell with a padded sound on the stone floor.

"Blunder will be called for the Crown," he said. "I might cross-examine him on his financial position, but I don't see what good that would do—except to discredit him personally. It would react on Estelle. Above all things, mention of her whereabouts must be avoided. Whatever happens to me, she is safe—or at least, comparatively safe."

"Yes, I think so. I don't know what may happen if she recovers her reason, but probably it will be possible, in that event, to send her to a retreat somewhere until... afterwards. Meanwhile, we must establish your innocence. I came to offer my services for what they may be worth in that direction."

He took snuff. The young man's stride had lengthened and become more vigorous. He was a caged beast now, with the fury of the captive in his eyes.

"But how, how?" he exclaimed. "How am I to convince a jury that, though I was out on the cliffs at the time of the murder, I did not actually commit murder?" He added, after a moment: "You see, I carried on past the Hall, to the southward, so as not to go in until it was time to leave altogether. I would have gone farther than I did, and reached the next village—and an alibi—if I hadn't torn my hand on a barbed wire fence...."

"What! You wounded your hand?"

"Yes; and then found I had lost my handkerchief. I had to do the best I could to stop the bleeding, by pressing the wound against my coat. They mentioned at the police court that they had found a bloodstain on it."

"It is a cardinal point in the indictment."

They sat in silence for some time. Then Dr Hailey asked:

"What about the Vicar? You had tea with him on the night in question, I believe."

"Yes, but left him long before the critical time."

Derwick sat down again. He sighed deeply.

"It is extraordinarily good of you to try to help me in this way," he said. "Do, please, believe that I am grateful... whatever the upshot. I am, too, more than grateful for the news you have brought me about Estelle. Her disappearance was a terrible weight on my mind. I feared the worst. Bad as things are, she is alive and being cared for...." He looked up suddenly. "Would it be too much to ask you to visit Hazlemere again before the trial, and just see how she is getting on?"

"Not at all," said Dr Hailey. "I was going to do that in any case."

When he left the prison his heart was heavy. He could see no adequate defence—no defence, at any rate, which would convince an average jury. The evidence was purely circumstantial, but it was quite strong enough to secure a conviction, for if Derwick had not murdered Sir William, who had? That was the question which would be reiterated again and again by the prosecution. So far, there seemed to be no answer to it. His most careful enquiries had failed entirely to reveal any hostility to the lawyer in his village. On the contrary, he was beloved both as a squire and as a man.

Nevertheless, he resolved to return to Calthorpe and spend the weekend in going over the ground once more. Experience had shown him that trifles, overlooked in the first eagerness of search, were sometimes observed on a later occasion. No trifle could be too insignificant to merit attention in this case.

CHAPTER 22 THE FINDING OF THE EYE

There is no place where the opinion of a neighbourhood is so faithfully reflected as the village inn. Dr Hailey had not been long at the "Black Bull", Calthorpe, before he discovered that, in the opinion of its patrons, Jack Derwick was already as good as hanged.

He overheard scraps of conversation to this effect through the open door of the proprietor's office, to which, as a personage in the case, he had been admitted soon after his arrival.

"What I asks you," one of the voices demanded, "is this: if *he* didn't do it, who did?"

No answer was forthcoming to this challenge, and the listener's heart grew heavy as he realized that, in all human probability, no answer would be forthcoming. The picture of Derwick's dark handsome face, strained with anxiety and anticipation of death, rose terribly in his memory.

Another voice declared: "Derwick was after her money, of course. When he saw he wasn't going to get it, he went blind mad. It's as simple as ABC."

There was a shuffle of beer-mugs on the counter, then the patrons of the "Bull" passed to discussion of the execution. They seemed to regret that it would take place in Newcastle, and not in Calthorpe. Their voices were entirely unmoved. Dr Hailey recalled a phrase he had read somewhere: "There is a cool something in the Englishman's make-up which makes him regard a criminal as other than a human being." It was apparently true.

He went to bed early, and got up before breakfast. He walked over the ground between the village and the Hall once more, lingering a long time beside the fatal tree where the murder had taken place. The dawn was red over the sea, a great splash of colour which seemed to open the heavens. The shapes of the tall pines made a dark lattice across this window of morning.

The sun rose and the mists which lay on the headlands vanished in diaphanous web-like wisps, which seemed to curl themselves into the ground. An exquisite clearness came into the air. Far away he heard the plaintive calling of a curlew.

It was such a Sabbath morning as only the North Country can afford, when Heaven and earth seem to have drawn very close to one another in a silence ineffable and full of light. Death and crime had no part in this sacrament of dawn.

Yet there, on the bole of the tree, were the marks of death, mute witnesses of crime! the little hole made by the ferrule of the victim's walking-stick, the scars which testified to his head-long fall.

He stood contemplating them, wondering at the secret they held. Again he passed his little magnifying glass over their surfaces. There were still a few grey hairs entangled in the rough bark.

He glanced at the round hole and then, as if attracted by some irregularity in its shape, which he had missed on his first inspection, magnified it also. His attention appeared to become concentrated progressively from moment to moment.

The light was not yet very strong, and he had to peer closely to satisfy himself, but at the end he had no sort of doubt. The hole which he had taken in the first instance for an imprint of the ferrule of a walking-stick was, in fact, nothing of the kind. It was a deliberate stamp on the wood by some instrument designed for the purpose.

And it represented, without any doubt, a rude figure of a human eye.

He stood back in extreme astonishment. He had seen just such a figure before in a museum of ethnology which was opened in London for a short time before the war. The curator of the museum told him that it represented a charm against the evil eye which was once in wide use among the English peasantry. He recollected his very words:

"If a cow or a sheep died, or if a mysterious human death occurred—even, I believe, if lovers quarrelled—this sign was resorted to. It was supposed to protect against the baleful glance of man or fiend which had wrought the trouble."

He made a further most minute examination. The mark had clearly not been cut. It had been stamped in a single stroke—a very powerful stroke it must have been, for the bark of the tree was cut right through. Within the circle of the eye there was a second, smaller circle, radiated like a human iris, and possessing a tiny embossed pupil. That could only mean that the author of this sign possessed some ancient instrument of the sort in use a couple of centuries ago, unless, indeed, Sir William had had his walking-stick shod in this strange fashion to gratify some whim. Biles had told him that the walking-stick had been recovered, but probably it was now in the possession of the prosecution, as an exhibit in the case.

He walked back towards the hotel, and then turned to make another inspection of his find. Was it possible that, after all, its presence was unconnected with the murder? It was, undoubtedly, a new mark, for the bark was freshly broken, yet it might well have been made on any day within the last two months. Lovers were addicted to imprinting strange devices on the boles of trees, and doubtless those of Calthorpe were not different from their fellows elsewhere.

But the coincidence between this device and the wounds in the dead man's eye was too remarkable, surely, to admit of such an explanation. Again he magnified the strange lines, asking himself whether, after all, he might not be mistaken about them. Some sticks possessed ferrules with a serrated surface to increase their "grip" of the ground. Could not this impression—so like an eye—have been made quite accidentally in this fashion? But for those museum specimens, he might have accepted that explanation. The thought came into his mind that a jury, not having seen the specimens, would accept it without question.

At breakfast he wondered again and again how he could convince ignorant men of the truth of his observation. He would try to discover where the ethnological specimens had been obtained, and where they now were. Possibly, the curator of the museum might be able to give expert evidence on the subject. But so much depended on Sir William's walking-stick.

Then he asked himself what, in any case, his discovery proved. Who would believe that Sir William met his death at the hands of some maniac unknown, with a taste for the darker aspects of folklore? Where, in any case, was the man? The sense of despondency which, in the excitement of his find, had passed away for a few minutes, returned with new force.

The landlord came into the coffee-room just as he finished his meal, and at once began discussing the crime. At another time, Dr Hailey would have tried to get rid of him as quickly as possible. Now, however, he wanted information, and bore with the wearisome recital. When it seemed to have concluded, he asked in casual tones whether there were any witches left in Calthorpe.

The worthy hotel-keeper stared.

"I never heard tell of any," he said decidedly.

"Only that I have been told that North Country folk are still full of old superstitions," the doctor explained. "I thought, perhaps, the village might number some old man or woman among its inhabitants with enough second sight to explain the mystery to us."

"Oh... I see."

The hotel-keeper laughed. He had not grasped that his guest was making a joke. He added heartily:

"No, we're too modern for that sort of thing nowadays. Besides, sir, what need of second sight in a case of this kind. Why, it's as plain as a pike-staff...."

He began to develop his opinions once again. Dr Hailey managed to reach the door. To his relief he saw that Superintendent Robson, of the local police, was entering the inn. He hailed him immediately.

It appeared that Biles had telephoned for some further particulars of the "ground" asked for by the prosecution. Robson had motored over from Belfort to collect them.

"In that case," said the doctor, "I will, if I may, accompany you on your work. I also came to make a fresh inspection."

"Found nothing new, I suppose?" said Robson, a little off-handedly.

"Er... not much. By the way, you recovered Sir William Armand's walking-stick, didn't you?"

"Oh, yes. It was washed ashore. It's lying at the Hall now."

Dr Hailey snuffed vigorously, in token of his satisfaction at this piece of news. He reflected on the carelessness of the police in not producing this, to his mind, important link in the chain of evidence.

"May I look at it?" he asked, in tones from which he tried to exclude the eagerness he felt.

"Of course. I'm going over to the Hall now, as soon as I've had a glass of beer."

Robson was not a fool though he had rather slow wits. He confessed to his companion as they walked along the cliffs, that he was not entirely satisfied with the evidence against Derwick. In his homely phrase, "it wanted punch somehow".

"I agree with you," said the doctor cordially.

"And yet... if not him, who?"

That question was assuming nightmare proportions. Unless some really convincing answer to it was discovered, it would hang the unfortunate young man. The doctor demanded sharply:

"You are quite sure that the neighbourhood contains no half-crazed fellow who might murder for the mere sake of doing it? Such cases are common enough, you know."

The police officer shook his head. "I know what you mean," he declared, "and it seems to me a good idea, but we've nobody of that sort around here… not a soul. There used to be an old man near Belfort, who was supposed to have murdered his son years before, but he died in the summer, and anyhow there was no real evidence against him."

They reached the Hall, a picture of quiet beauty in the glowing sunlight. Dr Hailey marked the fine sweep of the lawn and the comfortable arrangement of the shrubberies which enclosed this rather severe mansion in a warm embrace. But his eagerness did not permit him time for enjoyment. As soon as the front door was opened, he stepped briskly into the hall and took the walking-stick which Robson drew from a rack, and handed to him.

Bitter disappointment was in store. The ferrule of the stick was marked with a double circle on its road surface.

Yet he would not relinquish his hope until he had proved the matter by actual examination. With the policeman's consent, he took the stick back to the wood, and actually fitted it into the hole in the tree. He uttered a cry of joy as he did so. The ferrule was considerably smaller than the hole.

CHAPTER 23 THE HOUSE OF SILENCE

At Calthorpe that clue had seemed of enormous importance. In Harley Street, its value wore a far less encouraging aspect. After all, imprints on the barks of trees are doubtful things at best.

Nevertheless, Dr Hailey had hope. He had made careful impressions of the mark and the ferrule in wax obtained on Monday morning in Belfort. He compared these now at his leisure, measuring the circles they contained with his compasses. The inner circles were almost exactly of the same size, but the outer ones differed by a definite fraction.

He sat down and wrote a careful letter on the subject to Jack Derwick, and despatched this at once to the Newcastle gaol. The date of the trial had been announced during the weekend. It would probably begin on the following Saturday morning. There remained therefore five days in which to continue his investigations.

He drove to Wigmore Street, and saw an official of the Medical Museum there, whom he knew to be an authority on charms of all sorts. He showed him the wax impression of the hole in the tree, and asked him his opinion of it.

It was not so decided as he had hoped.

"A crude representation of an eye, possibly," said the official. "But really, you know, it might be almost anything."

"What about the radial lines in the inner circle?"

"Yes; I see what you mean. That would be the iris, of course, if your theory is correct."

Greatly discouraged, the doctor presented his second impression.

"Could these two possibly have been made by the same instrument?" he asked.

The official examined them very carefully.

"Off-hand I should say it was improbable," he declared, "but the difference is not very considerable. Sometimes, too, a stamp slips a little in making its impression."

Dr Hailey drove back to Harley Street. So, of course, would the prosecution argue and the jury accept. He went to the telephone and rang up a friend at the British Museum, who might possibly know something of the ethnological collection. But he drew blank. The war had scattered so many small scientific enterprises. "Who is the best man on folklore in England?" he demanded, and was given the name of Professor Mildmay, of Oxford.

The next day he went to Oxford. Professor Mildmay proved to be a very old man, who looked exactly like an astrologer in one of the mediaeval prints; but he had a keen brain. Dr Hailey gave him a succinct outline of the case, and then showed him the two impressions. He awaited his verdict with almost breathless interest.

The old man pored over the wax for a long time; his shaggy eyebrows were drawn down so that it seemed as if his eyes were shut. His companion began to fear that he had gone to sleep at his task. At last, however, he raised his head.

"There is not the least doubt in my mind," he said, "that your scruples are justified."

"Thank God for that!"

"You see," continued the Professor, ignoring the interruption, "this impression—the one from the tree—is sharply made. The edges of the lines are clean cut, whereas the lines in the other are blunter—in spite of the fact that the ferrule is evidently a comparatively new one. That to begin with. Then look at the outer ring."

He indicated its slightly uneven character and its larger size. Then he got up and went to a shelf in his bookcase, from which he extracted a large volume. Very slowly and deliberately he turned over the yellowing pages until he came to the place he sought. Dr Hailey saw a number of woodcuts. He glanced at them, and exclaimed in astonishment.

"These," said his companion, "are types of the charm against the evil eye, which used to be worn by large numbers of countryfolk in this country. As you can see, they resemble your impression very closely."

"I do see."

"Unhappily, they also resemble, to some extent, the mark made by the walking-stick."

Dr Hailey's voice took on an anxious tone.

"But you would be prepared," he suggested, "to swear that a fundamental difference exists between them."

"Oh, yes. I have no doubt about it."

"That is all I want."

The old man shook his head.

"I'm afraid," he said, "it is a poor enough straw with which to rescue any drowning man. British juries are not easily convinced by minute scientific considerations."

Nevertheless, it was something to go upon. After obtaining the Professor's promise that he would give evidence at Newcastle, Dr Hailey returned to London in better spirits than he had enjoyed since his experience at Hazlemere. He took the night train back to Calthorpe, and next morning called at the Vicarage.

He had met the Rev Hargreave Willoughby on one occasion during his first visit, and so was already on familiar terms with him. He plunged immediately into a description of his mission, explaining that he had come to the only man who, he felt, might know the inside of local superstition.

The Vicar was in his gardening clothes—which were much shabbier than his ordinary apparel. He looked excessively destitute, but his fine cold face scorned all thoughts of appearance.

"Alas," he said, "I fear that I cannot help you at all. This parish is all too deeply imbued with the most material type of commonsense."

He folded his earth-soiled hands over his knee and looked up rather vacantly into the face of his visitor. Dr Hailey suspected that his mind had already drifted from a subject which, no doubt, he regarded as trivial.

"So you think my discovery is without significance?"

"No; far from it. Such a discovery must have a meaning. My difficulty is that I cannot find any interpretation of the riddle... unless, indeed, that poor young man carries a walking-stick with a bizarre shod on it."

Dr Hailey frowned. He had forgotten that possibility. He rose to go.

"It is kind of you to see me," he murmured in dull tones.

"On the contrary, I am glad to see you. A country vicar, I'm afraid, is always glad when a visitor comes. Our lives are rather lonely ones... especially in winter."

After he left the Vicar, Dr Hailey visited in turn the schoolmaster and the parish clerk. His enquiries in their cases were of a general character; but in each case he obtained nothing. There were no half-witted people in Calthorpe. He drove through to Belfort in the afternoon and renewed his enquiries there, but again failure met him at every turn. Next morning, Thursday, he returned to London. There seemed to be no hope whatever of following his clue any farther.

He reached King's Cross in the late evening, and drove home at once. There were no letters awaiting him, though, somehow, he had half-expected some communication—anxiety always breeds that feeling in highly-strung natures. He went to bed, and only then realized how deeply exhausted he was.

Nevertheless, he woke early with the thought in his mind that only one day now remained before the beginning of the trial. His man had brought the morning papers to his room, and he glanced at them with anxious eyes. They were full of the case, which promised to be a *cause célèbre* of the most sensational

162

kind. He flung them from him and got up.

He could do no more. So far as he could see, Jack's only defence was a flat denial. The burden of proof lay on the prosecution. They must bring their case home to him. If he could show—and in the grey of a London winter morning it seemed a slender enough hope—that there had been someone else present on the scene of the murder, it might avail to raise a doubt in the minds of the jury, and so to save him. That was the very most which could be expected of the clue of the evil eye. He prayed that Professor Mildmay might make the very most of his high reputation as an ethnologist.

There was only one service left which it was in his power to render the accused man, and that was to ease his mind about the welfare of the girl he loved. He had set apart this last day for his visit to Hazlemere so that, whatever might happen at Newcastle, Jack should face his accusers in the comfortable assurance that Estelle was safe.

He left London early in the afternoon, and reached Hazlemere two hours later. He directed the chauffeur to drive right through the village to the mansion and to go straight up the avenue.

The house, when he reached it, seemed even more desolate and deserted than it appeared on his first visit. He rang the heavy iron bell which hung down beside the front door. It sounded loudly within, but the harsh notes died away among their own echoes. There was no response.

He rang again, this time with greater vigour. Again only silence rewarded his efforts.

"Doesn't seem to be anybody there, sir," said his chauffeur, who had followed him up the steps and was looking into one of the rooms on the ground floor.

"I fear not."

"Shall I run round to the back and see if there's anybody about there?"

Dr Hailey consented. The man was absent a few minutes. When he returned, his face was blank.

"The house is all shut up—back and front," he announced, "but there's a window slightly open near the back door."

The window, doubtless, which he had himself opened! Dr Hailey walked round the house, and passed through the door in the wall which he had reconnoitred so carefully in the dark. The place was utterly deserted. He came to the open window, and threw it wide open. He shouted into the house. His own voice answered him,

"Wait here," he told his man, "till I return. I'm going to see if they've left any traces behind them."

He climbed into the pantry, the door of which stood ajar. The corridor beyond was dark and silent. He pushed through the baize-covered door, and entered the main hall. Not a sound was to be heard. After standing listening for a few seconds, he began to mount the stair. At the top of the flight he stopped again, but again there was no sound. He walked along the passage to the room where Blunder and the doctor had been seated when he found them.

He pushed open the door. The room was empty!

He glanced around him in consternation. Everything seemed to be exactly as it had been that night. The plate of sandwiches, now grown mouldy, still stood on the side table, with the syphons. The chairs remained in disarray—his own, Blunder's, the doctor's. The fender contained the ends of several cigars.

He passed into the sick-room, and exclaimed in bitterness. The tumbled bedclothes remained, but the woman they had covered was missing.

A tumbler stood on a small table at the bedside; it contained a few drops of liquid. He raised it, and smelt the odour of stale brandy. There seemed to be no other medicament in the chamber.

He returned to the anteroom and looked about him in the desperate hope of finding some indication of the time or manner of the exodus which had taken place, but Blunder was not, as he knew, in the habit of advertising his movements by the things he left behind. There was nothing.... Even the blotting paper on a pad on the table was free of any inkstains.

And yet, now that he came to clarify his memory, the pad itself was an innovation since his last visit. Neither it, nor the pen and ink which lay beside it, had been there before. He wondered what need the two men could have of writing materials.

He picked up the pad and examined it more from force of habit than from any expectation that it would yield him information. It was not complete; several sheets had been torn off since the holder was last filled. He looked in the fireplace to see if any of them remained, and found a small scrap which had escaped burning. It was unstained.

From its position, he judged that the fire must have been going out when it was thrown into it. It certainly looked as though the party had left within a short time of his own departure—otherwise there must have been changes in the arrangement of the furniture. It looked, too, as though they had gone away in some haste.

This would be terrible news, indeed, to take to Jack Derwick. An awful fear clutched at his heart that the fate of Sir William Armand had likewise befallen his daughter. He hurried downstairs and came out again as he had entered.

"I want you to help me search the garden," he said to his man. "Look out for any fresh signs of digging anywhere."

Between them they made a careful survey. The ground had certainly not been disturbed in any direction. Dr Hailey heaved a sigh of relief. At any rate, that immediate horror could be dismissed from his mind. He glanced at his watch. It was four o'clock. In another hour it would be dark. He determined to spend the night in Hazlemere.

He drove to an hotel, and enquired of the host the name of the most important local house-agent. He walked up the wide main street until he found the address which he had been given. A boy showed him at once into a back office, where a young man in a smart but cheaply-cut suit received him.

"What can I do for you?"

"I have called about the house on the Highdown Road—the

big one, standing back in its own gardens. I do not know its name."

The young man nodded. "I know, 'Dalswinter'. Unfortunately, we are not the agents. It is in the hands of a firm of London solicitors, I believe, Messrs Armand & Blunder."

"What?"

"Messrs Armand & Blunder; Sir William Armand's firm."

The agent looked knowing as he imparted this information. Apparently, Hazlemere people were proud of being connected, however remotely, with the sensation of the hour.

Dr Hailey controlled his agitation with an effort. He understood now why this place had been selected for the early stages of a drama, the end of which he could only dimly surmise. Blunder had the keys entirely at his disposal.

"But is it not the case," he asked, "that the house was in use a short time ago—as a nursing home? '

"I didn't hear that, sir, and I think we should have heard about it sooner or later."

"Do you mean to tell me it has been standing empty for a considerable period?"

"Oh yes, a year at least. Several parties came down to look at it —but they didn't seem to care for it much. Too big, probably."

"You don't happen to know if one of these... parties... was a doctor?"

"No, sir, I don't know. I did hear that a caretaker and his wife had been put in a short time ago to air the place, but of course, as we aren't handling the business, I was not interested."

CHAPTER 24
A DOCTOR'S
CERTIFICATE

The horror of the situation seemed to be entirely without relief. As it stared him grimly in the face... Hailey cursed himself for a dolt, a fool. How, with his suspicions wide awake, had he allowed himself to be thus bemused by the cunning lawyer? How had he so easily accepted that story of the nursing home at its face value?

And yet, when the first outburst of his anxiety had spent itself, he could not wonder that he had been deceived. There was the demented girl as a proof of what he had been told—a proof which even his professional experience was compelled to accept as authentic. How could he doubt the evidence of his own senses.

Nevertheless, his senses had betrayed him. There could be no reasonable question that his first suspicions of Blunder were absolutely sound. The journey to Hempstead had been undertaken solely for the purpose of ensnaring him—doubtless because the lawyer realized he was being observed and was certain to be followed.

How clever the plan had been! He was to suffer an accident, and if he didn't break his neck on the spot, was to be introduced to the respectable presence of Mrs and Miss Blunder, and then carefully and securely locked up for the night under the family roof. The telephone call was doubtless a device to allay the suspicions of the lawyer's wife when her husband should depart in the small hours.

Thus would he calculate on having at least twelve hours' clear start in his enterprise, and on having, moreover, a perfectly free hand. While his pursuers were attempting once more to hit off the trail, he would be bringing his business to a satisfactory conclusion.

The Ford car had evidently upset these well-laid plans. But with what magnificent sang-froid the scoundrel had countered that unexpected advantage of his enemy.... The more he thought of it, the higher rose the doctor's admiration. Even Blunder's tears were a triumph though they were probably quite genuine. A man, he knew, may weep and weep and be a villain—indeed weeping and villainy often go together. Then, suddenly, the recollection of the rather flamboyant nurse's uniform worn by "Dr" Parson's wife came to him. She could not have donned that costume for his benefit, seeing that, most emphatically and certainly, he was not expected to make an appearance at the midnight party at "Dalswinter".

For whose benefit, then, was she dressed up?

The conviction gradually rose in his mind that, though the conspirators were not expecting the visitor they actually received, they were, in fact, expecting some visitor.

That, probably, was the explanation of Blunder's presence in the house. He had come in order to be present at some important meeting at which the attendance of a nurse would be essential. Of what nature could such a meeting be?

And most, important of all, by what devilish means had they driven the girl insane in the first instance.

Surely someone in Hazlemere must have penetrated a little of the secret? Miss Armand had been at the house during several days, and her gaolers must have required food in that time. He resolved before sitting down to dinner to make a round of as many foodshops as possible.

He visited a dairy and a butcher's, but neither of them had

supplied "Dalswinter" for upwards of a year, nor did the shop-keepers know that the house had been occupied by other than a caretaker. The same blank ignorance awaited him at two grocers' and at another dairy. He had almost decided to abandon his quest, when he remembered the pen and ink and blotting pad. It was just possible that they had been bought locally.

And so it proved. The stationer's girl distinctly remembered the purchase. It was made by a woman, and she noticed that a man was waiting for her outside the shop. The strange thing—the thing which had fixed it in her memory—was that they had come before the shutters were taken down in the morning Actually they were on the doorstep when she opened the front door.

Dr Hailey thanked the girl and returned to his hotel. It was almost empty, and he had the long dining-room to himself. He sat pondering deeply the reason for this curious early-morning purchase.

When he went to bed he had found no enlightenment. He felt too agitated to sleep, and lay tossing from side to side in a vain attempt to rid himself of his thoughts. Then, for about an hour, he seemed to fall into a troubled slumber which, however, was without refreshment. Suddenly, he sat up in bed with an exclamation of astonishment. Asleep, his mind had reached out to a new solution. Of course, that was what had occurred.

He found his watch under the pillow, and consulted it. Three o'clock! He could not hope to do anything for several hours yet. He lay back and suddenly fell into a deep sleep.

When he awoke it was after seven o'clock. He rang for his bath and then dressed as quickly as he could. Before he went in to breakfast, he sought out the proprietor in his private office and asked him the names of the local doctors.

There were three of them, but one of them, it appeared, did not practice much. Dr Wellwisher—a young man—had the most considerable practice. He decided to visit him first, and called at his house immediately after breakfast.

The doctor was already in his surgery. He received his distinguished visitor with evident surprise, and hurried to offer him a cigar, but Dr Hailey would not smoke.

"You must forgive me for this untimely intrusion he apologized, "but the fact is that my business will brook no delay. You may have noticed from the newspapers that the trial of Mr Derwick, for the murder of Sir William Armand, begins today in Newcastle. It is about that that I am here."

Dr Wellwisher's eyes opened very wide. He began to think that the London physician had lost his mental balance.

"About the Armand case? My dear sir, how can I help you there?"

His visitor waved a large hand impatiently.

"Tell me," he asked, "were you called to Dalswinter Lodge a few days ago to see a young girl with mental trouble?"

The doctor's face became grave in a moment. He hesitated.

"I know," said Dr Hailey, "that it is difficult for you to answer me because of the promise you made; but I can assure you that when you know the facts, you will no longer hesitate."

"You are aware, then, that I gave a promise?"

"Well aware. You were told, were you not, that the utmost precaution had been taken to keep the tragedy secret?"

The doctor inclined his head. The gesture was rather equivocal nevertheless. It was evident that he had some doubts about the bona fide character of this enquiry. Dr Hailey lowered his voice.

"You cannot, I think, know that the girl you examined was Miss Estelle Armand," he said.

"What!"

"For whom the police all over Britain are at present searching...."

"Surely you can't be serious?"

"I was never more serious in my life. It may surprise you to know that I traced the girl myself to the house the night before you were called in. I saw her there."

Dr Hailey opened a picture newspaper he had bought on the way to the doctor's house, and pointed to a photograph.

"There is your patient," he added.

His companion almost snatched the sheet from his hands. He examined it with flushed face, and hands which trembled in spite of him.

"I confess," he exclaimed, "that it's very like her... I had no idea..."

His voice fell almost to a whisper:

"They told me that she had a delusion that she was Estelle Armand."

It was Dr Hailey's turn to gasp. There was a deftness, a sureness, about Blunder's methods which electrified him. The man was great beyond even his expectations.

"I suppose," he said, "that you gave this as one of the symptoms of insanity observed by you?"

The doctor admitted it. He had asked the girl who she was, and been promptly assured by her, in the intervals of her raving, that she was Estelle. That statement had continued him in his opinion that she was insane.

"The same reason, I believe, was given by Dr Parsons, who also signed the lunacy certificate. The gentleman who called her his daughter..."

"A short, fat man?"

"Yes. He explained that the case had unhinged her mind."

"He is Mr Blunder, of the firm of Armand & Blunder. I fear, doctor, you have assisted him to get rid of a very dangerous witness —from his own point of view."

Dr Wellwisher's agitation was now almost painful. No man fears a scandal quite so much as a country doctor, because no man stands to lose so much by it.

"She is confined in a private asylum," he stated. "I accompanied her there myself with her fath... I mean, with the man who posed as her father. He seemed deeply affected."

"He would be."

Dr Hailey drew out his watch. "How long will it take us to get there?" he asked. "I have a big car in the town."

"About an hour."

"Very well, can you come with me at once?"

The doctor was only too anxious to help to undo his fault. In the car he described the scene at Dalswinter Lodge, in which he had played an unwitting part. Blunder, it appeared, had called at his house early in the morning, and given the name of Colonel Herbert. He had explained that his daughter had been subject to mental trouble for some years, but had broken down completely a week before, when reading an account of the Armand case. He had taken "Dalswinter" and brought her down there from his home in Knightsbridge, under the care of a doctor and nurse. Unhappily, she had become so violent that they were unable to control her, and the doctor had intimated that he could not continue to take charge of the case.

"He burst into tears at that point in his story, and covered his face with his hands. I was genuinely sorry for him, and promised to come at once to the house."

"I can believe," Dr Hailey interjected, "that he showed you a suitable gratitude."

"Oh dear me, yes. He almost embraced me in his enthusiasm."

Miss Armand, when the doctor saw her, was still delirious, but she was able to answer questions if they were spoken in a loud voice. She did not appear to realize where she was, and showed no fear.

"I saw her alone, of course, and satisfied myself very soon that she was the victim of delusions. I thought it fortunate, at the time, that I happened to have a certificate of lunacy in the house. As soon as I had made my diagnosis. Dr Parsons, who had already examined her apart from me, filled in his portion of the document. After that I took the girl and the man I thought was her father in my car to the asylum." He added after a moment, "He paid me a fee of fifty guineas on the spot."

"In the circumstances, a modest fee."

"I think so."

The car reached a big iron gateway. Dr Wellwisher squeezed the bulb of the speaking tube, and directed the chauffeur to blow his horn. In response to it, a woman appeared from a lodge and opened the gates.

Next minute they drew up in front of a large red-brick house which belonged, Dr Hailey perceived, to the late Elizabethan period. Evidently, Mr Blunder had spared no expense in the matter of the type of retreat he had chosen for his victim.

And then, suddenly, there came to him the fear that, after all, Blunder might have been acting in good faith. If Estelle Armand was really insane, this surely was the best possible way of removing her permanently from danger of arrest!

Could it be that he had shattered a perfectly genuine scheme for saving this unhappy girl from shame and disaster?

He passed into the splendid oak-panelled hall of the old house, with a sense of growing anxiety at his heart.

The next few minutes must decide for him... or against.

CHAPTER 25 A FIGURE
OF TRAGEDY

The medical superintendent of the asylum inspired Dr Hailey instantly with a feeling of exasperation. He was one of those foolish, "safe" men, who are of all others the most difficult to deal with when emergency measures are called for.

He had a catlike face, and wore a long straggling moustache. His voice was loud and hearty, and when Dr Wellwisher explained the reason of the visit, he uttered a sound like the wind among trees—a gusty yet self-approving sound.

"Heu! my dear sirs," he exclaimed, "you trust your Hillman" (Hillman was his name). "I know insanity when I see it, and whatever the poor, dear, young lady may say, and whoever she may be, there is not an atom of doubt that she is certifiable."

He stroked his moustache as he spoke. Dr Hailey noticed that he had blue eyes.

"Have you examined her recently?" he asked, in tones which for him were unwontedly crisp.

"No... not very recently. But believe me..."

"It is not a question of believing you. We do that, of course. It is a question of fact only. May we see the lady at once?"

The superintendent frowned in a purely contemplative manner.

"It would be a little irregular, I think," he declared, "without her father's consent... I beg your pardon... the consent of the gentleman who brought her here. Lunacy Law is very strict, you know, on matters of that kind."

"Oh, blow the Lunacy Law."

"Alas, if only I could."

Two things were obvious. The first that Dr Hillman knew very little about the condition of his patients—that was probably the business of the nurses he employed, or of his assistant. The second, that he meant to obstruct by every means in his power.

Dr Hailey's manner changed.

"You leave me no choice," he declared, "but to report to Scotland Yard that you are defeating the ends of justice by harbouring a woman against whom a warrant is out. It is a serious matter."

"What?"

The long moustache seemed, somehow, to lose its aggressiveness. The catlike expression became timid.

"These are the facts."

"Of course, I had no idea of anything so serious. I'll send for the girl at once. If you will excuse me for a moment...."

Dr Hillman left the room and closed the door behind him—a heavy oaken door which nevertheless shut without the least sound. Heaviness and silence brooded over this place. Dr Hailey turned to his companion:

"I should say he hasn't examined her once since she came here," he declared bitterly.

"I'm afraid not."

His own responsibility in this very awkward and unpleasant affair was weighing heavily on Dr Wellwisher's mind. If only he hadn't been called in. He felt thankful that he belonged to a society for the legal protection of members of his profession.

"In any case, Scotland Yard will have to be informed."

"I suppose so."

The door re-opened. Dr Hillman entered, followed by a nurse and Estelle. The girl leaned heavily on the nurse's arm. She was deadly pale, and her beautiful eyes had a wild, hunted look.

"What are you going to do with me now?" she cried; "oh,

please, let me go away from here."

"My dear young lady, my dear young lady," came the soothing voice of the superintendent. It was evident that he sought to assure the doctors that the inmates of his asylum were people to be envied.

"Miss Armand?" said Dr Hailey gently.

"Yes, yes. Oh, thank God, someone believes me at last!"

She tottered towards him, and put her hands on his arms.

"Don't say that you, too, think I am mad, that you are only trying to humour me—like the nurses...."

"I am convinced that you are not mad."

When she heard these words, Estelle reeled, and would have fallen, had he not supported her.

"You had better sit down," he said.

He led her to an armchair and bestowed her carefully in it. She lay back and closed her eyes. Her eyelids, he observed, were waxen in their whiteness. There were wide dark lines under her eyes.

"Do not exhaust yourself by talking at present," he counselled. He left her and came back to the superintendent.

"The girl is perfectly sane, of course," he declared severely.

"Er... yes.... Today she seems to be very much better.... This place, the fresh air..."

Dr Hailey made an impatient signal that he would like to say something in private. When they had come out into the corridor he declared:

"You had better ring up Scotland Yard at once. The trial of Derwick began this morning in Newcastle, and she is undoubtedly a most important witness for the defence. There is not a moment to be lost. You had better give them an exact description of what has taken place, but you need not know the real name of the 'Colonel Herbert' who brought the girl to you unless you like."

"You think there is no other course?"

"Unless you wish to be arrested yourself, there is certainly no other course."

The superintendent went off to his telephone box. Dr Hailey returned to Estelle. She was looking somewhat better now, and smiled as he approached her chair. He sat down and took her hand in his own.

"Are you strong enough, do you think, to answer just one question?" he asked.

"Oh yes."

"Why did you leave Calthorpe with Mr Blunder in that mysterious fashion?"

"Because he told me that if I could not be found, they could not possibly arrest Jack. He said that there was no doubt my father had been murdered, and that Jack would be arrested. The body had not been found by that time."

The colour sprang to the girl's cheeks, giving her back for a moment all her beauty. She bent her golden head, and the light from the window rushed and flamed among her hair. She added:

"I was the only person who knew he had been in the wood at the same time as my father."

Dr Hailey's eyes had a grim expression as he replied:

"My dear child, at least two people saw him going into the wood. The fact was stated in all the papers. But I suppose he counted on your not having read any papers."

"I suppose so."

The girl's voice was ineffably weary. Her head drooped. The doctor realized that further interrogation was out of the question just now.

"You know that Mr Derwick has been arrested he said.

"Oh, no."

A moan of anguish broke from her lips. She sat up, endowed, it appeared, with a new strength by the knowledge that her lover might have need of her help.

"Tell me… everything… please."

He told her. During this time she remained impassive, a figure of tragedy, whose grief must have appealed to the sympathy of the most callous.

"Do you think that they will allow me to go to him?" she whispered brokenly, when he had finished.

"They cannot prevent you from giving evidence in his favour."

The superintendent returned to the room. He seemed excited now, and full of a fresh importance. He would certainly have blurted out his news, had not Dr Hailey signed to him to keep quiet until a more favourable occasion should arise. The nurse brought Estelle some beef tea, and stood beside her while she drank it. The doctors left the room, and went to the superintendent's private office. There Dr Hailey announced that he must return at once to London, and go to Newcastle by the night train, in order to see Jack on Sunday. He suggested that Dr Wellwisher should accompany the patient to Newcastle the following night, if the police consented to this arrangement.

"They are sending men down now to arrest the girl," Dr Hillman stated. "I can only trust that no scandal will attach to my asylum as a consequence."

"My dear sir, you will be wanted as a witness at the Derwick trial on Monday. I suppose you can make immediate arrangements to travel north?"

The superintendent had not contemplated this possibility. It filled him with consternation. When Dr Hailey left the house, he was still bewailing his misfortunes.

Before he went away, the doctor returned for a moment to Estelle. There were two further matters on which it was absolutely vital that he should obtain enlightenment, if he were to bring any assistance to the accused man.

CHAPTER 26 THE PROCESS OF JUSTICE

The Court House at Newcastle was packed to suffocation when the Derwick trial began. The judge, Mr Justice East, was perhaps the most severe figure on the Bench, a man popular as certain types of schoolmasters are popular—by reason of his unflinching sternness. He was called a "hanging judge", and the public in this country has a weakness for the breed.

Jack Derwick stepped into the box as he might have walked into his own chambers. His lean, athletic-looking body had suffered nothing from his stay in prison, but those in court who knew him—and there were a number of them—detected a change of expression which told its own story.

No man, however well fortified in the knowledge of his innocence, faces the capital charge with equanimity. There is a quality of the process of justice which human nerves are scarcely able to endure.

He pleaded "Not Guilty" in a firm voice. Then the jury were empanelled. He watched them closely, reflecting, with a sense of mingled astonishment and anxiety, that his fate—his, John Derwick's, very life, once so fully and splendidly his own—depended now on the view which these casual strangers might choose to take of it. What manner of men were they? It was not fair, surely, that a man's conduct should be pronounced upon by men he had never known, men who understood nothing of his character, his way of life, his ideas, his ambitions; men, in short, who might have nothing whatever in common with him.

The jurymen were obviously impressed by the importance suddenly attaching to them. They looked and moved and spoke to one another as Englishmen of their class always do in such circumstances. Every Englishman, he thought, is a Prime Minister or an occupant of the judicial bench at least. If the opportunity comes, it finds him ready—so far at least as becoming gravity and the sense of responsibility are concerned.

A faint smile flickered on his lips at this thought. It broadened slightly when one of the twelve, a very fat man with a face which recalled a harvest moon, began stuffing a big red handkerchief between his collar and the back of his neck. Derwick had a quick sense of the grotesque; he had once seen another fat man do the same thing in a Welsh church, and this incident rose in his mind. He wondered if all fat men... And then came that chill thought, which for an instant he had almost forgotten, that this was not a fat man, but one of his judges, holding in his two hands life—with all life's swift and actual magic—and death....

Taken as a group, his judges were not formidable-looking men. Most of them seemed to belong to the shop-keeping class, though he thought he detected an individual of a different type in the second row, an elderly man with a hungry-looking face, but rather kind eyes....

The voice of the prosecuting counsel, Sir William Broom, a man he knew quite well, cut across these ideas. He sat back on the hard wooden bench to listen. He folded his arms, as sooner or later all accused men do. How was it that, in his former appearances in criminal courts, he had failed to notice all the strange, bizarre details which now kept crowding on his attention? Sir William Broom's voice, for example—that terrible rasp in it which must literally have rip-sawed his way to fame through other people's nerves.

Sir William was speaking about that other Sir William, whose going out of life had brought them all together. He called him a "man of irreproachable honour, an ornament to his profession" and so on. It was certain that within a few minutes he would be speaking about "murder", with a horrid rasping of the "r" in that word. The prisoner sighed. But, nevertheless, his sense of detachment which had come upon him suddenly when he entered the court, left him again. He began to listen with close attention.

Sir William outlined the case in detail. He seemed to have been carefully coached in his brief. As Derwick had expected, his great point was the absence of the prisoner from Calthorpe Hall during the whole period necessary for the carrying out of the crime.

"Evidence will be brought," he told the jury, "that the accused man was seen entering the wood just before Sir William Armand entered it, that he was not seen again till he appeared, two hours later, at Calthorpe Hall, and that then there were stains of mud—and blood—on his clothes. Further, you will be told that it was an easy matter for him to obtain a spade, and that he knew by personal inspection that very afternoon that there was a new grave in the very remotely situated village churchyard...."

Moreover, a clear motive existed. Sir William was a very rich man. He had a beautiful only daughter, to whom the prisoner was engaged, and with whom, evidently, he was deeply in love. Derwick, on the contrary, was poor though highly ambitious. Could anybody doubt that he was counting on the Armand money to assist him to carve out a great career in Parliament?

The jury, Jack thought, certainly did not look as if they doubted it for a moment. Sir William Broom evidently had some knowledge of human nature as it is found behind the counters of small shops. The idea of wading to power through mud and blood seemed to be both familiar and attractive to such minds.... Already, it appeared, a picture of himself to this effect was forming in their imaginations. He felt a sense of new bitterness, but this was followed a moment later by the whimsical thought that this "learned friend" of his was being abominably rude to him, and would certainly have been turned out of decent society if he had made such infamous suggestions about him over, say, a private dinner-table.

"You are men of the world, gentlemen of the jury," the voice rasped on; "as such I shall appeal to you. All that I ask—all that the law asks—is that you use your common sense."

Sir William Broom resumed his seat. Derwick felt his own heart, quicken, just as it always did at a political meeting when the chairman was about to call on him to address the audience.

The first witness was Inspector Biles. He retold the story of his investigations in minute detail, and it was easy to see that his evidence produced a profound effect. This was the kind of story which a jury of business men could understand and appreciate. Derwick asked him but one question in cross-examination.

"You have said," he stated, "that you received most valuable assistance in your work from Dr Eustace Hailey of Harley Street. Is it not a fact that the whole credit of these investigations belongs to Dr Hailey?"

Biles reddened a little, but quickly recovered himself.

"I am prepared to admit that, he said coldly.

Evidence was then called to prove that Derwick had actually gone into the wood just before Sir William entered it, and then an expert from the Home Office described his investigations of the morphine found in the dead man's body, and of the blood-stain on the prisoner's coat.

"That stain might have been made by the wearer of the coat's own blood?" Derwick asked him.

"Oh yes, by any human blood."

"If the wearer, for example, had touched the place with a scratched finger?"

"Possibly. He would scarcely touch the back of his coat, though, would he, in these circumstances?"

"If he carried his handkerchief in a hip-pocket, and was attempting to find it, he might do so?"

"Yes."

The day wore on, and the light faded from the dim windows. Servants from Calthorpe Hall followed one another in weary succession. The jury were assured that it would be quite easy for the prisoner to take a spade from the garden tool house. They were told that Miss Armand and her fiancé appeared to be on very affectionate terms; they were further informed that on the night of the murder their mistress did not appear at dinner.

"So that no one dined in the house at all that night," Sir William Broom suggested.

"No one, sir."

"Had that ever happened before when the family were staying in the house?"

"Never that I can remember, sir."

The last witness of the day was Mr Blunder. He bowed to the judge as he stepped into the box. His round face looked as healthy as a ripe apple, and he gave his evidence in sprightly tones which made welcome contrast with the dreary responses of the servants. When Jack rose to cross-examine him, he bowed again, as though he, at any rate, was not the man to forsake a friend in adversity.

"You stated, Mr Blunder," Jack declared, "that Sir William visited you a few days before his death."

"That is so."

"Am I right in believing that on this occasion—or subsequently—he told you that he meant to terminate the engagement between his daughter and myself?"

There was a slight, but quite appreciable, emphasis on the word "subsequently". Blunder's small eyes gleamed as he detected it. He shot a quick furtive glance at the face of the accused man. Jack could see that he was asking himself whether or not it was possible that Dr Hailey had supplied any information. He hesitated.

"You do not answer my question."

The little lawyer contracted his brows.

"Sir William did tell me that he meant to terminate your engagement," he declared in rather low tones.

It was the first real hit which the defence had scored throughout the day. Sir William Broom raised his head uneasily. Several of the jurymen leaned forward in the box.

"Did he tell you the reason?"

Again there was a craning of necks. The slight murmur which had characterized the court hitherto, died away into absolute silence, so that sounds from the street outside were clearly audible. Blunder gripped the rail in front of him with both his hands.

"Yes."

"What was it?"

The last question came like a pistol shot. In the deep silence it sounded unnecessarily loud.

"That," said the witness, "I am afraid I cannot disclose. Sir William was not only my partner, he was also my client."

The silence broke in an uneasy shuffling. It was obvious that the audience in court resented this refusal keenly. Blunder turned to the judge as though to claim his protection in his refusal, but before he spoke he was answered.

"There is no privilege as between a solicitor and client, Mr Blunder, when his client is dead. I think you must answer the question put to you."

Again the silence fell. Jack watched the small eyes questioning his face—wondering what he knew, how much he knew. He understood exactly what was passing in Mr Blunder's mind. He would have given much to know whether or not Mr Blunder was an honest man, but with Estelle in her present position he could not afford at the moment to doubt it.

He stood awaiting his reply with exemplary patience. At last it came.

"Miss Estelle Armand was the victim on several occasions of epileptic fits of a severe character. No one knew of these but her father, because they always occurred in the late evening. Sir William felt that it would not be right to allow a marriage in these circumstances."

"Thank you, Mr Blunder."

Jack sat down at once, to the very evident relief of the witness. The feelings of the people in court found vent immediately in a fresh rustling and murmuring, but the judge suppressed the sound with a frown. He leaned towards the witness box.

"I fancy, Mr Blunder," he said, "that I shall have some questions to address to you on Monday morning."

CHAPTER 27 ESTELLE ARMAND EXPLAINS

Public interest in the trial had become enormously greater during the week end as a result, no doubt, of the dramatic admission of Mr Blunder. When, therefore, the court sat on Monday morning, there was a new tension in the air.

Jack entered the dock, his friends thought, with a firmer, more confident step. He turned before he took his seat, and exchanged a smile with Dr Hailey who was seated just behind him.

By the judge's direction, Mr Blunder was recalled at once. Dr Hailey observed him closely as he mounted the step to the witness box, and concluded that he had not heard, as yet, of Estelle's arrest. Some precaution had been taken by the police to avoid any publication of the news whatever, and the fact that the event had occurred on a Saturday, made this easier. The little lawyer, however, looked rather uneasy. His uneasiness increased palpably, when his eyes met those of the doctor.

"You said, I think, that Sir William Armand made you his confidant in the matter of his daughter's health," the judge began, after consulting his notes of the previous bearing. "Can you tell me why he took this course?"

"Because, my lord, we were very close personal friends, and because he desired me to arrange a consultation with a medical friend of mine who specializes in epilepsy,"

"He did not propose to tell the prisoner anything about the matter?"

"No, my lord. He stated definitely that he would on no account tell him."

The judge was about to dismiss the witness, when Jack rose and asked leave to put some further questions to him.

"What was the last occasion on which you saw your partner?" he asked in crisp tones.

Mr Blunder started. Instinctively, he glanced towards Dr Hailey, whose dull eyes were fixed on his face. The doctor was in the act of taking a pinch of snuff. He made no sign. The lawyer seemed to measure swords with him for an instant, and then to recoil.

"On the day on which he was murdered," he said in low tones.

The judge raised his head sharply.

"Do I understand you to mean that Sir William left Calthorpe on that day?" he asked.

"No, my lord. I came to Calthorpe to see him... at the village inn."

Amazement was stamped on every face, including that of Sir William Broom, who half-rose from his seat and then sat down again. Jack's voice rang out, putting his next question:

"Under the assumed name of Mr Sawyer, I take it?"

"That is so."

Mr Blunder extracted a large, dark-coloured handkerchief from his pocket, and wiped his brow with it. Again his eyes sought and found Dr Hailey's eyes, but his quick wits challenged that impassive man in vain. He received no token of recognition or of approval.

"Consequently, it was you who accompanied Sir William into the wood, where he was murdered."

"Yes."

"Did you see anybody lurking in the wood at the time?"

"Nobody. It was growing very dark, however."

The judge interposed:

"Why didn't you tell us all this on Saturday? It is surely material to the issue before the jury."

"Because, my lord, had I done so, I should have disclosed my dear friend's most carefully guarded secret."

There were no further questions. Blunder left the box, and was accommodated with a seat in the front of the court, not far from where Dr Hailey was sitting. He remained for some time bent forward, with his head between his hands.

This closed the case for the prosecution. Jack rose to address the jury.

"Gentlemen," he said in quiet tones, "it is one of the penalties of innocence that it is usually unready to defend itself. That is my difficulty in addressing you today. This charge took me unprepared, because I had no need, or so I thought, of any preparation. When I came to consider the question of my defence, I found that the number of witnesses who might be able to help me was very small indeed. So I can promise you but little evidence. My chief defence, indeed, must be with yourselves—with that instinct which enables honesty to recognize honesty, and innocence to recognize innocence, even when, as in my own case, a fellow being is apparently enmeshed in the web of circumstance and coincidence.

"I shall not," he went on, "attempt to deny many of the statements made by counsel for the prosecution. I believe that in my dealings with you I can afford to speak the exact truth. It is a fact that I entered the wood at Calthorpe just before Sir William Armand entered it. It is a fact also that I had ample time to carry out the horrible crime of which I am accused. Nor would I be telling the truth if I denied that I did see a new grave in the churchyard when I passed that way.

"I remember seeing it most distinctly. Only an hour had then elapsed since my engagement to Miss Armand was broken off. I was feeling sick at heart, sore, if you like, greatly depressed. The thought occurred to me as I looked at the freshly turned earth that the occupant of the grave was in a happier state then those of us who, without hope, must still continue our lives."

He paused a moment. The faces of the jury remained impassive. Though he was accustomed to court work himself, he felt the lack of response as a heavy weight on his spirit. Perhaps, after all, he had been foolish in trusting to his own personality. It might have been better to take the advice so many of his friends had offered him and left his defence in the hands of one of the big criminal advocates.

"But, gentlemen," he continued in quieter tones, "if I cannot call many witnesses, I mean to call one or two. The Vicar of Calthorpe will tell you that I took tea with him on the afternoon of the murder, and you will hear from his lips whether or not I conveyed to him the impression a man about to take the life of another might be expected to convey. Again, I shall call a very distinguished expert to explain to you that some of the marks found on the tree, beside which Sir William Armand was struck down, are of a most peculiar character, and actually tell a tale very different from that put forward by the Crown. You will, I think, realize, when you hear this evidence, that it must have been the hand of a madman and not the hand of a man in possession of his normal senses which perpetrated this crime."

He sat down. In the rather dim light of the court, he thought he detected an incredulous smile on the lips of the fat juryman. He drew a deep breath. There is, after all, no more unconvincing proof of innocence than the assertion that one is not guilty.

His first witness was Dr Hailey, and the arrival of that—to the public—mysterious character in the box, was an occasion of great curiosity. His evidence, so far as it related to the finding of the body, merely confirmed that given by Inspector Biles; but when he came to describe the mark which he had found on the tree, interest re-awakened.

Sir William Broom cross-examined him only on this point, and used all his powers to extract an admission that possibly the work might have been made by the ferrule of the dead man's or of the murderer's walking-stick, but the doctor was unshakable in his view.

"I reached that conclusion during my first visit to Calthorpe," he admitted, "but when I re-examined the tree, I abandoned it at once."

"Have you much experience in the study of old superstitions?"

"Very little."

Jack called the Vicar of Calthorpe. The Rev Hargreave Willoughby came into court very much against his will. The whole "atmosphere of justice", as he called it, was repugnant to him. Nevertheless, he made a good witness. He assured the jury, in his tense emotional voice, that he found it impossible to conceive that the prisoner had committed the crime imputed to him.

"A murderer," he added, "on the very threshold of his crime, could scarcely behave as my guest behaved. My experience of human nature repudiates such an idea."

This witness was not subjected to cross-examination but Sir William Broom devoted considerable attention to Professor Mildmay. He had small reward for his pains; the Professor's mind was made up.

"I repeat," he declared, after he had been severely pressed, "that in my opinion the mark was made by one of the old stamps with which, in past days, farmers and others used to 'protect' their fields against occult influences."

"But surely such an idea is, shall I say, rather imaginative. I put it to you, Professor, who would be likely to possess such an instrument?"

"Oh, there are still a number of specimens in existence in remote country districts."

"Then you think that possibly one of the villagers came out after the murder and branded the tree—as a measure of 'Safety First'?"

"Either that, or the murderer himself made the mark. I am not a criminologist, but it strikes me that there are many features of this crime which suggest the work of a disordered intellect."

"Do I understand you to say, Professor," the judge interpolated, "that in olden times murder by stabbing through the eyes was not uncommonly met with?"

"That is so. If a man or woman was suspected of possessing the evil eye and was not publicly burned for this crime, he or she was sometimes murdered, the eyes were 'put out', and a charm against the evil eye installed in the vicinity."

The Professor left the box. Jack glanced again at the faces of the jury. He saw, as he had expected to see, that these *minutae* of science bewildered without convincing them. He could almost hear their comments on this, to their way of thinking, desperate plea, when they retired from the court. He rose, and in clear ringing tones called:

"Miss Estelle Armand."

The excitement which followed this announcement was extraordinary, for descriptions of the missing girl had been diligently circulated by the Press, and the failure of Scotland Yard to apprehend her made the subject of a great deal of sarcastic comment. Everyone in court seemed to press forward to catch a glimpse of her as she entered the precincts.

At that moment Dr Hailey took occasion to glance at Blunder. He suppressed an exclamation as he did so. The plump red face had paled to a sickly white, and the small alert eyes were staring. The doctor continued to watch until Jack's first directions to the new witness hushed the court again to silence.

"Will you tell the jury, Miss Armand, all that you know about the case from the beginning."

The girl's voice was low at first. She seemed extremely nervous, and looked very pale, but her beautiful features were under complete control. They revealed but little of the torturing anxiety which, as Dr Hailey knew, she was suffering at that moment.

"My father," she began, "cordially approved of mv engagement to Mr Derwick. He was, indeed, very fond of my fiancé, and treated him as if he had been his own son. That continued right on until the day before he died."

She paused and sighed deeply. There was a murmur of sympathy for her in the court. Dr Hailey, who feared she might break down, half-rose from his seat. As he did so, he observed that Mr Blunder had quite recovered his normal appearance. He was making notes on a small writing pad which he had balanced on his knee.

Jack asked:

"It was on that day, was it not, that Sir William told you you must break off your engagement?"

"Yes."

"He gave you his reasons?"

"Yes."

"And you agreed with them?"

"Yes."

The girl's tones had fallen so low that even the judge heard her with difficulty. He asked her gently to try to speak a little louder. Jack noticed that the jurymen, without exception, were straining forward to catch every syllable.

"Did your father suggest that the disclosure he had made to you should be kept secret?"

"He made me promise him that I would tell it to no one—not even to you."

The personal pronoun slipped out inadvertently. Estelle flushed and turned from the dock, which she had been facing, to the jury box.

"He made me promise him," she repeated, "that I would not tell Mr Derwick. I did not tell him."

She went on to describe how she had sent her lover away the next day, adding that, before she took this step, she despatched notices to both *The Times* and *The Morning Post*.

"There was so very little time to spare, because at any moment the blow might fall."

Jack leaned with one hand on the front rail of the dock. His body was bent forward and his face had an eager intent look which indicated in advance the importance he attached to the question he was about to ask.

"What was the nature of that blow?" he queried.

Estelle answered in a voice suddenly grown clear and resonant, so that her words carried to the back of the court.

"My father, through no fault of his own, had become a criminal."

CHAPTER 28 SIR WILLIAM ARMAND'S SECRET

In the stillness which followed, every word possessed its full significance.

"My father went up to London," Estelle continued, "because he had noticed in the papers that Lady Windwest was ill. He and his partner, Mr Blunder, were her trustees and the estate is a very large one. He wanted to satisfy himself that everything was in order."

She broke off because, at that moment, she happened to see Blunder for the first time. A shaft of sunlight had fallen on his face, picking him out as a spotlight picks out an actor on the stage. She seemed to draw back to the furthest corner of the box.

"Was everything in order?" Jack asked.

"No...." The word trembled on her lips.

"I take it you mean that these trust funds had been tampered with?"

The girl bowed her head. The terrible moments which her father had lived through when he made this discovery were still fresh in her mind. She could see his face again on the night of his return from London, the expression in his eyes when he told her that he was ruined.

"Did your father tell you, Miss Armand," the judge asked, "that he had made this discovery in London?"

"Yes, my lord. He told me that every penny he possessed in the world would not be enough to make good the money taken from Lady Windwest's estate. He came back to Calthorpe to decide what he ought to do, because Mr Blunder had begged him not to act without consideration."

"And he decided...?" Jack asked.

"To inform the police at once, and offer the whole of his fortune as a part payment of his debt. It was that decision which he conveyed himself to Mr Blunder at the village inn."

"So you knew that the man who called himself Sawyer was Mr Blunder?"

"I knew that Mr Blunder was coming."

"Do you think your father wished him to adopt a disguise?"

"He didn't mention that to me. Personally, I should think not, but it may be so."

"You feel no doubt that at the interview at the village inn, Mr Blunder learned that he would be standing in the dock on a serious charge within a very short time."

"No doubt at all. My father told me himself that he also must be arrested, though he had not touched a penny of the money. That was his reason for my breaking off the engagement. Had I not broken it off, and had this blow fallen on us, you might have shared in our ruin."

During this passage in the examination, the atmosphere of the court had become more and more tense. Gradually, every eye had turned from the girl in the box to the little lawyer, whose reputation as a professional man and an honest person her pretty lips were blasting. He sat, bent down, as he had been sitting since the moment Estelle entered the court. In spite of the burning curiosity which he must have felt was everywhere about him, he continued to make notes on the pad before him. Dr Hailey, who had watched him for a considerable time, saw that now he was writing quicker than at the beginning of the girl's evidence. Was it possible that that fertile brain had yet another surprise in store in the shape of a new explanation?

Just as this thought occurred, Blunder raised his head and glanced towards the doctor. His face was calm and unmoved. Their eyes met and he smiled slightly: it might have been a chance recognition in a theatre.

After his last question, Jack had bent down to consult his memoranda. When he stood up again, the ray of sunlight, which was gradually travelling across the court as the day wore on, shone on him. He looked at that moment a good figure of a man, with his fine head and crisp brown hair which had a faint sheen of gold in it. His lean body seemed to be in perfect physical condition. Dr Hailey glanced from him to the girl who, in happier circumstances, would have shared his life. Her beauty, he thought, was not less distinguished than his. It was strange, dramatic, this meeting, after their separation, in the grim old courthouse, where he stood defending his life against the whole force of organized justice.

"It follows, I think," Jack's voice declared, "that Mr Blunder had a good reason for wishing your father removed from his path? You know, perhaps, that Mr Blunder is the sole trustee under his will?"

"I have heard it."

Estelle then told the story of Blunder's visit to Calthorpe Hall. He had assured her that her father must have been murdered, and that Derwick would be accused. If she were missing, however, no action could be taken by the police against him, and that argument had been decisive.

"I recognize now that I was foolish," she confessed, "but at the moment I was terrified because I felt sure something awful had occurred, and I knew you had been in the wood, or near it, at the time."

Blunder took her to Newcastle, and from there they went by train to Grantham. He had his car at a garage in the town, and they took the road to London. Just as they were leaving the city, she felt a stab of pain in her arm. She cried out, and her companion at once apologized, and showed her a pin sticking out of his coat, which he said he had put there because the lining had been

195

torn. After that, she felt very drowsy, and remembered nothing more until she found herself in Dr Hillman's asylum.

Sir William Broom rose to cross-examine, with an expression on his rather pompous face which betrayed the surprise he felt.

"I am correct, am I not. Miss Armand," he began, "in thinking that at the present moment you are under arrest?"

"Yes."

"On the charge of being concerned with the prisoner in the murder of your father?"

"Yes."

He moved his head in the direction of the jury, as though indicating that a woman in that position was assuredly not to be trusted. Then he leaned forward:

"Mr Blunder has told us in his evidence," he said, "that your father informed him you were a sufferer from epileptic fits and that this was the reason why your engagement was broken off. Have you, to your knowledge, ever suffered from epilepsy?"

A faint smile appeared on Estelle's lips.

"Never."

"Never, that is, that you know of."

"If you wish to put it so."

Sir William Broom changed his line of attack.

"Did it not strike you as a singular thing that your father should meet his partner at the Black Bull Inn to discuss intimate business affairs?" he asked.

"No. My father would not, on any account, have permitted Mr Blunder to enter his home again. He only consented to see him at all because he hoped that, between them, they might be able to procure the money necessary to pay these shameful debts in full."

"I see. That does not, however, explain the appearance of Mr Blunder under an assumed name. I may tell you that he has himself given the court an explanation of this."

Estelle hesitated a moment. "I do not know why Mr Blunder disguised his identity," she said simply.

Sir William consulted his notes.

"You possess, I think," he said, "a hypodermic syringe, and some tablets of morphia which Dr Brown, who gave evidence in this court on Saturday, says he supplied to you."

"Yes. They were for use when my father got neuralgia."

"Did you give your father many injections?"

"Only two."

"You mean you used only two of the pellets in the phial of twenty supplied to you?"

"Yes."

"Then how comes it that the syringe and the phial are both missing from Calthorpe Hall?"

Estelle opened her eyes in a little gesture of astonishment.

"Are they missing?" she asked.

"The police have been unable to find them."

She nodded.

"Oh, I see. But they would not be able to find them without assistance from me. I always kept them, for safety, in a secret receptacle at the back of the desk in my bedroom. It is an old piece of furniture. I have the key of that receptacle in my pocket now."

Jack Derwick rose.

"My lord," he said, "I venture to submit to you that someone should be dispatched at once to verify this statement of the witness

The judge assented, and orders were given. Inspector Biles was entrusted with the mission. Then Sir William Broom resumed his cross-examination. He put several questions about Estelle's flight from Calthorpe, her explanation of which he appeared to regard as a myth from beginning to end.

"Your suggestion, I take it," he said. "is that you were drugged."

"I am not quite sure of that. The doctors who attended me are of the same opinion. They will tell you so when they give evidence."

"It is unnecessary to anticipate the evidence of other witnesses," said the judge, in tones of admonition.

"Have you any idea of the nature of the drug used?"

"I have since been told it was probably Indian Hemp or 'Hash-ish'. It caused me to lose my reason completely, so that I was certified as insane and sent to a private asylum."

Sir William Broom started. He had not heard anything of this. But he recovered himself quickly.

"It has already been suggested," he reminded her, "that your mental state is not satisfactory. I submit to you...."

He got no farther than that. Suddenly there was a scream from the body of the court, and several men and women jumped to their feet. They were seen to be raising a man's body from the floor, to which it had apparently just fallen.

Estelle turned and looked, and saw the face of Blunder. She knew instinctively that he was either dead or dying.

CHAPTER 29 MR
BLUNDER CONFESSES

Dr Hailey forced his way to the side of his antagonist. Blunder still breathed, but he appeared to have lost consciousness. In all probability, he had been struck down by apoplexy.

But no, he opened his eyes and managed to force a smile on his livid trembling lips.

They laid him on the floor of the corridor, with a coat under his head to serve as a pillow.

"Is that you, Hailey?" he whispered.

"Yes."

He closed his eyes again. The ushers had begun to clear the court, and there was more air. The proceedings were for the moment suspended.

"Bring me some brandy, somebody," the doctor ordered.

"It's no use." Blunder's voice was now so faint as to be scarcely audible. "Cyanide of potash... ten minutes ago...."

His breathing grew slower. Dr Hailey felt his pulse trip over one of its beats, a sign he knew of evil significance in the circumstances. Next moment the breathing stopped. The face of the lawyer became distorted and he bared his teeth. Then a severe spasm of all his muscles shook his body.

And then, gradually, the muscles relaxed, and the pale lips fell back again in an expression of gentleness. Both breathing and pulse had stopped.

Dr Hailey rose from his knees.

"He's dead," he declared.

He turned away, and glanced at the place where the lawyer had been sitting. The writing-pad lay on the seat to which someone had no doubt restored it from the floor.

He reached and took it. The judge was still seated on the Bench, and he made his way forward and told him what had happened.

"I fancy, my lord," he added, "that I had better hand you this document, which Mr Blunder was engaged in writing at the moment of his death. It is probably material to the present case."

The Court adjourned for an hour to permit of the removal of Blunder's body to the mortuary. When the sitting was resumed, the judge told the jury that he proposed at once to read them the memorandum left by the dead man, and written by him in court.

"It's in the form of a letter addressed to myself," he said. It runs:

"Your Lordship:

I am about to take a dose of cyanide of potash, which for some time now I have carried about with me in readiness. When this letter falls into your hands I shall, therefore, be dead. I am writing it in order that one part of the mystery of Sir William Armand's death may be finally cleared up. About the other part, I can furnish no information whatever.

"Let me say at once that what Miss Armand has told the court is true in every particular. Her father did discover that I had acted for many years as a fraudulent trustee, and that the fortune of Lady Windwest was almost completely dissipated. He wished to communicate with the police there and then, but I begged him to consider his daughter and her fiancé, and give the latter a chance to escape the disgrace which was coming. He agreed to think matters over and meet me, later, at the 'Black Bull' at Calthorpe with his final decision.

"I knew my man, and urged this arrangement on him because I meant to murder him...."

The judge's voice hesitated a little at this point, but he resumed his reading in a moment.

"I shall not trouble you with my reasons, as you would scarcely understand them if I did. I obtained a good disguise at Messrs Clarkson's in Wardour Street, telling them it was for a fancy dress ball, and went to Calthorpe under the name of Sawyer. I took all the necessary precautions to hide my identity in every possible way—and succeeded, as I think, remarkably well. Indeed, nothing could have been more certain of success than the plan I had decided upon.

"Briefly, it was this: I would accompany Sir William some distance on the way home, ostensibly to importune him to change his mind, and show me mercy. At a suitable spot I would trip him up—I am somewhat expert at this rather difficult operation. It would then be the work of an instant to plunge the needle I had ready and filled in my pocket into his leg, and give him enough morphia to kill him in a few minutes.

"My one fear was that my dose might somehow miscarry, and that in consequence he might be able to reach home, or, at any rate, to communicate with somebody before it took effect on him. In that case, I realized, I should have to take my own life.

"But my position was so desperate that I had to accept this hazard. As it happened, there was no need for anxiety. The plan succeeded even better than I could have hoped. The old man fell like a stone, and, in falling, struck his head on a tree. My dose was administered without the slightest trouble. I waited for a short time, holding my victim down, until he began to be drowsy, and those, I can tell you, were anxious moments, for he had considerable strength, and attempted to shout for help. Happily, no one heard him. As soon as he became unable to move easily, I left him. Within twenty minutes of setting out from it, I was back again at the inn.

"You may or may not believe me, but, as a man about to die, I can assure you that I know nothing further about the case. Obviously, my own plan was complete. Sir William, had he remained as I left him, would have been found with a few scratches on his brow

—made obviously by the tree when he fell, but no marks of violence whatever on his body. Knowing what I do of the average post-mortem examination in a country mortuary, I am ready to wager that the true cause of death would not have been discovered, for I calculated that he would go on breathing for about half an hour, and in that time the morphia would be well distributed over his body, and well diluted by his blood. Only the tiniest needle-mark would remain—a mark almost invisible even to eyes searching carefully for it. The verdict would have been 'death from heart failure' without the smallest shadow of doubt.

"Judge, then, of my amazement and horror when I learned that the body had disappeared and, later, that it had been discovered. I knew then that someone else had reason to wish my late partner out of the way—though why he should have re-murdered a man already doomed I cannot think. Possibly, he supposed Sir William was merely ill, and took the chance afforded of making a quick end of him.

"In any case, it upset my apple-cart. Nevertheless, I might have escaped, had not fate sent Dr Hailey to vex me. Let me take this opportunity of paying a tribute to the cleverest analytical mind it has ever been my misfortune to encounter in a long life. Twice, as the doctor will tell you himself, I managed to throw him off the scent. But he was too keen for me, and a certain piece of information I received a few days ago from a friend, convinced me that my time was near at hand. Miss Armand, of course, was my chief danger—for she alone knew the facts about Lady Windwest's estate. If I could secure her permanently, I was safe, for I had become trustee of a large sum of money—about £100,000, belonging to my partner, and his insurance policy is worth not less than £50,000. Moreover, Lady Windwest had recovered. It was merely a matter of time to clear up the mess sufficiently to be able to leave the country with a competency, at least. I nearly succeeded when I had Miss Armand certified as a lunatic and committed to an asylum.

"But Fate, as I have said, was against me...."

"The narrative ends there," said the judge, "but he has managed to sign it." He turned to Sir William Broom. "Do you wish to recall Miss Armand?"

"I think not, my lord."

Just then. Inspector Biles entered the court. He was sworn and produced the syringe of pellets which he had found in the desk at Calthorpe. Only two of the twenty pellets were missing.

The rest of the evidence was soon taken. It merely confirmed Estelle's story. Then Jack rose to make his final appeal to the jury.

He found them in a very different temper from that in which they had been when he addressed them in opening his case. Yet their minds were still, he realized, prejudiced against him. Blunder's confession, while it explained much, did not explain everything. He perceived that he must exert all his strength to avert disaster.

His speech was listened to with profound attention. Indeed, the court was hushed when he asked:

"Is it likely, is it even credible, that a man in love with Sir William's daughter, finding him sick almost to death in those terrible circumstances, would kneel down and murder him brutally?" He added: "With what weapon, moreover, could he commit that murder?"

He continued:

"This, surely, as Dr Hailey suggested, was the work of some lunatic, some homicidal degenerate. Such men exist in every land, and in most districts. It may be difficult to find the monster. After all, Jack the Ripper, operating in busy, well-lit Whitechapel, was never found. Yet can you doubt that he exists? Is there not the mark of the Evil Eye on the tree to prove it."

He sat down, his task finished. He leaned back against the wooden partition behind him. It seemed to him as though the big policemen on each side of him drew a little closer. Sir William Broom rose and cleared his throat.

"Gentlemen of the Jury," he began, "one murder does not excuse another."

His voice was, if possible, more rasping than ever, his manner more didactic. Step by step, he went over the whole evidence, sifting it, analyzing it, re-arranging it. His conclusion was that Derwick and only Derwick, could possibly have committed the deed, for he alone of all the persons in the drama had a motive, however inadequate, was on the spot, and was in possession of the necessary knowledge and the necessary time."

"You cannot," he concluded, "get away from these hard facts, whatever sympathy you may feel for this misguided young man."

It was late—about 7.30 o'clock. Yet the judge decided to finish the case, and began his summing-up at once.

"I do not disguise from you, Gentlemen of the Jury," he said, "that the case is one presenting almost a maximum of difficulty from the point of view of those who are called upon to decide it. There are so many and so diverse elements. There have been, even in this courthouse, so many terrible incidents. Moreover, public interest has magnified the issue out of all proportion—almost out of recognition."

His cold voice grew a little louder.

"Nevertheless, you must perform your duty. The issue before you is clear enough from one point of view, and that is the only point of view which should concern you. It is this:

"Did the prisoner, in fact, stab Sir William Armand in the eyes so as to cause his death, and thereafter bury him in the Calthorpe churchyard?"

He went on to say that the fact that Sir William might have died of the poison administered by Mr Blunder was not to be taken into account. Equally true, would it be to say, that he might have recovered from it. Medical science was full of resource, and there was always a possibility that someone might have passed that way and found the sick man before it was too late. Nor could the fact that Miss Armand had clearly had no part in the attempt to poison her father be allowed to weigh.

"I may tell you," said the judge, "that, in all probability, no further action will be taken against this unhappy young lady. But that probability in no sense exculpates her lover. He was out, alone, in the grounds of Calthorpe Hall, long after she had gone to bed. He was, moreover, in complete ignorance of the reason for his dismissal, a reason which I think does infinite credit both to Sir William and to his daughter. There is his own evidence to prove that the blow which had fallen on him was one under which he suffered mental distress, and which, quite possibly, filled his spirit with resentment.

"In this condition of mind, it is suggested by the prosecution, he found the main cause of all his troubles lying unconscious in a remote, unfrequented wood. A fresh grave, as he knew—this again he admits quite freely—lay but a few hundred yards away in the village churchyard.... It was very dark, very desolate."

The judge went on to say that if the jury felt that, in these circumstances, Derwick might have yielded even for an instant to the sense of injury he no doubt experienced at the moment, they must unhesitatingly bring in a verdict to that effect. If, on the other hand, they believed the theory of the defence that some wandering maniac with a taste for folklore had committed the murder, Derwick must be acquitted.

"The difficulty I find in accepting that theory," he added, "is that, according to all the local witnesses, no such individual has ever been known in the district. Nor is the analogy drawn with the case of the so-called Jack the Ripper murders a wholly satisfying one. On the other hand, the evidence of Professor Mildmay is entitled to full respect. In any case, if you entertain any doubt whatever, you must give the prisoner the benefit of that doubt."

He finished his address at nine o'clock, and the jury at once retired.

They returned almost on the stroke of eleven.

The verdict was "Guilty".

With a dim sense of horror to come, Jack heard the judge express the view that he considered this verdict to be in accord with the weight of evidence.

Then he heard another voice order him by name to stand up and declare if he had anything to say why sentence of death should not be passed on him.

He did not speak.
The judge pronounced sentence.

CHAPTER 30 THE EYE REAPPEARS

On the following Saturday, Dr Hailey reached Calthorpe in response to an urgent request from Estelle.

The Crown had offered no evidence against her when she was brought up before the magistrate, and she was released at once. She had remained in Newcastle for several days, in order to be near Jack. Dr Hailey, on the other hand, had returned to London in the hope of persuading Scotland Yard that some further investigations ought, even at this eleventh hour, to be carried out. He had had no success in this mission.

"Nevertheless," Estelle cried, when he told her, "we must save him. Oh, promise me that you will do everything in your power to save him."

They were in the big drawing-room of which, in other days, the girl had felt so proud. A great vista of tossing waves stretched away before the windows. He thought that never before had he seen a woman's face in which courage and gentleness were so fairly mingled. In spite of all that she had suffered and was now suffering, there was no sign of weakness.

"My dear child, I think I am nearly as distracted as you must be. After Blunder's confession I made sure that no jury would convict. But the judge was against us from the outset. That is the worst of a man such as West; he has no imagination."

"Do you think the Court of Appeal will set this terrible injustice right?"

"I hope so, indeed."

She turned away from him. He went down to the hall, and walked out along the cliffs. Personally he had no confidence whatever that the Court of Appeal would reverse the jury's verdict. It was against all precedent that they should do anything of the kind. There was just a chance that the obvious bias against the prisoner shown by Mr Justice West might be regarded as an unfair bias, but he doubted that. After all, the judge had presented both sides of the case, and he was fully entitled to make up his own mind.

He stood watching the wild turmoil of the waves, enjoying, unconsciously, this great spectacle of Nature in travail. How puny were the struggles of men as compared with this mighty conflict! Then the thought of Derwick awaiting in his fearful cell the sound of the steps of death, drew his mind back to reality. He turned and looked towards the quiet little village nestling in its fold of the cliffs. There, somehow, if only he could find it, was the key to this mystery.

That thought inspired him with a strange hope. His whole experience had proved to him that no human act is ever carried out without leaving its effect somewhere. For those who had patience to investigate and eyes to see, there were always fresh clues.

With this idea in his mind, he strolled down the village street, scrutinizing everyone whom he met. Not a doubt remained with him that the murderer of Sir William Armand was hidden under one of these roofs, behind one of these rough walls. He walked into the bar of the "Black Bull" and called for a pint of beer. While it was being drawn, he glanced at the faces of the people who shared the taproom with him.

There were a considerable number of customers, for it was Saturday afternoon, and the labourers on the neighbouring farms had their week's wages in their pockets. The talk was all of the trial—as it would be, until after the day fixed for Derwick's execution.

As he expected, these Englishmen were unanimously on the

side of the law. One or two of them recognized him, but none of them ventured to speak. The North-countryman is the most reticent of all human beings. He listened to them for a short time, and then accepted the landlord's invitation to come into his private room.

The landlord shared his patrons' opinion that justice had been done, but he was anxious to make it appear that he was a man of open mind—possibly because Miss Armand was his proprietor. He asked in a very guarded way whether there was any hope of a reprieve being granted to "the poor young man".

"None, I should imagine," said Dr Hailey shortly.

"You think they'll hang him?" This in tones which were instinctively gloating.

"Unless someone proves him innocent in the meantime."

The doctor, however, had not come to discuss the future, but to delve into the past and present.

"The difficulty about this place," he said, "is that one never by any chance sees its inhabitants. They all seem to live behind closed doors and never come out. Consequently, it's impossible to say what sort of people they are."

The innkeeper, as he had done on a former occasion, entirely mistook the nature of the doctor's anxiety.

"You'll need to go to church, sir," he declared, "tomorrow morning. That is the only time the whole village turns out together."

Dr Hailey took his advice. He installed himself in a front seat in the right transept, just under the pulpit, from which he was able to command a wide view of the building. It was, he saw, a beautiful old Saxon church in a wonderful state of preservation. The Normans had "improved" it with a few arches, but the original fabric was unharmed. The thought passed through his mind that the so-called Gothic style of ecclesiastical architecture had been greatly overrated.

The congregation began to enter the building. They were well-fed, healthy-looking folk for the most part, with the shrewdness of the North in their eyes. He searched in vain for any face of the type he was looking for—a type so common in some of the western districts of Cornwall and Wales and the Highlands of Scotland. Northumberland possesses a stock of the hardiest, both physically and mentally—no doubt as a consequence of the many invasions both by land and sea to which it has been subjected in the course of its long and turbulent history.

At the moment when the service began, he had seen only one individual who might conceivably be regarded as a degenerate type—a young farmer, he judged, with a red, heavy face and rather sinister expression; but the idea of connecting such a man with a murder was grotesque on the face of it.

The service was very simple, but nevertheless it impressed him more than he had expected it would. The Rev Hargreave Willoughby possessed that rare quality of inspiration which makes even the reading of a collect significant. He had evidently been at immense pains, too, to make the musical part of the service as impressively devotional—in the best sense of that much abused term—as possible. When he entered the pulpit. Dr Hailey was aware of a sense of pleasurable anticipation.

Nor was he disappointed. The Rev Hargreave preached with very considerable power from the text "Thou shalt not kill".

He explained his singular choice on such a day by reminding his hearers that he was devoting a series of sermons to the ten commandments. He had not felt that the terrible events of the last few weeks should deter him from proceeding with this intention. On the contrary, there might be more than a mere coincidence in the fact that the sixth commandment should form their immediate subject. If they chose, they might see the hand of God in that occurrence.

He leaned over the pulpit when he had said this, and the tension of his voice increased.

"This week," he said, "it was my painful duty to be present in a court of law, and see a fellow creature condemned to death... for killing... for breaking this solemn commandment. On the same day I was witness also of the self-slaughter of another fellow creature."

He paused, waiting as it seemed for the effect of his words to be manifest. Dr Hailey scanned every face before him with diligent care. Surely such preaching as this must discover guilt if guilt existed among these people.

"We feel, do we not," the clergyman continued, "very innocent of these horrible crimes? Yet, I tell you, we are not so innocent as we feel."

His voice rose in swift crescendo, which somehow seemed to harmonize with the shrilling of the wind among the trees outside.

"Killing is a big word, and there are so many ways in which a man or woman may kill. They may kill the body; for that crime the punishment is death. But they may also kill the spirit—and in this world go unpunished."

Again he leaned towards his congregation:

"In my view, in God's view, as you may discover for yourselves in the Bible, it is a far greater crime to strike at the spirit than to murder the body. To betray the trust of a child, to prove unfaithful to a friend, to deceive those who have put their faith in us, to put the lust of gain before the dictates of the heart, to make the holy emotion of love a counter of merchandise—all these are murders most foul. In the Kingdom of Heaven, believe me, the punishment for all these is death."

A little later in his sermon he mentioned the Derwick trial again by referring to the theory of the defence that some madman with a lingering belief in the influence of the evil eye had wrought the crime.

"Grotesque, perhaps, in this age of science, with its wireless wonders, and its new powers of control of Nature," he commented, "yet, in another sense, these old beliefs had their bedrock of truth. Surely the slayer of a soul is indeed possessed of an evil eye which not even the love of God can restore: 'If, therefore, thine eye be evil, pluck it out!'"

As he spoke these words, Dr Hailey fancied that the coarse-faced farmer did look uneasy. A young girl in one of the front pews, also, seemed to hear the sermon with disquiet. But so, perhaps, must anybody with even the beginnings of a guilty conscience.

He came out into the churchyard in as deep perplexity as he had felt when he entered the building. Mists of night seemed to be gathered about this case, which not all the straining of his wits was sufficient to dissipate.

Around him, as he passed down the narrow pavement, were the graves of Calthorpe. He looked towards the place where he had made his first great discovery in the case. The earth on the new grave had become darker; already an obliterating Nature was smoothing away all traces of that ghastliness. Then his eyes strayed further to another new grave under a great tree, which he realized must be that of Sir William Armand.

He turned from the pavement, and walked across to it. There were still a number of faded wreaths lying on the raw earth. One of them, he saw, bore a card inscribed "From the members of the Athenaeum Club", of which Sir William had been a member for many years. Another was from a well-known ornament of the Judicial Bench.

In a few days, doubtless, they would be taken away. And then the earth of this grave also would be smoothed away by the same broad hands, and even the memory of it forgotten. He raised his eyes in dim regret to the tree which stood, like a living sentinel, among these dead. It, at least...

He uttered a sharp exclamation, and took a quick step forward, round the head of the grave.

There, stamped on the trunk of this tree also, was the mark of the Evil Eye which he had found at the site of the murder.

CHAPTER 31 A FAMILY FEUD

The sight set his pulses throbbing with new excitement.

He glanced round. The churchyard was empty now. He could see the last of the congregation in the distance, going homeward to the village. He took out his glass, and examined the mark carefully. There could be no manner of doubt that it had been made by the same instrument as that used on the first occasion.

He knelt down and inspected the ground at the bottom of the tree, but there were no footprints to serve as a guide. The recent heavy storms had washed away any traces which might have been evident.

He left the churchyard and took the path across the fields to the Hall. One thing was certain. That mark had been made since Jack Derwick had left Calthorpe for ever. It had been made, too, at a considerable interval of time from the first mark, because Sir William's grave was a new one. The old family vault in the churchyard belonged to the last owners of the estate and was, he had been told, quite full. No one could possibly know where this new squire would be buried until the actual decision about his grave was taken.

It followed that the maker of those strange marks was at large in the neighbourhood, just as he had suspected. That fact must certainly be presented for the consideration of the Appeal Court, though probably they would merely take the view that it pointed to the presence in the neighbourhood of some superstitious person bent on warding off the evil spirits which might be supposed to have prompted the murder.

He told Estelle of his find as soon as he reached the Hall, and for the moment the news seemed to cheer her; but she, too, recognized that this clue, unless it could be followed up, supplied but a slender chance of attaining their object.

"Did you make any progress at all with your search?" she asked.

He shook his head. "The people here are not murderous by nature. They look honest and steady, all of them."

He went out for a long walk alone, returning in time for dinner. But still the key he sought eluded him. When bedtime came, he was no nearer any conclusion. Estelle had retired early because she was going to Newcastle again the next morning, and had need of all the rest she could obtain to enable her to endure the ordeal without flinching.

He sat in Sir William's study, with a book on his knees which he was not reading. A great fire burned in the big open grate. The subtle comfort of the room held him back from his intention to go upstairs. His mind seemed to drift away....

When he awoke, the fire had gone out, and there was a chill in the air. He glanced at his watch. It was four in the morning. With an exclamation of annoyance, he rose and took the book back to its place on one of the shelves.

Just as he was putting it in, he paused and stood a moment with an intent wondering look on his face. Somehow, during his sleep, his brain had gone on working. There had come, out of the darkness, a glimmer of a new light.

He moved along the big, well-stocked bookcase, searching its contents with eager eyes. Suddenly he came to the volume he was looking for. With hands which trembled, he drew it from its shelf and carried it to the table in the centre of the room. He found the place he wanted, and bent over the table reading intently. Then he stood up again with a puzzled expression on his face as though he was attempting to recall some far-off incident to his memory.

The next morning he travelled with Estelle as far as Newcastle. She told him that she believed there would be enough money to set her father's affairs in order, when the total of Sir William's estate, including his life insurance, had been realized.

"I shall have to sell Calthorpe, of course, but now I should do that in any case. I could not bear to live there permanently in the future."

He travelled straight on to London, and drove to Harley Street. Two hours later he caught the Cornish express. The next morning he breakfasted in Penzance. Then he drove out to the little village of Pensilian, which lies at the extreme western point of Mount's Bay.

The considerable resemblance between this hamlet and Calthorpe struck him at once, though the distinctly Cornish qualities of the landscape remained to make the likeness superficial. He told the driver of the hired car to wait for him, and took his way up the rough little street, which was unfit for any wheeled traffic, to the cottage of the registrar of the parish, the location of which he had previously discovered in Penzance.

He found it easily enough, and strode up through the small garden to the door. His knock was answered by an old woman who hobbled to the door with a stick. She declared that her son was within, and bade the visitor enter. Dr Hailey took off his hat and stepped down into the small kitchen where a man in middle age was eating a belated breakfast. The doctor introduced himself as Mr Smith, of Edinburgh, and said that he had come to consult the parish register, if that might be possible.

"The fact is," he declared, "I am writing a book on the parish registers of the country, and the strange stories which many of them contain. I am now going about gathering material for it."

Mr Ward—that was the name of the registrar—did not appear to regard the idea with much favour. Nevertheless, he invited his visitor to share his meal. Dr Hailey refused, but accepted a cup of tea.

"You have had, I suppose," he queried, "your own share of

queer happenings here in Pensilian?"

The registrar raised his heavy eyebrows. He nodded in an equivocal sort of way. He went on to say that the old registers were kept at the church. Only the more recent volumes were in his custody.

"Oh, it is the recent volumes in which I am interested; those for the year 1915 in particular. Let me see, was I rightly informed in Penzance this morning that during that year a mystery of some sort occurred in the village?"

Mr Ward glanced at his visitor keenly.

"Do you mean the case of Farmer Robin?" he asked, in his deliberate tones.

"I fancy that is the case I do mean. He disappeared, did he not, quite suddenly?"

"That he did, sir; and was never seen or heard of again, though there were those as had their own suspicions."

Dr Hailey took out his snuff-box and offered it to his companion who, to his very considerable surprise, accepted it with alacrity. They snuffed together, while the old woman refilled their cups with her very excellent tea.

"I wonder if you could tell me something more than I know already about that case. I can assure you that such mysteries interest me very deeply—indeed, they are exactly what I am looking for for this book of mine."

The registrar shook his head.

"There isn't much to tell," he declared. "Robin, he was an oldish man with a good farm. Had a tidy bit of money, so they said, though he didn't spend much. But his horses was fine beasts, and he used to drive to church in his own gig every Sunday. A well enough liked man, and very quiet living."

The man paused to raise his cup to his lips.

"Had he any family?" Dr Hailey asked.

"Yes, he had. Two sons and one daughter. The boys have the farm now, but the girl's married and gone out of the place to Camborne. There's no dealings between her and her brothers, I can tell you."

"Really? Why should that be?"

"For a good reason, sir. She married a man that her father had forbidden her to have any dealing with." He glanced uneasily at the door and window as if fearing that what he said might be overheard. "I may mention," he added in a lower tone, "that I believe her scamp of a husband might have thrown light on what became of the old man if he had cared to do it. That's all I say— there's more what thinks as I do."

Again the doctor took snuff. He awaited further information with an eagerness which he restrained as best he could.

"Anyhow," added his companion, "he was killed in the war, so maybe he's made atonement by this time. God knows; and it's not for us frail human creatures to judge, anyhow. But I do know that, for all she's a widow with two young children, her brothers will have nothing to do with his wife. There's the curse of their father still between them."

"Did Mr Robin, then, want his daughter to marry someone else?" Dr Hailey asked.

"He did, and a fine man too, one of the biggest farmers round about Pensilian. He's left the place now, for he was mad to make Kate Robin his wife, and when she refused him he joined up and went straight away to the war—though he needn't have gone, being a farmer, at all. They tell me he's back at the land again somewhere in Devonshire."

"Um; I suppose he made the old mistake of asking the father before he asked the daughter, whereas his rival asked the girl first."

The registrar shook his head.

"It wasn't quite that way," he declared. "You see, Kate and the man she afterwards married, were engaged for about six months before Mr Drew—that's the name of the farmer as wanted her —came to the place. Up till that time Farmer Robin was agreeable to the marriage. Then one day he and John Trevanin had a wild set-to about some private matter, and he ordered him out of his house and said he would never marry daughter of his. Nobody ever heard the truth of that quarrel, but, of course, all the tongues was busy. They said that Robin wanted a rich man for a son-in-law and picked a quarrel for the purpose of getting rid of the poor one, and I'm not denying it may be so; but Trevanin was a wild scamp, all the same."

"So that if Mr Robin had not disappeared, his daughter would now be Mrs Drew."

"Most like. Kate was a bold girl, but she was afraid of her father for all that, and had hardly dared have crossed him. Sure it is, she didn't see aught of Trevanin from the time of the quarrel till she was free to make her own choice; and they say Drew was visiting the house near every day."

"Was that in the Spring?"

"No, it was the month of November. I remember the time well, because my own wife died just the week before Robin was missed.... She died on the Sunday, and it was the following Saturday night that he was last seen coming out of the post-office there, from buying the weekly paper. He used to walk over from his farm every Saturday night to get his paper, for he was a great reader of the war news."

When the old lady had cleared the table, Mr Ward fetched his register. Dr Hailey glanced at one or two entries, including that relating to the registrar's wife who died, he saw, on 15th November, 1915, of "acute pneumonia". Then he closed the book, and rose to go away after having slipped a handsome fee into the man's ready palm.

"I suppose," he said, "that if a man were to fall over the cliffs about here, his body would be carried away by the tide and lost for ever."

"Oh yes. That was the conclusion the police came to—that he had missed his footing in the dark. There was a bit of a fog that night, you see. But it's one thing to miss your footing, and it's another thing..."

Mr Ward shrugged his broad shoulders expressively.

When Dr Hailey left the cottage, he walked up to the churchyard, which stood rather higher than the village, on the back of a rolling hillock. He entered it and looked about among the gravestones, till he came to one bearing the inscription:

In Loving Memory
of
HANNA GRANTHAM
Beloved Wife of John Ward
Who departed this life 15th November, 1915
"Thy Will be done".

He marked the position of this grave, now grass-grown and rather deserted, with great care, seeming to memorize its exact whereabouts in the churchyard. Then he advanced to the headstone and inspected it with the most meticulous care.

A look of profound disappointment spread over his face at the result of this examination. Could it be that, after all, he was mistaken, and that he had embarked on what was little better than a wild-goose chase? But no, he refused to believe it. He repeated his examination, this time with even closer attention.

"Ah!"

It appeared that he had found what he came to find. A look of lively horror was in his eyes as he turned away from the grave and went back down the village street to his car.

CHAPTER 32 A TRYST WITH THE DEAD

Two days later Dr Hailey alighted from the Scottish express at Carlisle. He caught a local train half an hour later, and so came to Appleby in Cumberland. From that remote place, he drove to Hendred Castle on the high moors.

It was after one o'clock when he reached this latter place. He sat down at once to luncheon in the George Hotel, which is certainly one of the best hostelries in this land of good cheer and solid comfort.

The room was empty, for in winter Hendred Castle has few save commercial visitors, who travel between Cumberland and Yorkshire by the branch railway from Appleby. He finished an excellent meal and went out at once into the wide market square of the little town, with its huge rough cobbles and its air of immemorial tranquillity.

He crossed the square and walked up High Street till he came to a house beside the door of which was displayed a metal plate announcing that it was inhabited by "John Cossar, Registrar of Births, Marriages, and Deaths". He rang the bell, and asked for this individual. He was shown into a small but very neat office, which appeared to be full of very large books arranged on broad shelves round the walls. When the registrar appeared, he took a small notebook from his pocket and consulted it.

"I should like to consult the volumes covering the month of February, 1905," he declared—"the deaths, if you please."

The man went to one of the shelves and drew out the required book.

"Is there any special name you wish to see?" he asked.

"No, thank you. What I want are the deaths which took place in the week beginning February 4th. Ah, here they are!"

He bent over the book, and then jotted down the four names which were given as having died in the time mentioned.

Were all these people buried in the churchyard here?" he asked.

"No, sir. Only two of them. The first and third. The others were buried in the small villages where they died."

Dr Hailey paid his fee and left the office. The weather had cleared, and it was a beautiful afternoon. He stood entranced at the loveliness of the old town, with its fair church and quaint overhanging gables. A bit of the wall which, at one period, had surrounded it, stood up grimly in the background.

He strode through empty streets, on the pavements of which his footsteps sounded strangely loud, to the church. The iron gateway leading into the yard was open, and he entered at once.

He spent the next hour among the graves, locating the two which he had marked in the registrar's office. One of them appeared to be the vault of a substantial local family, for it was railed in, and covered by an immense slab of stone. The other was an open grave, marked only by a cheap cross bearing the letters EAM. These, he knew, were the initials of the name, Elizabeth Anne Martin. He examined the cross as he had examined the headstone at Pensilian. The fact that it yielded nothing to his inspection did not, on this occasion, seem to cause him any disappointment.

When he had completed this task, he walked from the grave to the end of the churchyard which, at this point, abutted on the wall of the town. From here, he obtained a wonderful view of the church itself, a very beautiful example of the larger type of twelfth century edifices. The high gables of a distinctly modern vicarage showed to the left, peeping out from a screen of big trees.

He strolled slowly in the direction of the house. There was, he observed, free access to the churchyard from its garden, which was separated from the tombs by nothing more substantial than a shrubbery.

He returned to the street, and climbed further up the hill on which the old town is built, till he came to a long low building, standing back from the road in its own grounds. From this point a wonderful view of the Westmorland and Yorkshire hills is obtainable. He stood for a few minutes and watched the sunset develop over the lowlands to the west. Masses of smoky fire seemed to roll in the valleys. The breasts of the mountains were already shrouded in night.

He entered the building, and found himself in a wide hall, the centre of which was full of strange-looking machinery. Round the walls were innumerable glass cases containing all sorts of objects of all sorts and sizes.

He had often heard of this museum—which is one of the town's most treasured possessions—and he knew that some of the early pattern hand-looms he was now looking at were regarded as the finest specimens of the kind in the world. But it was not interest in the history of weaving which had occasioned his present visit.

The curator of the museum, an old man with a hard square face, came out of his office, at the entry of this unexpected visitor. Dr Hailey greeted him.

"You possess, I think," he said, "a collection of charms and suchlike?"

"Aye, sir; and if I say it myself, one of the finest in England."

The man led the way to a row of cases at the far end of the building.

"Most of them were picked up locally," he explained, "but our friends send us specimens occasionally.... This piece from Cornwall, for example...."

He indicated a rough-looking piece of iron, which seemed to have been moulded at one end. The doctor examined it closely through the glass of the case in which it lay. It was unlike the other objects surrounding it.

"You have a Society of Antiquaries in the town, haven't you?" he asked.

"Yes, sir. This collection really belongs to them, though it has been here now so long that we have come to regard it as our own."

He went to his office and came back with a booklet which he presented to the visitor.

"That's the list of members, past and present," he said. "You may care to keep it."

Dr Hailey thanked him and went away. At half-past six he left his hotel again and returned to the church to evening prayer. The large building was nearly empty, though he saw a few old people scattered about the dim nave. The voice of the officiating curate made echoes in the roof. He took a seat far back, and remained until the service was over. Then he slipped out past an old doorkeeper, and turned sharply into the churchyard, with the object of re-visiting the grave he had located in the afternoon. It proved a task by no means easy of accomplishment.

He carried a heavy stick in his hand. When finally he reached his destination and had satisfied himself that he was quite alone in the darkness of the winter's night, he unscrewed the head of this. It came away from the shaft, drawing with it a long, rapier-like blade.

He laid the sheath down carefully beside the stone cross, and then, after judging his distance as well as he could, pressed the blade down into the turf which covered the grave.

Five times he repeated this operation, before his probe encountered any greater resistance than that of the earth itself, but on the sixth occasion he felt the steel strike against some hard substance. He released the point slightly, by drawing it back, and tapped gently against this body. Then he pressed the point firmly downwards again.

After that, he withdrew it and re-entered it about an inch from the last place. He had to determine that distance by touch, for he did not wish to risk attracting any attention to himself by lighting his lamp. Again, at the same distance, the same solid obstruction was encountered.

He withdrew the rapier once more and tried again. The obstruction was met with in the same way. Clearly, it was of very considerable size. He took a small tube from his pocket and, having removed the rapier from the earth, smeared some of its contents on the point, which he then thrust back, till the steel struck the obstacle he was investigating.

He withdrew it and wiped the blade on a clean handkerchief which he had brought with him for this purpose. He folded the handkerchief very carefully, and put it in his pocket. Then he screwed up the walking-stick, and made his way out of the churchyard, along the wall of the church to the vicarage garden. He left the precincts by the vicarage gate which, as he expected, was unfastened.

When he got back to the "George", he asked for the use of a bedroom to change his clothes in, before dinner. As soon as he was alone, he took the handkerchief from his pocket and spread it out under the light of the electric lamp on the dressing-table.

There was a stain on the cloth made by the solution which he had applied to the blade of his rapier. Adhering to this wet surface were two white hairs.

The horror which had filled his eyes in the graveyard at Pensilian, crept into them again. He refolded the handkerchief, and put it away in a leather wallet. Then he packed his walking-stick carefully in his kit-bag, and went down to dinner.

At eleven o'clock he drove by car to Penrith, covering the twenty odd miles in a little over an hour. He was in ample time to catch the Glasgow-London express which stops at this station. A berth had been reserved for him, and he went to bed at once and slept until the express was running through Watford the following morning.

As soon as he reached Harley Street, he went to his little laboratory. He took one of the hairs from the handkerchief and put it under his microscope. He saw that it was eaten away in several parts of its length as though it had been subjected to rough usage, or to the long process of time in damp surroundings.

Later in the morning he went down to Scotland Yard, and sent his card in to Inspector Biles. The messenger returned at once, and asked him to go upstairs. He mounted the broad flight which, for so many, has proved to be a *via dolorosa*, and came to Biles's room. Next moment his friend was shaking him by the hand, with the joy of a schoolboy restored to the company of his best friend.

"My dear doctor, where did you go to after the trial? Everywhere I searched for you to pay my homage. Even the Chief here was ready to fall at your feet. Wonderful! Wonderful!"

Dr Hailey sat down and attempted to recover his breath, which was a trifle short after his climb.

"Spare me," he begged, "the necessity of abominating my stupidity more, even, than I do at present. Do you realize, Biles, that until Sunday last almost every conclusion I reached in connection with this case was wrong—wrong in essence, wrong even in circumstances and in facts. Pursuing Blunder so diligently, I lost sight of the real issue altogether."

Biles laughed.

"Remember, I have heard you speak like that before," he declared.

"But never before have you seen me so overwhelmed. If only I had studied the details with a little more care."

He got up and came to the fireplace where the detective was standing.

"I have a favour to ask of you," he declared.

Biles's face clouded. He knew that the doctor still believed Derwick innocent, and feared that what he was going to demand would be impossible to grant.

"If I possibly can, I will do anything you want," he said a little faintly.

"I want you to take me to your Chief."

"Now?"

"Yes, immediately."

Biles strode to the door and opened it. He was absent only about two minutes.

"Come with me," he said.

The room into which Dr Hailey was shown was like many another in the various Government offices, a little bare... a little formidable, but the welcome accorded him could scarcely have been more cordial. The Chief of the Criminal Investigation Department went out of his way to be gracious.

"The help you have given us," he declared, "is really beyond praise. But for your exertions, or so Biles assures me, the Armand mystery would remain a mystery still."

Dr Hailey raised his hand in protest.

"Forgive me," he said in low tones, "but that is precisely what it does remain... at this hour."

"My dear doctor, when a British jury has pronounced finally and firmly on it? Come now, you're joking."

"I was never more serious, never in my life."

The Chief knit his brow. He seemed not to know how to take this declaration. He glanced at Biles. The detective looked uneasy.

"Surely," he asked, "you can't mean that you think there has been a... a mistake...."

"I do not think—I know."

The doctor spoke so earnestly that both men felt uneasy. Had it been anybody else in the world, they would have dismissed the matter instantly from their minds, but this man they had learned to respect above anyone else.

"You came to ask something of me," said the Chief, anxious apparently to give the conversation a practical turn.

"Yes. A very great favour, I'm afraid."

"What is it?" The tones were rather less than encouraging.

"That you and Inspector Biles will accept my hospitality for one single night."

"What!... that is no favour at all."

The relief in the great detective's voice was most marked.

"Stop a minute. The night must be this one; and I warn you we shall travel some distance."

Again the detectives exchanged glances. They guessed their destination to be Newcastle. The enthusiasm which had flickered up a moment before, died out of their faces.

"To what place?" the Chief asked.

"To Cornwall. To Penzance in Cornwall."

Relief was again apparent. After all, then, their fears had been groundless. It was not to attempt to reopen the Derwick case that Dr Hailey was inviting them—at least, not ostensibly. The Chief went to a calendar on his desk, and looked at his list of appointments for the next twenty-four hours. He frowned slightly and then nodded.

"Very well," he said, "I'm your man. I can just do it, I find, if you promise to let me return first thing in the morning. What about you, Biles?"

"Yes, sir, I can manage it also on the same conditions."

Dr Hailey bowed. His manners, as the Chief remarked to Biles afterwards, were reminiscent of the Victorian age.

"The conditions are agreed," he promised. "But I also have a condition to make: that during the time of our excursion you will acknowledge my right to lead and direct operations."

The Chief shrugged his shoulders. If he didn't altogether relish this prospect, at any rate he was not going to make any more bother.

"I'll risk that," he declared, "on behalf of both of us."

They caught a midday train to Plymouth. At the station a big motor car was awaiting them. By ten o'clock they were in Penzance installed in their hotel and sitting down to an excellent hot supper which had been ordered earlier in the day.

"So far," said the Chief, "the favour which we are supposed to be conferring on you, doctor, has been rather difficult to discover."

"Wait. The night is to come."

Dr Hailey had scarcely spoken, when the hall porter came to announce that the car was in readiness.

"Have you put my long bag into it, as I directed you?" the doctor asked him.

"Yes, sir."

He turned to the Chief and Biles:

"Come, gentlemen. Time presses, and we have a considerable journey before us."

They went without a murmur. A big closed car stood at the door. It was brightly illuminated inside. The three men accommodated themselves on the broad back seat, and the chauffeur drew a rug over their knees. Then Dr Hailey switched out the light. The car moved off slowly down the main street of the town in the direction of St Michael's Mount.

"Are we permitted to ask questions as to our immediate destination?" the Chief inquired, as they rolled along the shores of Mount's Bay.

Dr Hailey sighed deeply, reproving, as it seemed, the flippant tones of his companion.

"My dear sir," he replied, "we are going to seek an answer to one of the darkest mysteries of crime which ever baffled human intelligence.... Our immediate destination is a graveyard, and we are about to keep a tryst with the dead."

CHAPTER 33
THE SECRET OF
THE GRAVE

There was a half-moon in the sky. St Michael's Mount, when they passed it, seemed like a grim hag's tooth set in the silver of the sea. The Chief, who was aware now of a sense of uneasiness he had not felt in the beginning of their enterprise, looked at it with dubious eyes. Was it here, he wondered, that the mysterious object of their adventure lay?

But no, the car swept on noiselessly past the end of the causeway leading to the Mount, and so into Marazion. A few minutes later they were running across the high land above the village, between empty cornfields which, in September, as he remembered from a former visit to this district, are bright with poppies.

They came to the cross-roads, where the byway leading to Pensilian tapers off. The car stopped, and the man descended and opened the door. Dr Hailey got out and spoke to him while his companions were alighting. Then he received his bag, and announced that from this point they must proceed on foot.

The village, when they reached it, seemed strangely quiet. None of them had spoken during the short walk, and now even the possibility of speech seemed ruled out. The long characteristic landscape, with its shadows and lights, held a weird aspect which in some curious way affected the senses. Inspector Biles found himself thinking that it was small wonder the inhabitants of such districts betook themselves to bed at sundown and stayed there till wholesome day was again in possession of the world.

He had puzzled his brains for hours now to read the riddle of this excursion, but he had failed to read it. There could be no connection, he felt, between the place they were going to and the churchyard at Calthorpe to which Dr Hailey had led him on that grim enterprise a few weeks ago, which had been fraught with such terrible consequences. Yet he knew that the doctor, once his mind was made up about a case, never really relinquished it. If this visit were not directly concerned with the murder of Sir William Armand, it had assuredly an indirect bearing on it.

There he was forced to leave the matter. His own mind was at peace about the whole affair, because he cherished not the faintest doubt that the guilty man had been brought to justice. It was an axiom with this clever detective that the obvious explanation is nearly always the true one. In his experience amateurs failed here, as in other departments of life, by trying to be too clever. They always favoured the complicated as against the simple, whereas life, generally speaking, was a simple business.

He glanced up and saw that they were approaching the church. Its square tower stood out darkly against the pale sky. The moon was reflected from some of the panes of its heavily-leaded windows. The ghostly forms of the tombstones were clustered about its base.

The gates were closed. Dr Hailey lifted his bag on to the top of the low wall, and climbed up easily beside it. He held out his hand to the Chief, inviting him also to ascend, but the latter seemed to hesitate.

"Is it really wise, my dear doctor," he expostulated, "to violate the sanctity of the place in this fashion?"

"It is essential."

"I confess I don't like it."

There was a moment's silence, then, mindful of his promise,

the Chief climbed the wall. Inspector Biles followed him. They walked up the steep slope of the churchyard together, allowing Dr Hailey to precede them by a few yards.

"What can it mean?" the Chief asked in a low whisper.

"I have no idea, sir," replied Biles, "but knowing the doctor, I should think it probably means a good deal. There's no doubt at all that he's found something pretty big."

Dr Hailey reached the grave of Mrs Ward, and set down his bag. He waited for his companions to join him. When they came up, he pointed to the grave and turned the rays of a small electric lamp on the headstone.

"There lies buried here, as you see," he told them, "the body of the wife of a local man who, as it happens, is the Registrar of Births and Deaths. The grave otherwise, as I have been at pains to assure myself, is empty—at least, so far as is known."

He pronounced these last words slowly and very deliberately. Though neither of his companions knew what he meant, they both experienced a thrill of uneasiness. The eeriness of the place, the silence, broken only by the occasional discordant scream of a seabird, the bewilderment of the pale, shifting light, oppressed their spirits with nameless dread.

"What are you going to do?" the Chief asked in a whisper.

"I am going to call you to witness to the truth," was the enigmatic reply.

As he spoke, Dr Hailey bent down and opened his bag. The moon was riding bare in the sky at the moment, and immediately they caught the gleam of a metal object. Inspector Biles, who was standing nearest, saw that this was the iron of a new spade. He uttered an exclamation of amazement. Dr Hailey lifted the spade out and moved round to the top of the grave.

"For God's sake, Hailey," protested the Chief in anxious tones, "don't do such a thing. It's horrible...."

He turned as though he thought of leaving the churchyard at once. Biles saw that his expression had become very grave, as though he considered that all bounds of decency, and even of law, had been overstepped.

"You will not regard it as less horrible when you know truth," the doctor's calm voice assured him. "Let me remind you that, as the chief criminal expert of this country, it is your duty to face even the darkest realities of human nature. I can assure you that the revelation you are about to experience will fully deserve that title."

He drove the spade into the turf as he spoke, and, with a heave of his shoulders, released a large clod of earth, which he set down carefully by the graveside. Then he began to dig in a wide circle which seemed to embrace the upper portion of the grave. The two detectives watched him at this gruesome task with ever increasing horror. Nothing, they told themselves, but his signal services to the cause of justice in the past would have induced them to allow him to continue so great an outrage on decent conduct.

"Ah!"

Dr Hailey stooped down and gleamed his torch into the hole he had made. Then he returned to his bag and took from it a small trowel. With this in his hand, he knelt down beside the grave and continued his excavations.

He worked now very slowly, removing only small quantities of earth at a time. The two men watching him shivered in the chill night, but they did not move from their positions near the front of the grave. Whatever he might be doing was his own business, until he chose to ask them to participate in it. They were there, as they felt, by a kind of trick; but since they had promised not to interfere, they would endeavour to keep their promise.

At last the doctor rose to his feet. He turned and beckoned them to approach. They came beside him, one on each side of the grave. He pressed the button of his lamp, and threw the yellow beam of light into the hole in the ground which he had made.

"Oh, my God."

The Chief started back. Even Biles felt himself chill with swift fear.

From the bottom of the hole, a human skull, pale, ghastly, grinned up at them.

Dr Hailey extinguished the lamp and gripped the Chief by the arm.

"That," he said in a tense whisper, "is not the skull of Mrs Ward. Her body is at least three feet further down, within its coffin."

There was no reply. Both the detectives felt sick, unnerved by this horrible discovery, the meaning of which one of them at least was still entirely at a loss to understand.

"It is necessary that you should make a more detailed inspection," the doctor continued. "I wish particularly to direct your attention to the eye-sockets of the skull, which, as you will see when I turn the lamp on again, have been pierced in several places."

He re-illumined the grave, calling on the Chief to observe the points indicated. The detective bent down and followed with his eyes the movements of the stalk of grass which Dr Hailey used as a pointer. He saw that each of the bony eye-sockets in the skull was perforated in several places. Biles, who was also bending over the hole, exclaimed in amazement.

"That is exactly how Sir William Armand was murdered."

"It is, exactly. The instrument, knife or dagger, whatever it was, reached the victim's brain through these wounds in this case as in that. And the murderer in this case, as in that, buried his handiwork in a new grave. Mrs Ward died on 15th November, 1915. The day was Sunday. On the following Saturday evening a farmer named Robin, who had just broken off his daughter's engagement, left the village here to return home, and was never seen or heard of again. You will admit that the two cases present many points of similarity."

The Chief stood erect, and drew a deep breath. He seemed to be overwhelmed. Dr Hailey again extinguished his lamp.

"And now," he said, "I propose that we return at once to our hotel. The further handling of this problem is your duty, rather than mine."

He bent, as he spoke, and replaced some of the turf on the grave, so as to hide its grisly contents. The Chief waited until he had completed this task, then he said:

"I fancy, my dear doctor, that our debt to you is a bigger one than any of us were able to realize."

He did not speak again until they were seated in the car on their way back to Penzance. Then he declared that he would give immediate orders for the investigation of the whole matter, adding:

"The disturbance of the grave is bound to be noticed tomorrow."

He turned to Dr Hailey.

"By what amazing process of reasoning," he asked in tones of the deepest respect, "did you reach this place."

"By no process of reasoning. By an accident only. Chance, a few days ago, put into my hands the connecting link I had failed myself to discover."

The doctor lay back on the cushions, and closed his eyes. After a few moments, he opened them again and asked:

"Do you remember the case of the missing rector of Hendred Castle, in Cumberland?"

He spoke very quietly, but both his companions uttered exclamations of horrified amazement at his words.

"What! You cannot possibly suggest..."

The Chief's voice thrilled.

"It is my experience," said Dr Hailey, "that murders of the kind we have just been investigating are never single murders. I mean they always belong to a series committed in the same way by the same hand. In this matter, perhaps, as a doctor, I have the advantage of you. In order to understand such cases one must have delved deeply into the foundation of human conduct, both normal and abnormal. One must know something of those mysterious sources from which proceed the streams of impulse and emotion."

He extracted his snuff-box as he spoke, and took a large pinch.

"At the beginning of every human nature," he declared, "there is love, but that early fountain is easily contaminated by the bitter waters of jealousy and hate and despair. And so character is determined. In the language of modern psychology 'a conflict' is produced. This conflict demands solution with such insistence that neither law nor honour nor decency are strong enough—in many instances—to prevent disaster."

He waved his hand as though the matter were too difficult for casual discussion.

"There is, from one point of view," he added, "a scarcely appreciable difference between the emotional lover who flits from mistress to mistress without ever achieving happiness, and the maniac whose life is made hideous by a long series of crimes. Both are the wretched slaves and victims of love—that fire which may burn with ineffable glory, or, being released from the control of reason, may consume and utterly destroy. What is still more astonishing, it is always the same immediate cause which leads to each of the philanderings or crimes in the series. The cast of an expression, the sound of a voice, the set of a pretty head, a sentiment expressed or hinted at in a particular way—these are the 'switches', so to speak, which release the pent-up violence of the unbalanced lover, and so urge him to plunge into a new entanglement. The homicidal maniac is in just the same bondage to circumstance and chance. Sooner or later the command, which he cannot but obey, will ring in his ears, and then he will go out. a wild beast, with the old bloodlust of the dawn of the world in his eyes. In his own way—and the manner varies—he will kill, and so satisfy for a moment, at any rate, the demon which possesses him."

The car reached Penzance, and drew up at the hotel. They found a cold supper spread for them in the coffee room. Dr Hailey invited his guests to be seated.

"I have a further request to make," he said, "which perhaps, in the circumstances, you will not refuse me. I want you, if it is at all possible, to travel back with me to Calthorpe, when I shall have one more piece of evidence—the most vital of all—to lay before you."

CHAPTER 34
FOOTSTEPS

The wind howled dismally in the chimneys of the old house, and the thudding of the heavy waves on the shore beat time to that sound. Dr Hailey glanced at his watch.

Had the storm, he wondered, delayed the coming of his visitors. The way to Calthorpe Hall is exposed, no matter from what direction one may approach it. Yet he thought that, in spite of the weather, they would not disappoint him.

His expression was rather grimmer than usual, and once his hand strayed to the pocket of the roomy smoking coat he was wearing, and closed for a moment round the barrel of the little pistol, which reposed there. He meant to run no risks.

On the other hand, he meant to make his demonstration a complete one in every respect. Though he had not complained at the time, he had resented a little the way in which the police had taken this case out of his hands as soon as he had provided them with the necessary clues. The arrest of Derwick had been, in his opinion, an act characterized by high-handedness—in relation to himself—as well as by precipitation. Always, he reflected, it was the same thing. As soon as a crime was committed, the newspapers began to shriek for a victim, and the police lost their heads. They put haste to satisfy the clamour above all considerations of certainty.

He had not relished the position into which he had been thrust by this policy of theirs. Instead of directing an investigation with the resources of the law behind him, he had been compelled to work single-handed, in the dark, without assistance. If he had reached a conclusion satisfying to his own ideas and instincts, he had no reason to thank them.

He was standing in the library before a big fire which crackled cheerfully, making a pleasant contrast with the dismal sounds of the elements outside. The heavy curtains were drawn close and the room glowed with warmth and comfort.

His reflections were interrupted by the faint sound of a motor changing gear. That meant that the car was entering the lodge gates. He listened until he heard it again. Then he went to the front door and stood behind it waiting. He did not wish to open the door until the last moment, on account of the boisterous wind.

The headlights swept into view round the final bend of the avenue. They cast a beam of silver on the glass fanlight over the door. He turned the handle and stepped out, meeting the heavy gust, which swept past him. When the car stopped, he opened the door. The Chief of the Criminal Investigation Department stepped out, followed by Inspector Biles.

"I'm afraid you have had a terrible night for your journey," the doctor cried. "I began to fear you might have been blown over on the way from Belfort."

He conducted them into the house and handed them over to the butler, Travers, who took them up to their rooms. When they came downstairs again, dinner was announced.

"I am to apologise for Miss Armand's absence," Dr Hailey said, in tones which were a trifle studied. "She is, as you may imagine, unwilling to leave Newcastle for the present."

He watched the Chief narrowly as he spoke, and saw that distinguished man redden a little. The butler was in the room, and so he made only a conventional reply, but a moment later, when they were alone, he raised his head and looked the doctor in the face.

"Remember," he said, "that we are obeying your orders now. Events might possibly have moved faster but for that."

"I think not."

The conversation turned to general matters.

When the servants had retired. Dr Hailey rose and placed himself in front of the fire.

"There are one or two points which I wish to make quite clear before... before anything happens," he said, "But in the first place, I should like to know how your side of the matter has been progressing. I presume the body of Farmer Robin was identified without much difficulty."

The Chief nodded.

"His watch and chain were still there; that alone was sufficient. The affair, I understand, has created a tremendous sensation in the neighbourhood, where the general idea prevails that the murder was committed by a son-in-law, who was killed in the war. There appears to have been some bitter dispute between him and his prospective father-in-law."

"There was. The old man broke off the fellow's engagement to his daughter in the first instance. She only married him after her father's disappearance."

"The police, of course, have been given strict instructions to take no action whatever until they receive further orders from headquarters."

The Chief's eyes fell to the tablecloth as he made this last statement. There was, in his manner, a faint suggestion that he was aware of standing on the defensive where the doctor was concerned. He raised his glass of port to his lips and sipped it slowly.

"And Hendred Castle?" Dr Hailey asked. "Have you had any communication from that quarter?"

"We have—a long telegram, which was re-transmitted from London, to catch us at Newcastle this evening."

The Chief's voice thrilled. "My God, Hailey," he exclaimed suddenly, "you are absolutely uncanny. It was exactly as you foretold it would be. The old Rector was found in the grave you indicated. He had been buried in his surplice, just as you anticipated."

"And his eyes?"

"As you foretold… exactly as you foretold."

Silence fell between them. The storm seemed to be growing fiercer and the big windows rattled in their frames. The thudding of the waves was like the knocking of mighty subterranean hammers.

"You agree, then, that the same hand wrought all three murders?"

"It must be so. Coincidence could not extend to cover that wide range."

Again there was a pause. Then the Chief rose and came towards the fireplace, carrying his wine glass in his hand.

"No doubt," he said, "in a day or two now we shall possess the complete answer to the riddle."

Dr Hailey took snuff. He realized that the last remark was a challenge, but he had his own reasons for ignoring it. Three days had now elapsed since their visit to Cornwall, and yet, even in that time apparently, no inkling of the truth had reached them. A sense almost of bewilderment overwhelmed him. Then he reflected it is easier to test a theory than to interpret it from a record of experiments conducted to prove, or disprove, its value. In the place of his companions he might not, himself, have fared any better.

"You have no suspicions, then?" he asked them, permitting himself just this one small revenge.

The Chief shook his head.

"So far, no. But do us the credit, my dear doctor, of remembering that the work at Hendred Castle only took place this morning, that at Pensilian only the night before. There are certain necessary preliminaries to the disturbance of graves in consecrated ground. We do know this, however," he added in lower tones, "Derwick has never visited either of these places, so far as can be ascertained. He was little more than a lad when the Rector of Hendred Castle disappeared, and in 1915 he was in the army in France."

"His appeal comes before the court tomorrow, I understand?"

The Chief's face assumed, suddenly, a very grave expression.

"I am sorry to say," he declared, "that it was heard today. There was a change of arrangements at the last moment. We had another message at Newcastle to the effect that it was dismissed. Until our investigations at Hendred Castle had been carried out, we felt that no interference on our part was warranted —though I wish now we had acted in advance of knowledge."

It was evident that the hitch in the process of justice which he foresaw to be inevitable, weighed heavily on the spirit of this distinguished policeman. Dr Hailey reflected that, to the official mind, all things—even life and death—are official. These men were not inhuman or lacking in sympathy. That charge, so often brought against them by the ignorant, was grossly untrue and unfair, but they were nevertheless parts of a machine which exists at all only because, on the whole, its smooth working can be relied on. Every failure of the machine to function threatened a little that public confidence which was its main support and strength. He glanced from the Chief to Inspector Biles and realized that, though as honest men they must rejoice in the vindication of innocence, as detectives the fact that innocence had been placed in peril was a very serious blow to them. It meant endless criticism, endless rebuke from those very newspapers which, had they failed to "do something" at once, would have been their fiercest detractors.

The position of a member of the Criminal Investigation Department was not, he decided, an enviable one. In the circumstances, the record of that remarkable body reflected the very brightest credit on those who directed its operations.

"I suppose," he said, "that a petition for a reprieve is certain to follow tomorrow."

"Yes, quite certain. In a case of this sort, where a romance is interwoven with a story of crime, the public imagination is always deeply stirred. Women, especially, seem to be affected. The affection they bear to good-looking men who are accused of doing murder on behalf of one of their own sex, is truly astonishing."

Dr Hailey glanced again at his watch. It still wanted ten minutes to nine o'clock. He nodded his agreement.

"Women," he declared, "have a different code of honour from men, perhaps, in a sense: a nobler, more exalted code. I have yet to meet the woman who would stick at crime, except possibly the one crime of murder, to save the man of her heart or the child she loved. Our laws and our law courts are still entirely masculine in their attitude, in spite of women jurors."

They heard footsteps on the gravel outside.

These passed the window and reached the front door. The bell rang in a vigorous peal.

"Come," said Dr Hailey to his companions.

He led them across the hall to the library and closed the door behind them. They heard the footman approaching to open the front door. He crossed the room to the window, and flung back the heavy curtains which covered it, exposing a deep embrasure.

"It is essential," he declared, "that you should remain out of sight for a little time…. If you step in here I will draw the curtains over you."

Biles glanced at his Chief, who had started slightly at the idea of concealment, but his expression indicated that he was ready to follow any instructions given him. Dr Hailey covered the two men from sight, and then seated himself in front of the fire.

The door opened, and the footman announced:

"The Rev Hargreave Willoughby."

CHAPTER 35 THE TIGER SPRINGS

The Vicar of Calthorpe advanced into the room with firm, active stride. His usually pale cheeks were glowing from the whips of the wind. Raindrops gleamed on his face.

He greeted Dr Hailey cordially.

"I trust I am not late. What a fearful night; on the cliffs once or twice I thought I must be blown off my feet."

He selected a cigar from the box which the doctor offered him, and cut it very carefully with his pocket knife.

"I do hope," said Dr Hailey, "that you will forgive my abrupt summons. Nothing, I can assure you, but the urgency of the case would have made me send it. But the Court of Appeal, as I have just heard, has refused Derwick's application, and there is therefore not a moment to be lost in launching our petition. I felt that it was of great importance to have your name at the top of the list of local signatures."

The clergyman inclined his head.

"In that matter," he declared, "I am entirely at your disposal. Personally, I have always been opposed to capital punishment, which I regard as barbarous and useless, quite useless. On that ground alone I should be ready to sign any petition which you may have drawn up."

"And I, too. But this case presents other features, I think, which enormously strengthen the case for a reprieve." The doctor's voice became a little more earnest. "I do not know what you think, sir," he added, "but it appears to me that only a madman, in Derwick's place, would have attacked Sir William. What possible motive could he have for the crime?"

The question came sharply. The Rev Hargreave did not answer it at once. He blew a coil of smoke from his thin lips and watched it rise in widening circles above his head.

"His engagement had been broken off, of course," he declared at last. "That may have temporarily unhinged his mind. Love, I have observed, comes to different men in different ways. And the loss of love, also, is apt to exercise a more severe effect on some than on others. It may restore to one individual his ambition in a new and more alluring form; it may rob another of all desire to succeed in life. Again, it may drive a man to solitude or send him headlong into the vortex of pleasure and gaiety. In this matter, what may seem to one but a slender motive for an extreme course of action, may, in the eyes of another, justify almost any excess."

He spoke precisely, with a trace of his pulpit manner and enunciation. Dr Hailey nodded agreement.

"I have met with cases of all sorts myself," he agreed. "The longer I live, indeed, the more I become convinced that woman is the real touchstone of character. We know but little of a man until we know how he has fared in relation to the opposite sex."

He got up and crossed the room to a side table where a decanter and some syphons had been placed.

"Do let me give you a drink?" he urged.

The Rev Hargreave turned to watch his tumbler being filled. As he did so, his face was fully illumined by the lamp hanging in the centre of the room. Dr Hailey noticed that his eyes were very bright, whereas the colour had almost entirely vanished from his cheeks. His cold features seemed to have taken on a sterner aspect. He brought the two tumblers to the fireplace and set them on the mantelpiece.

"Some time ago," he said, "I happened to hear of a most remarkable case which, were the facts not known to me, I should certainly regard as entirely beyond credence. It concerned a member of your own profession."

The Vicar looked up, treating his companion to a glance which was hawk-like in its swiftness.

"Ah," he said, "my profession includes men of the strangest, as well as men of the noblest, character."

He half-rose from his chair and took his tumbler in his hand.

"The ministry of religion," he added, "attracts a certain temperament irresistibly. That is why apparently worldly men are so frequently found in holy orders."

Dr Hailey nodded.

"In this case, however," he said, "the principal actor in the drama was by no means worldly. He was a young curate of most ascetic cast of mind, working in a large north-country parish on the edge of the Yorkshire moors. I believe that the people to whom he ministered made an idol of him. When he preached, the church was always crowded, and large numbers of women, especially young women, used to hang on his lips. One of the latter was the daughter of his rector, a very beautiful girl, with masses of golden hair and eyes of that dreamy spiritual quality which so greatly attracts a certain type of man—a girl, I imagine, not unlike Miss Armand."

He paused and took a pinch of snuff. The Rev Hargreave had bent forward while he was speaking, and now sat staring into the fire. His face was so still, so rigid, that his features seemed to be carved in marble. The cigar he was holding burned in a thin wisp of smoke which rose straight into the air above his head. The long line of smoke might have been drawn with a ruler so unwavering was it.

"Naturally enough," the doctor continued, "the young clergyman fell desperately in love with this beautiful child. They exchanged vows, and he poured out all the passion and fervour of his spirit in his wooing of her. Love, as he soon found, was his supreme gift. In the intoxication of that discovery, no obstacle seemed insuperable.

"Nevertheless, obstacles of a formidable character existed, which must have impressed any man less sanguine by nature with the difficulty of the enterprise on which he had embarked. For one thing, the girl was a distant relation of his own; for another, his family history was a sombre one. Both his parents had died in asylums. This fact was known, of course, to the girl's father."

Again Dr Hailey took snuff. The motionless figure of the clergyman afforded no sign either of interest or the lack of it.

"It was inevitable, in the circumstances, that consent to a marriage should be withheld. The lovers, however, were too deep in their new happiness to pay heed to this difficulty. They promised each other that nothing should come between them and that, as soon as the girl attained her majority, they would get married in spite of family opposition.

"But the girl, as it turned out, was not a very strong character. The strain of her father's disapprobation weighed on her spirit, and she became ill. The doctor ordered her away to the South. At first she wrote her lover daily, but after a time her letters became less frequent. In three months they had ceased altogether, and then, one morning, he learned that she had become engaged to another man—the younger son of a very wealthy peer.

"The curate, strangely enough, showed no sign of the blow he had received. He went about his duties as usual. It was assumed that he had accepted the inevitable in a Christian spirit. The rector showed him all the kindness and consideration possible, even to the extent of arranging that the marriage should take place in London."

Dr Hailey's voice assumed a more serious tone.

"And yet," he went on, "I have reason to know that, at the moment when the blow fell on him, he became a madman. The intense egotism of his nature, an evil inheritance from his parents, brought forth delusions of persecution. He saw himself, not as a suitor rejected on quite legitimate grounds, but as a martyr sacrificed to sordid and wicked motives. As always happens in these cases, he believed that the powers of darkness were arraigned against him.

"His nature was fine in many respects and chivalrous. Moreover, he was a profound student of the superstitions of earlier days, an antiquary and ethnologist of distinction. There came to him the feeling that he had been singled out by Divine Providence to make war on the enemies of the holy spirit of love. He was a new St George, a new St Francis; he possessed the power to cast out devils, the right to adopt any means to secure this glorious and righteous aim.

"Naturally, however, the Kingdom of Darkness must exert its whole force against so tremendous an antagonist. Persecution was in the air around him. Spirits of evil dogged his steps by night, fearful shapes of horror haunted his sleep; the evil eye, that immemorial token of malignancy, cast its wicked spell on him. The need to strike at these assassins of his soul grew more urgent every day.

"And added to that need was the need to purge the temple and body of Christ of the profane persons who defiled it—the wolves in sheep's clothing, who violated the sacred spirit of love in order to sell their daughters for money and position. He would rid the world of all such, he, the new saviour of society, the new knight of the Cross. Beginning with the Rector himself, he would work swift destruction on every father who set his face against a daughter's love....

"You see, a madman's mind is the most logical instrument in the world...."

The doctor raised his tumbler to his lips. Still the bent figure remained in stony immobility.

"One winter night, after evensong, when the rector was returning alone from the church to the vicarage, his curate, who had been hidden among the shadows of the buttresses of the great building, struck him down. As the old man pitched forward under that blow, ten thousand devils were released in the young man's spirit. Snarling like a dog, he sprang on his victim. There was a flash of steel, once, twice, as the bloodthirsty knife descended, smiting out the Eyes of Evil.

"It was over in an instant. The madman lifted his poor victim and bore him down the hill among the ghostly tombstones to a new grave, still covered with half-withered funeral flowers. He had a trowel with him. He scooped a hole in the loose earth, big enough to hold the frail old body. He buried it...."

Suddenly Dr Hailey sprang to his feet. The clergyman had turned upon him and there was such a look in his eyes as even he had never before seen on a human face. He moved back behind the chair on which he had been sitting. His hand travelled swiftly to his pocket.

Biles, who had a clear view of the room through a slight tear in the curtain in front of him, saw the Rev Hargreave crouch like a wild animal before it springs. He moved his face round slowly, and even the hardened detective caught his breath. The eyes seemed to be suffused with blood. They were staring. The thin lips were drawn back from the big teeth in an expression, sardonic, sinister, horrible. Then the fearsome sound of a maniac's laugh rang in the room.

He saw Dr Hailey raise his pistol and cover the clergyman. The doctor's face was rather pale, though his movements were deliberate enough.

"If you move, I shoot—remember."

Again the horrible laugh rang out. The Rev Hargreave drew himself up to his full height.

"Your weapons," he cried in a great voice, "cannot prevail against me, for I come in the name and the strength of God Himself."

He made the sign of the Cross on his brow. Then, in an instant, with such agility as seemed beyond the power of a human frame, he leaped on his victim and bore him with a crash to the floor.

The pistol was flung violently across the room.

CHAPTER 36 AS IN A DREAM

The two detectives sprang from their hiding-place. They flung themselves bodily on the struggling men, who rolled backwards and forwards in what was obviously a death grip. Biles caught a glimpse of Dr Hailey's face, and saw that it was dark and suffused as though his breath were being strangled in his body. Then he noticed the thumbs of the clergyman pressed into his friend's eye-sockets. He clasped his own hands round the assailant's throat and drove his fingers deeply inwards, where the great blood vessels run up the neck to the brain.

That old and well-tried method of self-defence was instantly successful. The clergyman's hands grew feeble—he released his terrible grip. The detectives dragged him back from the body of the doctor. With a swift movement, Biles applied the self-locking handcuffs, which he invariably carried on his person.

Dr Hailey lay gasping on the floor, where he had fallen. The Chief came to his assistance and raised his head. When his breathing had grown a little easier, he went and fetched the tumbler of whisky.

"Thank God, you were near at hand. I had no idea how strong he was...."

Biles stood guard over the prisoner, who lay quite still, with his eyes closed and the colour entirely gone from his features. After a time. Dr Hailey staggered to his feet, and came and joined them.

"I have arranged," he said, "that the car shall be ready to go to Belfort at once if you wish it. It seems, I think, the best solution in the circumstances."

He gazed at the cold beautiful face of the man who had so nearly proved his undoing. Every trace of the demoniac fury of a few moments ago had passed away, smoothed out of sight, as it seemed, by gracious and effacing fingers. He bowed his head and sighed deeply. The clergyman opened his eyes and a smile flickered for an instant on his lips. Then suddenly his brow contracted in a look of utter bewilderment. He tried to rise and felt the irons bite on his wrists.

"Where am I?" he murmured, "and what has happened? What is the meaning of this, gentlemen?"

His eyes were sincere in their expression of wonder. The Chief glanced uneasily at Dr Hailey.

"You have had a very violent fit," the doctor declared; "we had to secure your hands for your own safety. Please lie still and do not talk."

The Rev Hargreave, however, was in no mood to listen to this advice. He struggled to his feet, and then sat down in the chair which Biles wheeled towards him.

"I have had such a frightful dream," he told them. "I dreamed actually that it was I who murdered Sir William, and not that poor young man. I found him lying asleep in the wood, and I stabbed at his eyes with my pocket-knife. Then I went back to the Vicarage, and got one of the old iron stamps I used to collect and marked the tree where he fell with the sign of the Evil Eye; and after that—will you believe it?—I carried his body to the churchyard and buried it where it was found in poor Miss Anderson's grave..."

His eyes closed again as he spoke, and his head bent forward. He had fallen asleep.

"That is the usual thing," Dr Hailey said, "after an attack. He will be drowsy now for many hours."

He poured himself out a stiff whisky and swallowed it at a gulp.

"It was his sermon last Sunday," he told the detectives, "which gave me the clue. He mentioned the Evil Eye in a way which, when I thought it over, seemed rather extraordinary. And then suddenly at night in this room the truth dawned on me. I consulted a reference book of the clergy, and found that he had been curate of Hendred Castle and Pensilian. I visited both places.... You know the rest."

CHAPTER 37 OUT
OF THE DEPTHS

Estelle had received several telegrams from Dr Hailey during the period covered by his investigations. They gave her hope, and enabled her to bear up better, when she went to the prison to see Jack, than she might otherwise have been able to do. But, in spite of them, a terrible fear haunted her mind. When the news that the Court of Appeal had dismissed her lover's petition reached her, her heart quailed.

Could it be that, after all, the doctor's optimism was not justified? Had he failed in some critical moment of his quest?

She went to bed, and lay awake all night, not even trying to woo the sleep which, if it came, must be filled with anxieties and horrors not less terrible than those which afflicted her waking senses. At an earlier hour than usual she rose and dressed and went down to breakfast.

But she could not eat. The hotel waiter brought her a morning newspaper, and she read the judgement of the Court with uncomprehending brain. They seemed to think that everything which could have been said in the prisoner's favour had been said—she flung the sheet away from her. How blind, how stupid all these men were. Could they not realize that the truth stared them in the face in the eyes of a good man?

At half-past eight a boy brought her a telegram. It was from Dr Hailey, from Belfort, and ran:

"Jack innocent—have no fear."

Somehow it failed to convince, or even greatly to comfort, her. He had been hinting at the same thing for a week now. She set forth for the prison, where she was expected at 10 o'clock.

But today the usual order of her entry within these grim doors seemed to have changed. The official at the gate received her with deference. He said that the Governor desired her to call immediately at his office.

Next moment she was shaking hands with that rather solemn official. He motioned her to a seat.

"I have strange news for you, Miss Armand," he said, in very gentle tones. "Pray try to compose yourself, to hear it."

For an instant she thought he was going to say that all hope must be abandoned. Then a glance at his eyes reassured her; they were almost happy. He touched a bell, and a man appeared. He made a sign. Then he rose and moved to the door.

"If you will wait a moment," he said, "you will be fully enlightened."

He went out and closed the door softly behind him. She heard the click of a latch behind her, and turned her head sharply. Another door, just behind her, had opened. Jack, dressed in his ordinary clothes, stood in the passage-way.

A cry broke from his lips when he saw her. He sprang across the grim little room. She stood up and suddenly felt herself sway. If he had not caught her in his arms she must have fallen.

*

They returned to Calthorpe the same evening, when all the formalities of Jack's release and vindication had been completed. As they drove from Belfort through the quiet woods neither of them spoke a word. Their hearts were too full, in this wonderful, sacred hour, for speech of any kind.

The car turned into the main avenue and glided to the door. Estelle saw Dr Hailey's tall figure advancing down the steps to meet them. She came to him with both her hands extended and tears gleaming in her beautiful eyes.

"My friend," she whispered, "my friend."

DR HAILEY SERIES
BIBLIOGRAPHY

1. *The Mystery of the Evil Eye* (Hutchinson & Company, London 1925). US title: *The Sign of Evil* (J.B. Lippincott Company, Philadelphia 1925). Serialised weekly in *Flynn's* between 29 November 1924 and 3 January 1925.

2. *The Double-Thirteen Mystery* (Hutchinson & Company, London 1926). US title: *The Double Thirteen* (1926). Serialised weekly in *Flynn's* between 5 and 26 September 1925.

3. *The Horseman of Death* (Hutchinson & Company, London 1927 /J.B. Lippincott Company, Philadelphia 1928). Serialised in *Flynn's*, 17 and 24 September, 1, 8 and 15, 1927.

4. *The Mystery of the Ashes* (Hutchinson & Company, London 1927/J.B. Lippincott Company, Philadelphia 1927). Serialised weekly in *Hull Times* in October and November 1926 and in *Flynn's* between 20 November and 11 December 1926, as *Tiger's Spring*.

5. *Sinners Go Secretly: Being Pages From the Diary of Dr Eustace Hailey* (Hutchinson & Company, London 1927/J.B. Lippincott Company, Philadelphia 1927). Short story collection.

6. *The Dagger* (Hutchinson & Company, London 1928/J.B. Lippincott Company, Philadelphia 1929).

7. *The Red Scar* (Hutchinson & Company, London 1928/J.B. Lippincott Company, Philadelphia 1928).

8. *The Fourth Finger* (Hutchinson & Company, London 1929/J.B. Lippincott Company, Philadelphia 1929).

9. *The Room with the Iron Shutters* (Hutchinson & Company, London 1929/J.B. Lippincott Company, Philadelphia 1930).

10. *The Blue Vesuvius* (Hutchinson & Company, London 1930/ J.B. Lippincott Company, Philadelphia 1931).

11. *The Yellow Crystal* (Hutchinson & Company, London 1930/ J.B. Lippincott Company, Philadelphia 1930).

12. *Murder of a Lady* (Hutchinson & Company, London 1931). US title: *The Silver Scale Mystery* (J.B. Lippincott Company, Philadelphia 1931).

13. *The Silver Arrow* (Hutchinson & Company, London 1931). US title: *The White Arrow* (J.B. Lippincott Company, Philadelphia 1932).

14. *Case of the Green Knife* (Hutchinson & Company, London 1932). US title: *The Green Knife* (J.B. Lippincott Company, Philadelphia 1932).

15. *Case of the Red-Haired Girl* (Hutchinson & Company, London 1932). US title: *The Cotswold Case* (J.B. Lippincott Company, Philadelphia 1933).

16. *The Case of the Gold Coins* (Hutchinson & Company, London 1933/J.B. Lippincott Company, Philadelphia 1934).

17. *The Loving Cup* (Hutchinson & Company, London 1933). US title: *Death Out of the Night* (J.B. Lippincott Company, Philadelphia 1933).

18. *Death of a Banker* (Hutchinson & Company, London 1934/J.B. Lippincott Company, Philadelphia 1934).

19. *The Holbein Mystery* (Hutchinson & Company, London 1935). US title: *The Red Lady* (J.B. Lippincott Company, Philadelphia 1935).

20. *The Toll House Murder* (Hutchinson & Company, London 1935/J.B. Lippincott Company, Philadelphia 1935).

21. *Murder in Thin Air* (Hutchinson & Company, London 1936/ J.B. Lippincott Company, Philadelphia 1936).

22. *Death of a Golfer* (Hutchinson & Company, London 1935/J.B. Lippincott Company, Philadelphia 1937). Reprinted with alternative title: *Murder in the Morning* (Hillman Periodicals, New York 1937).

23. *Death of A King* (Hutchinson & Company, London 1938). US title: *Murder Calls Dr Hailey* (J.B. Lippincott Company, Philadel-

phia 1938).

24. *Door Nails Never Die* (Hutchinson & Company, London 1939/ J.B. Lippincott Company, Philadelphia 1939).

25. *The House on the Hard* (Hutchinson & Company, London 1940/no US edition).

26. *Emergency Exit* (Hutchinson & Company, London 1941/ Julian Messner Inc, New York 1944).

27. *Murder in a Church* (Hutchinson & Company, London 1942/ no US edition).

28. *Death of a Shadow* (Hutchinson & Company, London 1950/no US edition).